The Vampire Files

The Vampire Files

BOOK SIX

BLOOD ON THE WATER

P.N. ELROD

ACE BOOKS, NEW YORK

This book is an Ace original edition,
and has never been previously published.

BLOOD ON THE WATER

An Ace Book / published by arrangement with
the author

PRINTING HISTORY
Ace edition / June 1992

The Penguin Putnam Inc. World Wide Web site address is
http://www.penguinputnam.com

ISBN: 0-441-85947-X

Check out the Ace Science Fiction/Fantasy newsletter,
and much more, at Club PPI!

ACE®
Ace Books are published by
The Berkley Publishing Group, a member of Penguin Putnam Inc.,
375 Hudson Street, New York, NY 10014.
The name "ACE" and the "A" logo are trademarks
belonging to Charter Communications, Inc.

PRINTED IN THE UNITED STATES OF AMERICA

10 9 8 7 6 5 4

Thanks to
Julie Malik
for the technical help,
and special thanks to
Margaret Summy,
for getting me "centered!"

IT WAS WAR, THEN. The quiet kind that you notice only as an impersonal paragraph in the paper you read over the morning coffee or in the evening relaxing, after work. Bold black letters might spell out "Shooting Victim Found," and then go on to give some sparse details of the person's age, where they lived and died, and that the police were following some promising leads. Most of the time you never learn if they turned up anything or not. Life moves forward and new paragraphs on other casualties appear in the paper. New, but with a dreary similarity to all the others, as in any war.

In my case I might not even get that much of an epitaph. Vaughn Kyler's enemies tended to simply disappear. Without an inconvenient body to trip over, the cops couldn't be expected to make an arrest.

I gripped the wheel more tightly to control the tremors in my hands and took a second look in the rearview mirror. The Cadillac was still there and following close enough to make it obvious that the men inside wanted me to know about it. The side windows were smoked over, but I could make out four vague figures through the windshield, though little else. Maybe one of them was Kyler but that wasn't very likely. The wide streets of Chicago, even at night, were far too public for him.

Last August he'd taken control of the Paco gang, and since Frank Paco himself was confined to a lunatic ward and his brothers and cousins were missing and probably dead, no one was around to object. In six months Kyler had doubled the earnings and spread the profits around so his position was that much more secure, but he was always on guard against any threats to his authority, which, unfortunately, included myself.

In no uncertain terms he'd ordered me to leave town or die. His attitude at the time indicated that he didn't really care about my choice as long as one or the other removed me from his sight. I suppose from his point of view he was giving me a better break than I deserved. That or he was just being careful. Sooner or later he could overstep things enough so that the cops would no longer ignore the situation and be forced to officially notice him.

But last night's many events had crowded his threat right out of my mind and I hadn't left, much less even thought of alternatives. On the other hand, he'd had a long full day to recover from that particularly busy evening and decide what to do about me. Sending some of his boys in one of his Caddies to play tag had to be part of it.

I made a few turns just to be sure and the big black car echoed my course in a leisurely manner. They had enough power under that hood to make mincemeat of anything my humble Buick could do. If I wanted to get away with a whole skin, it would have to be with brains and not speed. I just wished that I felt smart instead of scared. Kyler had that effect on me.

They didn't seem to be in much of a hurry to push the issue. I could figure that they'd planned out what to do and were only waiting for me to make it easy for them with a wrong move. They didn't quite hug my back bumper, but kept close enough to edge up my nerves. Not a good idea on their part; a nervous man is liable to do anything. It would have been far better to tail me at a discreet distance until I'd arrived at the Top Hat Club and then pick me off as I left the car. They wanted to frighten me before moving in; Kyler apparently had no reservations against letting his boys have some fun.

Even as the thought occurred, my hands abruptly stopped shaking. I drew a short breath, releasing it as a brief, taut laugh that flushed away my vague fears. I suddenly knew exactly how to handle them and had only to find the right spot for it.

The setup was important. I'd have to let them think they'd succeeded in rattling me. Shifting into the right lane, I cut a sharp turn at the next corner and put my foot down. The Buick had enough in it to accelerate away at a good clip, and I left them behind for a few hopeful seconds.

Traffic was light in the area, which was just as well since I didn't want any bystanders or cops getting in the way. I hadn't seen a patrol car yet, not that I was remotely interested in involving the law over this. If the men in the Caddy ran to type they'd have no qualms about bumping off a cop to get to me. I was content to leave Chicago's finest out of the immediate line of fire and take care of these clowns myself.

I continued the illusion of a chase for several long blocks. At one point I thought I'd genuinely lost them, but the familiar pattern of their headlights swung into view again and caught up. Losing them without having to try anything fancy would have been just fine, but that kind of luck wasn't working for me tonight. I took the next corner fast and tight, the wheels squawking until they bit the pavement with a quick lurch. The Cadillac easily kept pace.

The corner coming up was to be my last one. Sooner or later I'd have to run into a traffic stop that I couldn't beat through, and this was it. The driving lane ahead was blocked with cars waiting for the next signal change. The curb was lined with parked vehicles. Oncoming traffic prevented me from making a U-turn, so I stood on the brake and stopped just short of the guy in front of me. For effect, I tapped the horn, but no one bothered to move out of the way.

Since I was giving the impression of a nerved-up and frantic man, it was time to do something desperate. I cut the motor and launched out of the car on the right-hand side, sparing only one glance back at the Caddy. They'd been ready for that move; the front and rear passenger doors opened and two guys in dark coats bowled out after me.

I slipped between the parked cars and darted a dozen yards along the sidewalk. The street was well lighted, but that didn't matter as long as I managed to get out of their sight for a few seconds. I ducked around the corner of a building and vanished. Period.

My forward movement slowed, stopped, and reversed, but by then they'd pounded past and were just starting to wonder what had happened to me. Their puzzlement wouldn't last all that long, so I whipped back the way I'd come like an invisible cloud, hugging the side of the building for guidance. I couldn't see at all, which made it hard to gauge distance, but tried my best guess. It worked out. When I re-formed into a solid man again I was twenty feet behind their car and in a position to do myself some good.

Vanishing was one of my more convenient talents—acquired, not inherent—though at first it had taken some practice to get it right. I'm one of the Un-Dead—a *nosferatu*—a vampire—pick your own name. Any one of them is close enough to the truth, but I tend to ignore them all because of the dramatically bad press associated with such words. In my own mind, I have a condition; terrible in some ways, great in others, but not something to be lightly overlooked.

I wouldn't show in their rearview mirror, but crouched anyway as I ran up to their right rear tire. The cold wind blew the exhaust right in my face, but I don't breathe much except to talk; it was annoying mostly because it made my eyes water.

Fumbling out my pocketknife, I buried the sharp point into the side of the tire with one strong jab. It deflated in a most satisfactory way, getting the immediate attention of the people inside. The guy in the backseat rolled down his window to see what had happened.

He wasn't Kyler, though it would have been nice. I popped his unfamiliar face once on the chin and he dropped out of sight without a sound. The driver said something, but I missed it when I vanished again and poured through the open window into the car. Just as he turned around to check on his fallen buddy I went solid. There was an even chance that he never knew what hit him. In this case it was my left fist, the punch pulled enough so as not to break his jaw.

The car started to drift forward and I had to scramble over the seat to grab at the hand brake. I killed the engine, yanked the key, and tossed it out the rear window into a pile of gutter trash.

The other two would be coming back any second now. I quit their car for my own, gunned it to life, and made that belated U-turn into the oncoming lane. Happily, no one got in my way, but I was beyond noticing such details, being in too much of a hurry to get back home again to see if Escott was still alive.

We were partners, sort of; he had a small business as a private agent, which meant that he didn't do divorce work, and I helped him out whenever he needed it. The last case had involved a search for a diamond-and-ruby bracelet worth fifteen grand that sparked off three, almost four murders. Escott and I still had the bracelet. We couldn't return it to its owner without implicating ourselves in two of the deaths. Escott was innocent; I wasn't, but he was my friend and doing what he could to protect me.

In essence, Kyler was at the bottom of it all, and Escott was trying to figure a way of pinning things to him. He was planning to use the bracelet in some way, only it looked as if Kyler wasn't going to give him the chance. As far as Kyler was concerned the bracelet and the money it represented belonged to him now, and too bad for anyone who happened to get in the way.

There's a deep cold well inside all of us where we keep our blackest fears. Mine had cracked open and was pouring stuff out like Niagara as I turned onto the last street and saw a twin of the Cadillac I'd disabled parked in the alley behind our house. This was a quiet little middle-class neighborhood where such cars are dreams just too good to be true. The smoked windows confirmed its ownership and the threat it represented.

I left my car on the street and tore around the empty Caddy to the back of the house. The narrow yard was silent. The garage was closed tight, but the roof of the Nash was visible through a side window. Escott had been home when they'd come calling. I vanished and seeped through the crack at the bottom of the back door and assumed a more or less vertical position just inside the kitchen.

Unable to see, I concentrated on listening, but heard nothing in the immediate area. I swept the room once to make sure it was empty and cautiously re-formed. Nobody stared back at me.

The place was wrecked. Every drawer and cabinet was open, their contents dumped out. Escott wasn't too interested in cooking or it might have been worse, but it was bad enough. The refrigerator was open and humming away, trying to keep its stripped insides cold. I shut the door very quietly, my hands shaking again. This time with rage, not fear.

A variety of indistinct sounds were coming from all over the house. There were at least two men on the ground floor and two others upstairs. Nobody talked much. They knew their business.

Peering around the edge of the door, I could look through the dining room to the front parlor, where I'd left Escott listening to his radio. He wasn't in sight, but I did catch a moving glimpse of a dark hat and coat that didn't belong to either of us. I dropped back.

The bedrooms were on the second floor and my instinctive urge was to take the high ground first. Any other time I'd have used the stairs; now I vanished again and rose straight up through the ceiling. The room I materialized in was my own. I was prepared for a mess and they hadn't disappointed me. The barely used bed was torn apart, my books and papers and clothes scattered to hell and gone. It was just my good luck and his bad that the thug who'd done the tearing was still there.

With something like joy I grabbed him by the scruff of his neck, lifting him away from the bureau he was ransacking. He was too surprised to cry out, and then he didn't have the chance to as I slammed him face first into the nearest wall. The first time wasn't satisfying enough, so I did it again, and once more because I was feeling mean. He left a bloody smear on the faded paper as he slid to the floor, a bundle of loose bones held together by his clothes.

It had made enough noise to draw the attention of his partner, whom I could hear in the bathroom next door.

"Arnold, what the hell was that?"

Arnold, being in no condition to answer, said nothing. The man in the bath emerged cautiously into the hall. He could see Arnold's fallen body from there. I waited behind the bedroom door for him to come in for a better look, only the guy was too wise to try that one. He crossed the hall to the top of the stairs and called down.

"Chaven, something's wrong."

Chaven's voice, familiar to me, answered, "Like what?"

"I dunno, but Arnold's out cold. The boss said to watch for anything weird and this is it."

I expected a derisive reply but was disappointed. "Okay, come down."

"But what about Arnold?"

"Come down, *now*."

He did.

Shit.

It meant they knew more than what was good for me.

Their conversation drifted up from the foot of the stairs.

"What happened, Tinny?" Chaven asked.

"I dunno. I hear a thump and look in one of the bedrooms and Arnold's lying on the floor there."

"Out or croaked?"

"Jeez, I dunno. I din' like the feel of things so I stayed out."

"All right, we'll check on it together. You two stay back and cover us."

There was some shuffling followed by floorboard creaks as Chaven and Tinny slowly came up the stairs. I could have played more games, taking them out one at a time, but not knowing what had happened to Escott left me with a need to force the issue.

"Stop there, Chaven," I called from my room before he was halfway up. I made it sound as if I had a gun. I abruptly realized I did, since Arnold was sure to be carrying one.

The floor creaks ended. "Fleming?" Chaven's tone held equal amounts of caution and doubt.

"Yeah, and I've got your boy, so let's talk." I dug at Arnold's inert body, looking for the kind of argument that would be sure to work against these jerks.

Chaven used those few seconds to regain his balance, recovering too fast for my peace of mind. "Okay by me. Come out where I can see you."

"Sure." Maybe the ready answer surprised him since anyone else in my position would have been leery of getting his head blown off. But I finally emerged—holding the unconscious Arnold in front of me. Bullets can't kill me, but it hurts like hell to get shot, so I was only taking sensible precautions. I was also holding the gun I'd just salvaged.

Unimpressed, Chaven steadied his revolver on me, eye level. The sharp lines of his body and the set of his thin, hard face told me he was more than ready to use it. From ten feet away he wasn't about to miss. It flashed through my mind that I ought to go ahead and let him shoot since faking my death might get them off my back for a while.

Of course, Escott would then be stuck with them . . . if they hadn't gotten to them already.

Neither of our guns had gone off in the last five seconds but that could change if I even blinked wrong. I kept still and kept quiet. By letting Chaven be the first to speak it would give him the illusion that he was in control of things.

Tinny spoiled it by trying to be helpful. "I can get him from here." He was on the stair just behind Chaven.

"So can I. Lay off." Chaven never once looked away. "The bracelet," he said to me in the same annoyed tone.

"It's not here," I lied.

"Go get it."

"When you and your boys leave."

He had a sense of humor, if the noise he made was a laugh. "We go when I get the bracelet."

"What do I get?"

He thought about it for only a second. "Another chance to blow town."

"Like hell."

"Take it or die."

"Your boss has already decided that. Tell me another one."

"We can make it easy or hard, Fleming."

"You can't do anything to me or you lose the bracelet. Does Kyler think my hide's worth losing fifteen grand over?"

"You're worth nothing to him." But he was just talking to get the last word in and to think some more. "Besides, there's still your partner."

"Except he doesn't know where it is."

"He'll know, all right. He's too careful not to know."

"Then why don't you ask him?"

"With you here I don't have to. Now hand it over."

So Escott had managed to get away in time. They wouldn't have bothered ripping the place apart if they'd had him to question . . . unless they'd made a mistake and killed him outright. If they had, then none of them were leaving this house alive.

"Okay, but everybody get back. Crowds make me nervous."

At an invisible signal from Chaven, Tinny and the other two thugs retreated down the stairs to the landing. I could just see them through the banister. They still had their guns out and pointed in my general direction.

I hefted Arnold a little higher and took a step forward. Chaven didn't seem to notice that holding up all that extra weight with one arm wasn't bothering me much. He backed off a pace, but to the side, not down the stairs. His mind was on other things, then. We locked eyes at the same moment of realization, only I was just an instant faster as I pushed Arnold straight at him and ducked.

Chaven's gun roared out in the confined space of the upper hall. He snarled something and tried to bring the muzzle down, but Arnold was in his way long enough for me to get my feet set and launch toward him. For a few seconds it was all blind pawing, thick coats, and elbows, then I took a chance opening and clobbered Chaven in the head with the side of Arnold's gun. He stopped moving. I tore the revolver from his hand.

Tinny and his two chums came up out of nowhere. I shoved a foot into Tinny's gut. He grabbed at it, dragging me free of Chaven, but lost his balance and fell backward, his arms suddenly wide. One chum tried to catch him at the same time the second tried to get out of the way and they all tripped each other and took a partial roll down the stairs. By the time they got themselves pulled together, I was up again and looking like William S. Hart with a borrowed gun in each fist.

I suddenly had their full attention. Except for myself, everyone was breathing hard and red in the face, some more than others, as they realized I had them square.

"You! Put it on the landing."

Tinny knew I was talking about his gun without having to ask, which made him a bright boy. He did as he was told, and so did the others when it was their turn. I kicked everything through the open door into my room.

Chaven began to groan and push at Arnold as he came around. He snapped abruptly awake and glared. I expected him to start cursing once he took in the altered situation, but nothing came out. The look on his face and especially in his cold, stony eyes was eloquent enough. We both knew what we thought of each other.

"You stand up slow," I said, and he followed my directions carefully. He lifted one hand to check where I'd hit him. His fingers came away with a little red on them.

"Yeah," he said, as though agreeing with some inner voice.

I waved a muzzle at Arnold. "Get him. Everyone downstairs."

They got him, struggling clumsily with his uncooperative body. Chaven let the others work while he watched me, no doubt making plans on what to do at our next meeting.

I herded them through the kitchen and out the door. They slow-marched to the Cadillac and got in. Chaven was the driver; I made him wait until the others were settled.

"You can tell Kyler that I got his message about the bracelet."

"I'll do that, Fleming."

"You can also say that I want a better deal before I hand it over."

"What kind of deal?"

"I'll talk that over with Kyler. Have him call me here. The number's in the book."

That was the end of our business for tonight. I hoped. He got in the car and quietly drove away with the search party. He was visibly frustrated and anyone else might have expressed it in their driving, but not Chaven. He could have been out on a Sunday jaunt with his granny for all the care he took over signals and speed. Maybe he wasn't in such a hurry to return to his boss empty-handed.

Trotting back to the house, I checked the place from the attic on down. It was still a wreck, but unoccupied. The last spot I checked, primarily because it was so well hidden, was the walled-off section of the basement where I slept during the day. I disappeared, flowed through the familiar pattern of bricks to the alcove beyond, and re-formed.

The small room was in total darkness. My night vision is excellent except in those rare spots protected from all outside light, like here in my private sanctum. I usually left the lamp over my desk on for that reason, but now it was off. The complete claustrophobic blackness pressed on me as it would anyone else, and I instinctively started to back out again when a low, soft sound stopped me. A heartbeat.

"Charles?"

"Jack . . . thank God you're all right." It came out in a rush along with his pent-up breath.

With a click, the small light over the desk flashed to life. I winced and squinted painfully against the sudden brightness until my eyes adjusted. Escott was sitting in my work chair with my bathrobe draped over his clothes and a relieved expression on his bony face.

"You've been down here the whole time?"

He gave me a "what do you think" shrug and put the .38 he was holding back in his pants pocket.

"And with no light?"

"Out of necessity, I fear. It seemed preferable not to give them a lighted target if they chanced to find me."

Set in the ceiling above the folding bed was a trapdoor, visible on this side, but only a normal part of the kitchen furnishings on the other. It was centered under the old oak dining table and covered by a tacked-down throw rug. To unlock it, you had to open one of the cabinet doors back all the way. Once lowered, the trap automatically relocked. Escott had a penchant for such devices and the talent to design and construct them. Not for the first time was I glad that he'd indulged the theatrical side of his nature.

"You couldn't duck out of the house?" Given the choice of running or hiding in a dead-end bolt hole, I knew what my preference would have been.

"With them coming in both doors I was caught in a classic pincers movement. As it was, I barely made it down here. I'd just time to slide under the table and drop through the trap. It slammed down over me as they broke open the back door, then I had a few bad minutes waiting to learn if they'd seen or heard any of it. For a while I was beginning to feel altogether too close in kinship with the unfortunate fish trapped in a barrel."

"I see what you mean."

He glanced at his watch. "Heavens, I would have sworn that more time had passed than this."

"It was long enough for them to tear the place apart."

"Looking for that bracelet, no doubt."

"And not finding it. You put it in the safe, then?"

"I didn't have it."

"But I gave it to you last night." A little wave of cold puzzlement washed over me.

"And I returned it to you before I had to leave." He held up his hand as I started to object. He took off the robe and pulled a black velvet bag from one of the pockets. A fortune in diamonds and rubies linked together by bright platinum spilled out and twined around his long fingers.

"Jeez, I don't remember." Then again, I really didn't want to remember. Escott had mentioned that I'd been in pretty bad shape and I was ready to take him at his word and leave it at that, but the sight of the bracelet started to bring things to the surface. I recalled its weight in my own hand and the way the light made the rubies look like fresh blood. A whole new tremor ran up my spine. Escott noticed and slipped the thing back in its bag.

"I'm not in the habit of searching pockets that do not concern me, but when I borrowed this for protection, I couldn't help but find it." He hung the robe over the back of the chair.

"Protection?"

"Yes. Despite its proximity to the furnace, this . . . ah . . . haven of yours was a bit chilly for me."

"Is it?" Since my change I'd developed a certain indifference against most temperature extremes. "Guess I better get you out of here."

"I was rather hoping you'd say that. Would you object if I bought a folding ladder to store here against any future emergencies of a similar nature? Just in case I must make an unassisted exit."

I told him to go right ahead, then vanished to float up to the kitchen. I pushed the cabinet door back until the catch clicked, then hauled up the trap. The big table had to be shoved to one side this time to give us both room to work. Escott reached high and I was just able to grasp his wrist and pull him out.

"Good heavens," he said the second his head cleared the floor. It was for the mess he saw, not the acrobatics.

He stood, his shoes crunching against a sea of spilled sugar, salt, coffee grounds, and milk. He walked slowly into the dining room and surveyed the broken liquor cabinet, the scattered bottles and glasses. He went on to the front parlor to find the overturned radio, tumbled furniture, and slashed cushions. I followed him upstairs, where the mess was worse. Drawers had been dumped, their contents pawed through. The books and souvenirs in his library/study were torn from the shelves. The overwhelming sick rage at the invasion hit me all over again; I could only imagine what Escott felt.

He was an extremely neat and organized man; Kyler's people couldn't have picked a better way to get him angry. He didn't show it much, only by the hardening of his eyes and the knife-edge thinning of his mouth.

"I'm sorry, Charles."

"Hardly your fault, old man. Looking at this, I can get an idea of what they might have done to me had I not been able to drop out of sight in time."

"I should have seen this coming. I could have stuck around and stopped all this."

He shook his head. "I wouldn't worry about it now. One cannot anticipate everything, otherwise life would be very dull, indeed. What *did* inspire you to return?"

I told him about the tail, how I'd slipped it, and what had happened when I found Chaven's party.

"You took care of all five of them? And by yourself?"

"With some help from Sam Colt." I pulled the guns I'd taken from my coat pockets. "There's more in there." I nodded in the direction of my room. That's when he laughed, actually laughed, out loud.

"I could almost wish to be a fly on the wall when Kyler questions his henchmen on this bit of business."

"They'll be back."

"I don't doubt it. I suppose he'll be calling any time now, unless he decides to forgo negotiations altogether after this. What will you say to him?"

"I'm still working on it, but I figure if he wants the bracelet this bad maybe we should give it to him."

"And you think you can convince him to leave us alone?"

I shrugged. "Unless you've got any better ideas?"

"Not at the moment, no. I see that surprises you."

"I thought you had a plan to plant it on Kyler and then call the cops down on him."

"Initially, yes, but I've had time to think it out. There's little chance of successfully pulling that off without drawing undue legal attention to ourselves. While I may be able to weather such a storm, you are ill suited to spending any time in jail."

"You mean you can't just make an anonymous call?"

"The authorities in this city would require something more than that to justify issuing a search warrant against someone in Kyler's position. Nor can I really approach Lieutenant Blair on this. He's far too intelligent. If either of us turn up waving that bracelet about . . . well, I should not care to dwell on the consequences. And if Kyler took it into his head to talk, even a partial telling of the truth of what happened last night would place us in a terribly precarious position."

"What do you call this? We're already there, if not with the law, then with Kyler."

Our problem was the fact that one of Kyler's lieutenants had murdered a girl and that I, in turn, had murdered him. It wouldn't take much for Kyler to twist the events around to suit himself, and he had enough power and influence to get away

with it. At the very least, Escott would lose his license and probably serve hard time for his part in things. On the other end,
Kyler could probably save himself a lot of trouble by having
Escott just disappear like too many other people before him. At
this time of year Lake Michigan made for an awfully damned
cold grave.

"You might want to pack some stuff," I said.

"And run?"

"If I can't make a deal with him we're both up shit creek."

He nodded in reluctant agreement. He'd had plenty of time to
think things through sitting in the darkness. "We might require
a bit of breathing space before our next move," he admitted.

I started to ask him what he had in mind, but let that one lie
for the time being. Neither of us could really do or plan anything until we heard from Kyler.

The call came about thirty minutes later. I was in the kitchen
sweeping up some of the mess and answered.

I'd been expecting Kyler, but Chaven was on the other end of
the line.

"Get a pencil," he snarled.

Escott always kept one close to the phone along with some
paper. I snapped it up in time to write out the phone number
Chaven dictated to me.

"You call there exactly at eleven o'clock, y'hear?"

"I hear."

He slammed down his receiver, but I'd been ready for that and
was holding my earpiece a safe distance away.

Escott had come downstairs to listen to my side of the conversation. I showed him the number. "Probably to a public
box," he commented.

"Yeah?"

"Lieutenant Blair is a remarkably efficient investigator; perhaps Kyler is worried about wiretaps on his lines in connection
with last night's deaths. If so, then this is one call that neither of
you will want to have overheard."

"Or traced. Think I better do the same thing. Just in case."

"And from another neighborhood," he added.

Chaven's phone call only traded one kind of waiting for another. Having a specific deadline to look forward to was slightly
less nerve-racking, but in some ways it was worse. My concen-

tration for even the simple task of sweeping up the kitchen was shot all to hell; mostly I moped around and peered out the windows. For a while I thought the clock was broken, but it matched my wristwatch minute for minute. Escott stayed busy upstairs. I wasn't sure if it was his way of handling the wait or if he was only avoiding my twitchy restlessness.

At one point I found myself dialing the number to the Top Hat Club to ask for Miss Smythe. I hung up on the first ring. Bobbi would be in the middle of one of her sets by now and the management might take a dim view of the interruption. Besides, what could I say to her that wouldn't leave her alarmed and worried?

She still didn't know that I'd almost died last night, permanently and horribly. She also didn't know how I'd gone over the edge and what had happened when I struck bottom. I could still feel the gun jump in my hand and see the blinding flash. It didn't quite blot out the man's last scream or the look on his face.

No regrets, remember?

Yeah, sure. Easy to say, hard to do. I was coming to realize that it wasn't so much that I had killed, but that I'd been out of control at the time. I was caught up in the not unreasonable worry that it could happen again.

Damn the bracelet. Damn everything and all its relatives.

I grabbed the broom and made an effort to finish the job. By ten-thirty the floor was clean of every grain and speck, but I was still sweeping for something to do. The mindless activity kept me from thinking so much. My thoughts weren't exactly comfortable.

Escott wanted to come along and I had no objections to offer, especially since he volunteered the use of his Nash. The big car was armored, with an engine powerful enough to match anything Kyler had. Much safer than the Buick.

Exactly at eleven, in an outdoor booth about two miles from home, I dialed in the last number Chaven had dictated to me.

"What do you want?" No introductions, no preamble. Kyler knew I'd recognize his voice.

"A truce."

"Terms." He made it a statement, not a question.

"You and your people leave me and all my friends alone. We do the same for you. For that, you get the item you want."

"What else?"

This seemed too easy, but I plowed ahead. "Your word on it."

"When?"

"As soon as possible. Tonight."

A pause from his end. In the background I heard muffled traffic noises, indicating that Escott had been right; Kyler was also
in a public booth. For all I knew, we could be only blocks apart.
"All right," he finally said. "And my word that we leave you
and your friends alone."

"Good enough."

"Double-cross me and all bets are off."

"Okay."

"Come to the warehouse at midnight."

I covered the mouthpiece with one hand and hissed at Escott,
who was just outside. "He wants to meet at the warehouse."

"Ask him why."

"Why the warehouse?" I said to Kyler.

"It's known to both of us. You'll be safe from me there. My
word on that, also. Agreed?"

I didn't like it, but said yes. He hung up quietly, as though
he'd eased a finger over the hook. The usual clicks of discon-
nection followed by the dial tone came a moment later.

"Not one for wasting words, is he?" Escott commented as I
pried myself from the cramped booth.

"Yeah. And he was awfully damn cooperative. It makes me
wonder what I just missed."

"He does seem to have you on the defensive. Why is that?"

"Why are people afraid of snakes?"

With no better way to spend the time, we went back home
again. Escott hung his coat on the hall tree and disappeared for
a moment, returning with a crumpled map of the city in one
hand. I followed him to the kitchen, where he spread it flat on
the table.

"I know where the place is," I said.

"As do I, but it is the surrounding area that requires my attention."

"You want to come along again, huh?"

"I have a more than casual interest in the outcome of this
business."

A half dozen objections ran through my brain in as many seconds. Escott would have already thought of them all and then

some and have counterarguments for each. "Okay, but I go in alone. If things go wrong, I'll need you in reserve to get us out of there."

We bent over the map. Escott was better at making sense of all the thin black lines and tiny letters and picked out a likely place to park. By eleven forty-five we were there. He rolled to a smooth stop on a side street about a quarter mile from the International Freshwater Transport warehouse.

"Good enough," I said.

"Not quite," he cautioned, and shifted into reverse. The car was now in an angle of shadow created by one of the many tall, ugly buildings in the area.

"You won't be able to see anything now." The high walls blocked all but a narrow view of the main street leading to the warehouse.

"Then, hopefully, they won't be able to see me."

Heavy winter silence closed hard upon us when he cut the motor. Each little tick it made while cooling down sounded like a firecracker to my sensitive ears.

"Have you a gun?" he asked.

"I've got the one I took from Chaven. I'm not planning to do anything with it, but can figure on a search; it'd be a shame not to give them something to find."

"And if anything should go awry?" His tone was matter-of-fact, but still expressed a reasonable concern.

I shrugged a little. "If I'm not back by half past, then assume something's fishy, find a hole, and pull it in after you. Same thing if it looks like you've been spotted. Take off and stay away from the house and the office. If that happens and we get separated, I'll leave a message with your answering service."

"Presuming that you are in a condition to do so," he muttered. He wanted to go along, but we both knew that on my own I stood a better chance of bringing it off and getting out with a whole skin. There wasn't much they could do to me, and, if necessary, I could always vanish.

"I'll be careful."

Escott handed me the black velvet bag. I checked the contents out of nerves rather than any lack of trust and shoved it deep into a pocket.

"Good luck," he said.

I got out, shut the door, and started walking.

2

MY RUBBER-SOLED shoes made soft padding noises on the pavement as I covered the quarter-mile distance in short order. I was dressed to blend in with the neighborhood and the night with dark pants, shirt, no tie, and an old pea jacket borrowed from Escott's disguise closet. A cloth cap was pulled low over my forehead and I'd wrapped a wool muffler several times around my face and neck. Since winter had set in I'd found it a necessary item to conceal the fact that I only breathed while talking. Most people probably wouldn't notice what was missing on cold, damp days, namely the usual dragon's puff of vapor, but why take chances?

This kind of worry coming from a man about to walk into a lion's den. Correction: snake pit. Kyler was anything but warm-blooded.

I got within a block of my destination without seeing anything worth notice. One car went by, but I avoided it by slipping into a deep doorway until it was long gone. At the cross street I cut to the left, away from the river, then right at the next corner. Opposite the IFT warehouse was yet another large building and I was now walking behind it. The place had a back entrance for the heavy trucks; I hopped up on the loading platform and went straight for the nearest door.

It was locked, but I vanished and went inside anyway. My eyes adjusted quickly to the large dim interior once I re-formed. I took an experimental sniff of the place, catching the good clean smell of cut wood. Huge stacks of lumber loomed around me. So far, so good, as long as none of it avalanched down on my tender skull. I took great care not to bump into anything.

I crossed all the way to the front of the place but stood well back from the windows. They gave me an adequate, if somewhat grimy, view of the IFT warehouse across the street.

It looked empty. No cars were parked anywhere near the place and even the outside light over the office door was off. I could just make out the glint of a new hasp and padlock, probably installed by the cops to keep people away from the scene of last night's crimes. Perhaps Kyler planned to make our exchange in the street.

Something snuffled and growled behind me. Claws clicked over the bare concrete floor. Turning, I immediately spotted a large pair of glowing green eyes winking balefully in the faint light from the windows. They were spaced very far apart. Below them was an endless row of shark's teeth, and from a vast chest came a continuous rumbling like an extra-large diesel engine. That's about all I really noticed about the dog in the half second that passed before it charged.

I suppose I could have handled it, could have used my special influence to calm it down and make friends, but logical, friendly ideas like that are for people with the time to think them up. When a mastiff the size of a calf with a mouth like the Grand Canyon comes barreling down on you, the first thing you really want to do is try to get out of its way. My abrupt disappearance was more of a knee-jerk reaction than a planned escape, but whatever works.

The thing bored through the space where I had once been solid and I heard a muffled crash as it slammed into the front wall. The sound it made was more irritation than pain as it recovered from the shock and turned. It yelped in sudden confusion when it butted into me again and sniffed frantically, trying to pin me down. Its claws dug at the empty patch of concrete where I had stood, gouging up chunks of it for all I could tell; the damn thing was big enough.

I'm a dog lover, but know when I'm outnumbered. Rather than argue with it, I floated up until I bumped into a scaffolding about ten feet overhead, and sieved through. It was the floor to an upper office I'd noticed on my way in and had the advantage of putting a locked door between me and the dog. The monster was still furiously investigating below as I became solid by slow degrees and in absolute silence.

By cautiously craning my neck I had the same view of the warehouse, just a slightly different angle, and could see more of the street. The wait was more uncomfortable since I didn't want to move around much. The dog was the persistent type, and if it got a clue to my location it would certainly follow. I didn't trust the door all that much, or the dog to be quiet about trying to break through to get to me.

With that comforting thought, I stood very still, indeed, and used my eyes and ears. The walls muffled my hearing somewhat, but some motor noises came to me. The vast dark bulk of the Chicago River supported some slow boat traffic, and thanks to my new perch I was able to see some of it. A couple of boats chugged lazily past and I did not envy their crews having to work on a cold night and at such a late hour. They reminded me that Kyler also had a boat and might even use it for his transportation, so I divided my watch between the street and the river.

At five to midnight I saw, but did not hear, Kyler's two Cadillacs pull up before the warehouse. The motors were very finely tuned; a cat's purr would have been loud by comparison. They cut the lights and I counted ten men as they emerged and crowded by the door. The cars blocked a lot of my view and I couldn't pick Kyler from the group. There was a brief pause as they did something to the padlock, then the door opened and they filed inside. So much for the police sealing the place off.

The outside light came on, then an inside one. Silhouettes bumped and thinned out as the men trooped through the office into the warehouse proper. I hadn't noticed any weapons, but all their lethal hardware would be easily concealed by their long, heavy coats. Kyler wasn't going to take any chances with me if he could help it. Maybe I should have felt flattered by all the preparations, but it was an honor I'd just as soon skip.

I pulled on a pair of gloves and checked the velvet bag again. The bracelet glinted, not evil in itself, but certainly an inspiration and a focus for the darkness in all of us. I polished it a little and hoped that it would be enough to buy me and Escott some freedom and peace.

Drifting down through the floor, I sailed past the dog, who was stubbornly on guard at the spot where it had last seen me. It whined once in puzzlement, but stayed put. I floated on a straight course between the stacks of lumber, brushed against the back wall, and was out again. It was just on midnight when I walked around the building and emerged onto the street.

No one seemed to be hanging around outside, which struck me as odd since Kyler was the cautious type. They were probably hiding somewhere, then. Yet another comforting thought.

The front of the warehouse was a blank, giving no clue to what was going on inside. Like the bracelet, it could be innocent or sinister. In my present mood I knew which one to pick. I walked slowly to the door and opened it. The mechanism sounded unnaturally loud to my keyed-up senses.

No one leaped out at me. So far, so good, again. Two hard-looking men I did not know stared back at me. One stood up from his seat on the desk, the other continued to lean a little too casually against a file cabinet. I kept the muffler in place. The fewer people who saw my mug, the better.

Neither of them moved. It was like a zoo when you walk past the exhibit with the big cats. You know the bars will keep them in place, but there's always that shiver of uncertainty in the back of your mind that they just might not be up to the job. The only restraints here were the invisible ones of Kyler's word.

I went through the inner door into the warehouse. The lights were on, but I was very aware of all the men I couldn't see. At least eight of them were lurking out there among the stacks of crates. One of them stepped into my line of sight. He said nothing as I moved forward. He waited for me and became my escort, leading me deeper into the building.

The line of crates ended, leaving free an open space, or it would have been free except for the ropes the police had left behind. Off to one side an abstract chalk design sprawled at the base of a crate. In the middle, near a closed trapdoor that led down to a river landing, was another. The latter was more recognizably the outline of a man's body, like a flat ghost. Next to the head was a spray of dark stain. In my mind I could still smell the cordite and blood.

I tore my eyes from the memory and made myself look at the man standing in the center of it all. Vaughn Kyler regarded me with equal amounts of tension and expectation.

He was in better shape than when I'd last seen him. The cut on his forehead had been neatly patched over, and either the vicuna coat had been cleaned or he was wearing a new one.

Chaven stood next to him, arms hanging free, his lean form all but vibrating from unspent energy. His forced retreat earlier had left him with a serious grudge against me.

The next few steps were difficult. The warehouse was partially built out over the river and the force of the free-running water below made an invisible but effective barrier to someone with my special condition. It was worry making. Kyler had warned his men earlier to beware of anything unusual when they'd searched the house. I wondered if he had chosen this spot because he'd sensed this weakness in me and wanted to test it further. I pushed hard against the opposing press of the water and hoped that it wasn't too obvious. Once past the first yard or so, it wasn't so bad, except for all my back hairs standing at attention.

Kyler, Chaven, and the guy next to me—now, where were the other five? Two of them closed ranks about twenty feet behind us. Another stood off to the left, partially hidden by some loading equipment. The two remaining were to the right, concealed by crates.

I kept going until only a few feet separated me from Kyler. From the very first, he'd given me the panicky creeps, and time had not mitigated that reaction. He looked ordinary, just another businessman nearing his fifties in well-dressed affluence. I was beginning to realize that it was the absolute *stillness* of the man's manner that made me think of poisonous reptiles, that and his cold, unblinking eyes.

"You bring it?" His voice matched his eyes, cold.

I nodded. My mouth was dry. He waited for me to make the next move. I slowly pulled the black bag from my pocket and held it high. "Straight deal?" I whispered, hardly able to work up enough spit to talk.

"Let's see it first."

Right. Any promise he might give at this point was dependent on his taking delivery of the thing, and we were both very aware of it. I opened the bag and turned it over. The bracelet flowed and twined around my fingers, catching the distant lights, turning them into silver and red sparks.

It was his turn to nod and he held out his hand to take it. If anything was to happen to me it would be now. I was expecting either gunfire or a guarantee, war or peace, when I turned it over; anything except what did happen. The only warning I got

was Chaven's mouth curling into a nervous twitch of a smile as
the bracelet finally slithered into Kyler's possession.

A blinding explosion of white light froze everything in place
for that instant. It came from the left, from the guy by the loading equipment. It was incongruous, yet horribly familiar to
someone with my journalistic background. My eyes seemed to
take an age to recover, but I didn't have to see to know that he
was slotting in another film plate for a second photo. He
knocked the spent bulb free of the flash. As if in slow motion, it
spun to the floor, scattering into a hundred glass slivers as it
smashed against the scarred wood. The pop it made on impact
acted like a signal for everyone to close in. The man next to me
grabbed my arm.

They'd caught me flat-footed with this one. My instinct to
vanish nearly took me out of things as it had before with the
guard dog. I had to ice that for the moment, what with Kyler and
all his men looking on. The two behind us crowded in and the
other two on the right finally emerged from hiding. The me-
dium tall one in the leather coat wore his hat at a dapper angle
over his dandy handsome face. His unexpected presence here
only added to my shock.

The deal was off, but then it had never really been on. It was
a trap. Not Kyler's, though . . . the cops'.

The man walking toward me was Lieutenant Blair.

"C'mon," he said to the one holding me. "Let's have a look at
him."

Oh, *shit*.

The muffler was still around my face. He hadn't recognized
me and things were going to stay that way if I could help it. I
savagely shook off the guy's grip and bolted to the left. The
photographer was encumbered by the camera, but tried to block
me long enough to hold for his pals. I bowled past him and tore
to the right. I absolutely had to get out of sight, and my best
hope was to circle around to the stacks.

They were wise to that one. Blair and another man outflanked
me, the latter drawing his gun and ordering me to stop. I doubled back, making a feint for a side door on the other end. The
photographer left his camera and tried to tackle me. I caught
him before we both went off balance and swung him around
sharply. He lost his footing and stumbled, blocking Blair's rush

for a few precious seconds. I took the opening only to face two more men drawing their guns.

Cutting between them was not the best option, but the only one left. I was moving too fast to stop, anyway. A gun went off, probably by accident. I felt nothing and remained solid. Someone cursed and caught my arm again. I punched an elbow in his direction and got free. Blair shouted something, but I lost it as I gained the narrow opening between two long lines of crates. I was suddenly free of the uncomfortable pressure of the water below us.

At the far end and coming up quickly was one of the guys from the front office. Halfway along, he paused to pull out his gun and level it. Behind me, Blair and the others paused as well, abruptly aware that they were in each other's line of fire.

The crates stacked on either side were about four feet square, graduating to smaller ones on top like giant building blocks. I latched onto a narrow edge and heaved upward with desperation-inspired agility. Blair and his men suddenly closed in. One of them just missed grabbing my foot as I lurched up to the next tier. Blair ordered someone to run around to the other side of the stack to head me off.

I wasn't quite sure how, but I made it to the top of the wooden mountain about twenty-five dizzy feet up. A little belatedly, I remembered my fear of heights as I teetered on my uncertain perch. Blair yelled, telling me to come back before I got hurt. He stopped a man from following; evidently they were all cops except for Chaven and Kyler.

They were standing well back from the activity. Kyler had me in full view, still wearing a look of expectation on his normally blank face. He'd set me up good, and now I knew why.

Blair's voice cut through my disgust with the situation, reminding me that I had to keep moving. Fine, except that I was now limited to two directions, unless you wanted to count a sudden drop as a third. Cops were now on both sides of the stack, ready to nail what was left if that happened.

Fortunately, the boxes up here were small enough to be useful, as I discovered when I tipped one over and sent it crashing. The men scattered hastily as the thing tumbled down. Metal parts, shards of wood, and excelsior hit the floor like a bomb. Another gun went off—I couldn't tell from which side—and I ducked in reflex. Before he could get a second shot, I dropped

two more boxes, one left, the other right, and then plastered myself flat. With everyone rushing to get out of the way I figured
they'd be too busy to notice my disappearance. I also hoped that
the angle and height of the intervening crates would help block
Kyler's view of the stunt.

Two more random shots went off before Blair called for a
stop, followed by a long, confused pause as they tried to locate
me. I held my place, and figuratively held my breath, waiting
them out. Confusion gave way to frustration, and a man was
boosted up on the stacks for a look around. I flowed well away
from any chance contact and let them get on with the search.
After a time I eased my way down to the floor and tried to make
sense of their shouts and rushing around.

"Where the hell is he?" was the most frequently repeated
phrase. No one had an answer to it, either. Blair sent men to
cover all the exits and to check the street. The rest circled and
recircled the place. After several minutes of futile combing they
began to realize they'd been skunked.

Blair shouted a question at Kyler. Between the distorting
echoes and the natural muffling caused by my unnatural state I
could hardly make it out, and neither could Kyler.

"What?" he called back.

I zeroed in on Blair's voice. "I said, did he get past you?" He
was striding toward Kyler. I froze onto him and held tight, letting him carry me along. With his unknowing help I was able to
move out over the water again. Despite the heavy leather coat,
he began to shiver.

"We didn't see anything," Kyler answered. I hoped that he
was telling the truth.

"If you're trying a double cross, you may regret it."

"Lieutenant, I was only doing my civic duty. As you can see,
we got the bracelet back for you and I understand that it is a crucial piece of evidence in the case you are working on. This lunatic has killed twice, one of them a close friend and associate of
mine. I have told you before how much I want to bring this man
to justice; I think my cooperation tonight in informing your department of this meeting proves my sincerity."

"And were you able to identify him, then?"

Kyler let the pause drag out and I moaned inwardly.

"Were you?"

"I regret to say that I did not recognize the man," was his bland reply.

Now, what the hell was he up to?

"You're certain of that?"

"Yes, Lieutenant. He was wrapped up in that muffler, but I am positive that if I'd had any previous contact with him, I would have remembered it. I have a very good head for names and faces, you know."

Blair had nothing to say to that and called for a report from his men. The answers were all negative. He walked off to join them. I hung back to eavesdrop on Kyler.

"Where do you think he went?" Chaven asked him in a low voice.

"Who knows? He might still be here."

"This is crazy, Vaughn."

"But you saw what happened."

"I saw a guy go up who hasn't come down yet. What's with him? How does he do it?"

"I'm working that out. Are the boys in place?"

"Probably. Tinny was on his way just as the cops arrived for us. His girl's practically—"

"Shut up," said Kyler, not raising his voice, but still managing to express urgency.

As Escott sometimes said, *bloody hell.* I whipped away from them and threaded between the stacks and occasional cop, feeling my way toward the front. It was like blind man's bluff, except the goal was to avoid running into people.

I found the office almost by accident when I picked up half of a phone conversation. Blair was calling for reinforcements and giving out a description of me for the prowl cars in the area. He got the height and weight right and had noticed the clothes in detail, right down to the brown-and-blue stripe pattern on the muffler. Thank God he hadn't gotten a look at my face.

I slipped through the front door and bore left, moving fast over the flat plain of the street, using the curb as a guide. Whenever it curved sharply, it meant a corner, and I'd have to strike out for the other side and hope to hold a straight line. A car roared toward the warehouse; the buffet of wind from its passage threw me briefly off course.

A partial re-forming gave me fresh bearings and some much-needed orientation. I hadn't come as far as I thought and I was running out of time. Escott wouldn't wait forever and sooner or later a patrolman might pull up to ask him awkward questions. I dropped out of reality and sped along more recklessly than before, practically flying over the pavement.

The next time I went solid, I was within yards of his corner. Escott stood in a doorway covering the street and saw me melt out of nowhere.

"We're up shit creek," I said, slowing only a little. "Get the car in gear. We have to get to the Top Hat right away."

"Good lord, they're after Miss Smythe?" He darted around to the driver's side and threw himself in. I wrenched open the passenger door and chafed at the pause needed to start the motor.

"Something I heard from Chaven. Dammit, I thought she'd be safe from all this."

"No doubt Kyler has some excellent sources of information and an instinct for finding an opponent's vulnerable points," he said as he shifted and hit the gas.

"Hurry, but be careful. The cops are looking for me now." I tore off the cap and telltale muffler and dropped them behind the seat.

"What's happened?"

While he negotiated a route out of the district, I filled him in on things. "I guess you could say he kept his word; he didn't come after me, he only had to step aside and let Blair do the work."

"And yet he did not give you away to him."

"I think that whole fiasco was a test to see what I'd do when cornered. In one move he's gotten himself off the suspect list for the murders, shifted it onto someone else, and learned that much more about what I can do. He's probably figured there's no way to get a direct hold on me, so he'll try to get to Bobbi instead."

"Which indicates that he must want something of you."

"He wants me out of the way. Anybody who can do what I do is too dangerous to have loose. I'd just like to know what he meant about 'working that out.' "

"Perhaps he's researching the folklore section of the local library."

· "Oh, great." I had a nightmare vision of Chicago's underworld searching for me, armed with crosses and draped in garlands of fresh garlic. It was just as well those items only worked at the movies. On the other hand, a hammer and stake were also part of the vampire hunter's traditional arsenal, and I knew from experience just how terribly effective *those* were.

"What about the photograph?" he asked.

I shrugged. "I'm not even sure I'll show up on the plate, but first things first."

"Absolutely," he murmured, concentrating on his driving. He beat through a couple of stop signals while I kept an eye out for patrol cars. The street traffic was mercifully light at this hour, but it still seemed to take a long time to get there.

It was the middle of the week, but the place had a good crowd if we could tell anything by the number of cars in the parking lot. Neon lights spelled out the name of the club against the clear sky and a glowing red top hat danced endlessly from side to side below them. Both caused confusing reflections on the windows of the cars, making it difficult to tell if any were occupied.

"I'll go check things inside," said Escott as he found a place to park. I started to object, but was interrupted. "They won't let you past the door dressed like that," he pointed out.

He was right and my regular clothes were inconveniently packed away in a bag in the car's trunk. We'd both prepared for the necessity of having to drop out of sight in case things went wrong.

"Besides, you could alarm the ones we're after if they should see you. Since they know what you look like, your sudden appearance could lead to an unfortunate incident."

"I'll do more than just alarm them," I growled, but saw the sense of things. I described Tinny as best I could. Escott took it in, then slipped out to go to the club. I got out on my side to make a more thorough search of the parking lot.

All I found were some courting couples in different cars who were generating enough personal heat to ignore the low outside temperature. They also ignored me, but then I was going out of my way to be quiet. I'd retrieved the cap and muffler from the back of the car and had wrapped up again. They linked me to the search Blair was conducting, but that was a few miles away, and I felt safe enough using them here. Nevertheless, I was quick to duck out of sight when a police car cruised past on its rounds.

A street ran behind the club and was where I usually parked

while waiting to pick up Bobbi when she was through for the night. The manager and a few other employees also parked there, so I was familiar with their cars. The Olds on the end close to the back entrance was new to the spot, though, and there were two men sitting inside.

Maybe it was the jackpot, but I'd have to be sure first. There was no percentage in committing mayhem against innocent citizens. I assumed a casual walk and paused in front of it. The light was bad for them, but I gave them a chance to notice me and made a point of returning the favor.

The one on the driver's side turned on the headlights. The harsh glare was probably meant to discourage me; understandable, since I was more or less dressed like a suspicious character. I shaded my eyes against it and moved out of the way. The lights cut and they laughed a little. I nodded back in a friendly way and slapped my pockets for a battered pack of cigarettes, pulling one out.

"Gotta match?" I called so they could hear me through the windows.

Neither of them answered. I walked up to tap the driver's door and repeated my question. His hat was pulled low, so I couldn't see much above his hard jaw line. He rolled the window down and told me to scram.

"Kyler sent me," I whispered.

He and his partner exchanged looks. "Who?" he asked.

"You heard me. He said to say the deal's off and to get out of here."

"I don't get it. You trying to make trouble?"

"Just trying to keep you out of it. Let the cops nail you if you want, it's no skin off my nose, but I wouldn't want the boss to think I didn't know how to listen to orders."

The driver frowned deeply and I wondered if he'd recognized me despite the muffler. By now I was fairly sure he was one of the mugs who had invaded the house. I was ready for a hostile response; instead, he leaned forward to start the car.

"What about Tinny and Chick?" he asked.

"They're leaving with me. It's safer."

He nodded once, shifted the gears, and pulled out of his slot. As soon as he turned into the main street, he hit the gas and didn't stop for as long as he was in earshot.

I gaped after them and indulged in a laugh of my own. This was almost too easy.

Escott would have the front of the club covered by now, but he might not have been able to invade the backstage area. I trotted up the steps to the rear door and slipped inside. A tall curtain blocked the audience's view of the utilitarian walls, but when the stage lights were on it was filmy enough to see through. I had a fine backseat for the floor show.

The band had just started up a bright and brassy fanfare, which brought on an abrupt burst of applause. I got a filtered view of Bobbi making her entrance for a novelty number. She was dressed like a feminized version of Frank Buck in white satin jodhpurs, matching bush shirt, patent leather riding boots, and a sequin-trimmed pith helmet. The explanation for the costume came when she launched into her rendition of "The Animal in Me." She charmed her way through the first chorus, skipped to one side of the stage, and pretended to hunt around for jungle dangers. As she returned, a line of tap dancers wearing tinsel grass skirts and strategic coconut shells followed.

They scattered across the stage to the delighted hoots from the audience and hammered out the number. A few bars later, the girls screamed and drew back in mock terror as a guy in a gorilla suit strutted out of the wings. He wore a white tie and collar and carried a walking stick. Bobbi sang more lyrics to the gorilla, then joined him in a little soft-shoe, hamming things up like crazy. The gorilla dropped to one knee to present her with a bouquet of fake flowers that magically appeared in his paw. Bobbi pantomimed a show of flattery, but decided to turn him down. The gorilla roared to his feet, grabbed Bobbi, and threw her over his shoulder. She gave out with another chorus from there as he carried her around the stage.

Just as it looked like the gorilla would run off with her, a second gorilla appeared in their way. This one wore an apron and carried a comically large rolling pin, which she used to threaten her "husband." He hastily put Bobbi down, mimed unconvincing innocence, and got bashed on the head for his trouble. While he was still reeling, his "wife" grabbed his ear and marched him offstage. Bobbi shrugged elaborately, then she and the dancers went into another chorus. She eventually made her own exit on a papier-mâché elephant pulled by an unseen member of the technical crew.

Even from my spot the show looked slick and full of fun. The applause didn't die down until she came back for a short reprise, sung from the back of the elephant. She made a final bow and rode away, waving and blowing kisses.

I couldn't hold still after that and worked my way around to her, arriving in time to watch her climb off the elephant by way of a ladder built into its upstage framework. The satin pants suited her admirably, especially from where I stood.

She was flushed and grinning, surrounded by the other girls for a brief moment until she caught a glimpse of me and stopped. I suddenly remembered to unwrap the muffler and her smile returned like a burst of light when recognition came. She threw her arms around me in a bear hug and I lifted her off the floor in delighted relief. All the pressures of the last few nights, all the fears, major and minor, dropped away from my over-loaded brain at this expression of her honest, uninhibited joy.

For what seemed like a long time I'd been wandering blind and lost in one of the darker corners of my mind. I held on to her, feeling the warmth of her spirit and body soaking into my own. Maybe we both felt it, since neither of us was in much of a hurry to let go of the other. I kissed the top of her silky blond head, working my way down to her lips. When she finally came up for air my mood had undergone a considerable shift. My upper canines had started to bud.

She noticed right away. "Do I always have this effect on you?"

That raised a smile out of me, albeit a closemouthed one. "I've missed you, baby." I caressed the soft skin of her neck. Now was hardly the time or place for that sort of thing, but soon, perhaps.

A couple of girls whooped and whistled at this unintentional show until the stage manager told them to clear off.

"You too, Bobbi," he said. "Get your boyfriend outta the way or it's both our hides."

Bobbi's boss was not sympathetic to visiting friends, no matter what the circumstances. I put her down again and she took my hand, leading the way to her dressing room.

"Not that I'm not glad to see you, but why so early, and what's with the getup?" she asked.

"Charles and I are working late and there's been some trouble."

"It's that bracelet thing, isn't it?"

"Yeah, sweetheart."

"What kind of trouble?"

"You ever hear of Vaughn Kyler?"

She stopped short, her big hazel eyes freezing onto mine. "Yes, I have. My God, Jack, what have you gotten into?"

"Nothing I can't get out of, but he knows about you and I'm here to keep anything from happening."

"Me? What's he want with me?"

I explained the situation in a few quick sentences. The blood drained out of her face and the grip of her hand got tighter. "I already got rid of two of them," I said, "but there are at least two more right here in the club."

"Where's Charles?"

"Out front, I guess, but I'm not leaving you to go looking. He can take care of himself. Whether your boss likes it or not, you've got a bodyguard for the time being."

"And who's going to bodyguard you?"

"I'm in no real danger; that's why Kyler's trying to get to you, honey. We've gotta come up with a safe place for you to stay until the shooting's over."

"You're not exactly inspiring me with confidence when you talk like that. Are you serious about shooting?"

"Very serious."

She shook her head, not in denial, but with stretched patience. "Okay. Let's sit down and see if we can figure out what to do next."

"In your dressing room, I want my back to a wall."

"I think that's where you'd rather have me," she said. The situation may have been threatening, but she was still flying high from the show, and detached her hand from mine to make a playful swat at my butt. I took what was dished out and tried to return the favor, but she just managed to dance out of the way in time. Laughing, we reached her dressing room door, but she sobered and stood back so I could look inside first.

It was well that I did. I was all but nose to nose with Tinny. He'd found another gun and it was ready in his hand. The mutual surprise froze us both for a second. Possibly as a distraction from the unpleasantness, I found myself noticing every detail of his plain face. Sometime tonight since the scuffle on the stairs at home, he'd acquired a road map of fresh scrapes. One of them was still oozing and I caught a whiff of the bloodsmell.

"Jack . . . ?" Bobbi couldn't see anything, but had picked up that something was wrong.

Tinny jammed the gun under my jaw. I decided not to move. He shifted a little, caught sight of Bobbi, and grinned. "Hold it there, cutie, or I make a mess."

Bobbi gasped once and held it, doing what she was told.

"Go get her, Chick," he ordered.

His big partner, who had been standing well behind him, nodded. "Three birds with one trip," he said. I wondered what the hell he meant by that, then put it together with Tinny's scrapes and immediately understood what had happened.

Chick started to shoulder his way past us to the hall. It wasn't deserted, but no one had noticed that anything was off, yet. Just as Chick came level with us, I snapped my left hand up and grabbed for the gun.

Tinny might have been expecting something like that, but couldn't have anticipated my speed. As I moved faster than their eyes could follow, their own movements seemed to break down for me. It was like watching a movie with the projector running the film a frame at a time.

Chick saw what was coming and had just enough instinct to duck back into the room. My hand closed over Tinny's and smashed it against the doorjamb. He grunted out a pain-filled objection, but didn't drop the gun. My other hand was still on the doorknob; all I had to do was pull on it. Fast. The edge of the door caught him sharply on the back of the head. The whites of his eyes flashed and down he went.

He was in the way as I forced the door open to get at Chick. The delay provided him a moment to do some reacting of his own. By the time I was through, he'd hauled out a blackjack as thick as a baseball bat and was all set to use it. He raised his arm for a short, vicious swing, then nearly lost his balance in his effort to stop. He let the blackjack fall and raised his arms high. The sound he made had no words, but somehow he was able to express surrender and a plea for mercy in one inarticulate, horrified gurgle.

I looked where he was looking. Bobbi had plucked the gun from Tinny's slack hand and was aiming it steadily at Chick's crotch. Her teeth were showing, and it was not a smile.

"Back," she growled.

I knew she was on my side, but found myself backing up a step myself.

She came forward enough so no one in the hall could see what she was doing. "Jack, pull this lug inside."

I carefully kept out of her line of fire and got a grip on one of Tinny's ankles. Bobbi followed him in without taking her eyes from Chick or altering the direction of the gun's muzzle. She shut the door, giving us some very necessary privacy.

Chick started to babble out an idiotic explanation, reminding me of the gorilla from the dance number. I told him to can it. My attention was entirely focused on Escott's inert form. They'd dumped him onto the chaise longue at the far end of the tiny room and had him trussed up like a leftover Christmas package. While Bobbi kept Chick sweating, I crossed to Escott in two fast steps and checked for a pulse, drawing in and releasing a vast sigh of relief when I found one. He was groggy, but breathing regularly and didn't seem to be bleeding anywhere.

I nodded an all's well to Bobbi, then fastened my eyes on Chick. "You got lucky," I said to him. "Now I don't have to break your neck."

▲
3
▼

HE WENT WHITE at the lips. Despite my assurance, he saw something in me that frightened him more than the threat of Bobbi's gun. He started to bolt for the door, but I was on him too fast. I caught his collar and swung him against the wall, rubbing his face in it.

"Be careful, Jack," Bobbi warned. She wasn't worried about either of us getting hurt, but that Chick might see more than what was good for him. The mirror over her dressing table reflected all this side of the room.

I locked my eyes onto his. He had defenses up that he was unaware of, but those quickly crumbled beneath the tidal force of my own anger and fear. His pupils shrank to pinpoints and his mouth sagged as I began to tear into his mind.

"Jack?" Bobbi's voice was troubled with the first hint of alarm.

Part of me knew what I was doing to him and that I should stop, but it was easier for that part to simply get out of the way and let the terrors within rush free.

"What are you doing? Jack?" She touched my shoulder, then shook it, trying to reach me.

His legs started to go.

"Jack?"

It was the dust-dry scent of her fear that finally broke through and saved him. I shut everything down, pulling back before it was too late, pulling back and turning away from her until I had myself under control.

"What is it? What's wrong?"

Three nights now of uncertainties, frustrations, deaths, and near death, and no end in sight; Bobbi's presence had only eased the darkness, not removed it.

"You all right now?" She ran her cool fingers lightly over my forehead. I caught her hand and pressed it against my cheek.

"Yeah, I'm all right." For the moment, but it was enough. I flushed out my lungs with a cleansing breath and felt the stuff ebb away, leaving behind only a faint shadow on my soul. It could return or not. The choice was mine.

"Then what . . . ?"

It was safe to look up. Chick was still conscious, but confused. I told him to close his eyes and go to sleep. He did and I let him slide to the floor.

She watched him go, biting the inside of her lip. "This is part of that kind of hypnosis you do?"

I nodded. "When I'm upset it can get away from me." I tried to say more, to explain it somehow, and couldn't.

"It scares you," she said.

"Yeah."

She left the borrowed gun on a table and came over to hold me, which was exactly what I needed. It didn't last long, because we had to see to Escott, but it helped. She gave me a final squeeze, then found a towel somewhere and wet it down at a tiny sink in the corner. I fished out my pocketknife to cut away the bindings on Escott's wrists.

"What is this stuff, anyway?" I complained, sawing through the fabric with some difficulty.

Bobbi tried unknotting Escott's gag. "It used to be one of my stockings. If they're this tough, how come they get runs so easily?"

"Don't know, but at least they did him up in style. You okay, Charles?"

He made a glottal noise that sounded like an affirmative, but wasn't all that convincing. One of his eyes was starting to puff up and his knuckles were scraped. He winced as Bobbi finally tugged the knot loose.

"Looks like you've been to the war, buddy." I broke through the last strands of silk.

"Several, I think," he muttered thickly, working his sore jaw.

"You want a doctor?"

He shook his head. Cautiously. "I'll be fine." Bobbi dabbed his face with the towel and he was content to lie back and let her fuss over him.

"What happened?" I asked when he looked up to answering.

"I'd come backstage for a quick look round and discovered Tinny waiting here, ready to accost Miss Smythe at the first opportune moment. I'd almost settled things in my favor when the other fellow turned up. After that . . ." He shrugged and touched the back of his skull, wincing again.

I looked at the discarded blackjack and figured that Escott had gotten off very lightly. "We're going to have to get out of here. Are you up to it?"

"You've got to be kidding," objected Bobbi.

"Don't I wish, but those other two mugs I got rid of could be back at any time with reinforcements, and they're going to be pretty sore. There's no law that says Kyler's going to be busy all night making excuses to Lieutenant Blair. If he and his crowd turn up, I don't want you or Charles caught in the cross fire."

"Fine with me, I don't like this kind of roughhouse, but Charles is still—"

"Capable of moving if necessity calls for it," he told her. "The sooner the better, if you please."

She gave him a look of mixed exasperation and affection, then got a bag and began stuffing her street clothes into it.

"It won't bother your boss that you're leaving early?" I asked.

"We just did the last show of the evening when you came in." She paused. "I can't go home, can I?"

"Not tonight. We'll find a hotel somewhere."

She considered the two of us with a raised eyebrow. "*That* should be cozy."

Escott sat up, rubbing his wrists. "Might I suggest a safer haven for all of us?"

"Suggest away," she said, sweeping some odds and ends from her makeup table.

"The Nightcrawler Club."

She stopped packing. That place had a lot of memories for her and the bad ones were still fresh.

Escott was well aware of them. "This is something of an emergency."

"I guess so," she admitted. "But for how long?"

Neither of us had an answer to that.

"And my job here?" She correctly read our faces. "Forget I asked."

"Sorry," I said.

She shrugged. "Don't be. It's better than being with Tinny and Chick. Staying there is a very good idea, I'm thinking maybe Gordy can help us out. If anyone in this town knows about Vaughn Kyler . . . but what do we do with these two clowns? We can't leave them here for the janitor to find."

"We could try questioning them," said Escott.

My recent loss of control had spooked me so much that the last thing I wanted to do was get involved in a hypnotic version of twenty questions. Besides, I'd made a private promise to myself about avoiding that particular mental trap. Now was not the time to inform Escott of my decision or the reason behind it.

I shook my head decisively. "Uh-uh. We've got to get out of here before their friends come looking for them. We'll pass them off as a couple of drunks who tried to get Bobbi's autograph. Where's the club bouncer?"

Bobbi had completed her impromptu packing and pulled on a coat. "I'll take care of it." She whisked out, her boot heels making no-nonsense clacks against the floor.

"As I've said before, what a very remarkable girl," Escott murmured.

"One in a million . . . and I just let her out of my sight." I hastily started after her, but she hadn't gone far. At the other end of the hall she was explaining things to the stage manager, jabbing a thumb in my direction to emphasize a point. He nodded with a grim but satisfied smile and quickly moved off.

Bobbi returned, looking smug. "He'll be back in a minute with Udo and Jürgens."

"Udo and Jürgens?"

"Busboys."

The stage manager soon reappeared with a couple of large young men who were enough alike to be twins. The seams of their white work coats were strained to the limit and I could have sworn that some of their arm hair was sticking out of the gaps. "What do they clear away, real buses?"

"*Shh*, they're really very sweet."

The trio lumbered past to stop only a moment at her dressing room. When they returned, Tinny and Chick were each dangling bonelessly from a massive shoulder. The stage manager brought up the rear, carrying their fallen hats.

"Drunken bums," he muttered. "We'll dump 'em outside, Bobbi. They won't be bothering you anymore."

The twins laughed and I was suddenly very glad not to be one of their parcels.

In the dressing room, Escott was on his feet again and working a dent from his hat. "This establishment certainly employs an effective cleanup crew. Those two fellows reminded me of the giants that built Valhalla."

"In *Das Rheingold*?" asked Bobbi.

"Why, yes. Do you enjoy opera, Miss Smythe?"

"If it's done right. Back in school I was in some Gilbert and Sullivan. . . ."

"Are we ready to leave?" I interrupted.

"Wait a second." Bobbi got her bag of clothes and paused long enough to stuff Tinny's gun and Chick's blackjack into her purse. "You never know when one of these might come in handy," she informed us, then led the way to a side exit.

Once out of the building, my feeling of vulnerability became more pronounced with the abrupt slap of cold air. We hustled to Escott's car, crowding together on the front seat. Despite his protest that he was fit, I insisted on driving and told him to keep his eyes peeled for tails. Our route north was an indirect one and in the end I was satisfied that we hadn't been followed.

I stopped in the service alley that ran behind the Nightcrawler Club, cut the motor, and waited. The back door soon opened and a couple of mugs emerged to check on us. Escott rolled down his window and Bobbi leaned over to hail one of the men.

"Ernie? How you doing?"

The shorter man relaxed when he recognized her. "Hey, it's Bobbi. What're you doin' here, babe?"

"Come to visit Gordy."

"He's busy now, but he'll see you." Ernie made a point of noticing me and Escott.

"These are some friends," Bobbi explained. "They're okay." He squinted, doubtful. " 'F you say."

"Can we park the car here?"

"Yeah, but not for all night."

"Good enough." At that, we piled out and Ernie escorted us into the building.

The kitchen was more or less familiar to me, as were the stairs and upper hall. About six months ago Slick Morelli's goons had dragged me over the same ground for a little rough questioning and the memory of the event was still strong. The circumstances were happily different this time, but I had a shiver of discomfort to suppress all the same.

Gordy, Morelli's lieutenant, had taken over the operation of the club and whatever else his New York bosses had an interest in; the Nightcrawler was only part of the iceberg. Most of the businesses were entirely illegal, but like any other, in need of good management in these hard times. He ran the operation efficiently, profitably, and with a minimum of trouble, exactly as required.

We were ushered right up to the office with its pastoral landscapes and comfortable leather furniture. Gordy loomed over a desk piled high with stacks of loose cash and canvas money bags: that evening's casino take. A huge, phlegmatic man, his eyes crinkled when he saw Bobbi, his version of a delighted grin. He nodded a greeting to me and Escott, then gave us all a second look, taking in Bobbi's flashy costume and bag as she removed her coat, my informal working clothes, and Escott's by now obvious battering.

"What's the problem?" he asked.

"Vaughn Kyler," said Bobbi.

Behind us, Ernie muttered something unintelligible. Gordy fastened his small eyes on him and jerked his head. Frowning, Ernie shut the door, his steps retreating down the stairs. Gordy gestured for us to take seats. Bobbi and I huddled together on the couch, Escott sank into its matching chair. Gordy came around the desk and leaned one hip on it, ignoring the bundles of cash as though they were so much confetti.

"Give," he said, never one to wait on ceremony.

By silent consent, I was elected storyteller. Maybe my past journalism experience had something to do with it. I went through all of it, starting with the original job Escott had taken on to recover the stolen bracelet, and ending with the disposal of Tinny and Chick.

"Right now, what we need is to drop out of sight for a while until we can figure out how to settle things with Kyler," I concluded.

"Don't see how you can do it. Kyler's gotten pretty big in this town. I can help some, but not that much. I don't want to risk a war and neither will my bosses."

"Can you at least offer Miss Smythe a place of safety?" asked Escott.

"No problem on that, same for you if you want it. Kyler's real target is Fleming and I can tell you he won't give up."

Bobbi didn't like his answer. "But what about Jack? You can't just toss him in the street to get run over."

"Gordy's saying that he doesn't have much of a choice," I told her. "If Kyler catches on to where I am—"

"Who's going to tell him?"

"Nobody," said Gordy. "He's able to figure it out for himself."

Bobbi read him right. "You mean he's already . . . ?"

"He called me about ten minutes ago."

Escott leaned forward. "Has he now? What was his purpose?"

"He wanted to know everything I could tell him about Fleming. I said I didn't know much, but he wouldn't have bought that. From what's been happening, I'm thinking he's got other places to go for news."

"And what has been happening?"

"You remember the *Elvira*?"

Slick Morelli's yacht. The scene of my murder. I remembered. Too well.

"When it went up for sale, Kyler bought it."

We all exchanged uneasy looks. "Why?" I whispered.

Gordy gave a minimal, but eloquent shrug. "He's after you, kid. That's all you need to know."

Bobbi wrapped her hands around one of mine. "Are we so positive that Kyler wants to kill Jack?"

When I'd summarized things for Gordy, I'd mentioned the death of Kyler's lieutenant, Hodge, but had been circumspect about the details. "Sorry, baby, but I'm stuck with it. He had a chance to call it all off tonight and didn't, and the proof is the easy fifteen grand he gave up in the trying."

"Then what will you do?"

Good question.

"Perhaps a little information gathering of our own is in order," Escott suggested thoughtfully. "Does Kyler still make his home at the Travis Hotel?"

"He's got the top floor all to himself," said Gordy. "If you're thinking on a visit, think again. He's turned the place into a regular bank vault."

"What may one expect to find?"

"Steel shutters on the windows, bulletproof glass, and an army of guys just looking for trouble to come their way."

"What does the management of the Travis think of their guest?"

"What can they think? He owns it."

"Convenient for him, I daresay."

"You got an idea, Charles?" I asked.

"No. But doubtless one will turn up. Some research is required first, beginning with what kind of questions Kyler had concerning you."

Gordy's eyes turned inward to his memory and he gave us a succinct recounting of the conversation. The more I heard, the less I liked it.

"He's too damned interested in what happened aboard that yacht," I said.

"Not to mention what you've done since then," Escott added soberly, letting all the implications sink in. "You haven't exactly led a quiet life lately. You've been fairly invisible to the papers and the police, but there are numerous other places to go for information, and Kyler would have gleaned each of them clean by now. I don't suppose you would consider allowing Kyler to go ahead and kill you?"

"I hope you mean that the way I think you do."

"Certainly. Arrange things in your favor so that he thinks you've been eliminated. You've done it before."

"By accident, and I only got away with it because no one was looking for anything unusual."

"That's for damn sure," said Gordy, who had been a witness.

"I can't count on Kyler to fall for that. If he has an idea about what I am, he'll know bullets won't do the job."

"And you weren't able to influence him, either," Escott said, referring to the attempts I'd made to hypnotize Kyler the night before.

"Nope."

"So forced persuasion or driving him insane may be eliminated as options."

"Yeah, though with him it would have been a short trip."

Great. Now I was making jokes about it. Maybe I was getting used to the situation. Or maybe it was the way everyone was watching me, as if I had the easy answer.

Gordy shrugged again. "If you want any advice, I'd say change your name and get out of the country. That . . . or kill him first."

Bobbi's hands tightened over mine.

That was Gordy's easy answer, and the one I'd expected to hear. "Okay, say that I did it. I'd have to take care of his lieutenants, too, because they'd know who to blame and still be coming for me. Where does it stop?"

No answer.

"And I don't know if I can do it. Not cold. Not just walking in on him. Could you?"

His expression was unchanged, which made his reply that much more disturbing. "Yeah, kid, I could, but I don't want a war. This has got to stay between you and him."

Escott gave me a long, steady look, which I did not return.

"Does it bother you being back here again?" I asked, holding the door for her.

"Back in the club or this part of it?"

"This part." I gestured around at what had once been Slick Morelli's bedroom.

"It's just another place now that he's gone."

Some of the furnishings were still intact: the bed, a few pictures on the walls, tables, but it had the impersonal look of a hotel. Bobbi ignored it all to push open a second door leading to a smaller bedroom and went in.

"But this is where I'll want to sleep," she added.

It, too, had been stripped down, but didn't look quite so empty now that she was there. She put her bag on the dresser and let her overloaded purse drop next to it with a thud.

"They've got you backed into a corner, haven't they?"

I watched as she began setting her things out. "What do you mean?"

"First Kyler, now Charles and Gordy. It's like they're all pushing you into something you don't want to do."

"But may have to."

"It's already tearing you up. What happens to you afterward?"

I had no answer for her, not having one for myself.

She stopped unpacking and looked at me straight. "We can leave town like Gordy said. That would save everybody the most trouble."

"How do you figure?"

"I don't need to give you a list, Jack, you'll have come up with enough reasons of your own by now."

"Yeah, baby, and every one of them has an argument against it. We could take off and disappear, but then what happens to Charles? Kyler's after him as well. Say he decides to come along and we all start over some place else, we'll always have to be looking over our shoulder. I do enough of that already."

"Okay, but can you live with the other thing?"

"It wouldn't be any problem for me to float right into Kyler's steel-lined fort. He has no defense against that. If I know where he is, I can get to him. I've thought it all out."

"But . . . ?"

To kill. I'd done it before. Once by accident, while unused to my new strength, again, and quite deliberately for personal revenge, and again in a black moment of insanity. So much had happened in so short a time that I was afraid of that blackness returning, perhaps for good.

"But I think too much," I concluded.

"Just don't shut me out, Jack. I'm in this with you. No matter what happens, you're not alone."

I looked at her troubled face, remembering all the rough spots she'd pulled through, and felt something like a lump coming up in my throat. I drew her close, both of us clinging hard to one another and shaking a little. She started to speak, but I shushed her. "No more talk, sweetheart. I'm all talked out for now and running out of time. I just want to be with you while I can."

"Especially here?" she murmured. "Where we started?"

"We started downstairs in the casino hallway," I reminded her.

"And ended up here. Where we first made love."

"Not ended, I hope."

"Never."

I kicked the door shut. "Gordy better not shoot the lock off this time."

We suffered no inconvenient interruptions, during or after. We were quiet and intense, both needing the reassurance of touch, not speech. For me the little room filled with the sound of Bobbi's quickening breath and heartbeat and the susurrant whisper of my hands over her skin. As it often did for me, time seemed to slow between one beat and the next, my own movements slowing to match. Our leisurely dance took us to her bed once more and with no less passion than we'd known the first time.

I drew on her life, on all that she was and was willing to freely give. We drifted for ages, without thought or motion to disturb that perfection of sensation. When at last I pulled away enough to look down at her, she was shivering—not with cold or pain, she insisted, but from the aftermath of the pleasure.

"Your eyes are all red," she observed. We'd forgotten to shut off the light. "No, don't turn away. I like it."

"You sure?"

She chuckled. "My demon lover."

We settled against one another. Bobbi fell asleep in my arms; I stared at the ceiling and dreamed.

Times like this were the toughest.

Not that there was a lot of misery in my life, but now I would have given almost anything to be able to drop off to sleep—real sleep—with Bobbi and wake to see her in the morning sun. My condition gave me many advantages, but intertwined were restrictions that could never be ignored.

One of them was immortality. Or the next closest thing to it.

It sounds like a good idea, but what do you do in decades to come as your family and friends age and die while you stay ever the same? Life was so ephemeral—if not for me, then for everyone else. What would happen to Bobbi and me? We'd exchanged blood on many occasions. There was a slim chance she might change to be like me, but absolutely no guarantees, only equal amounts of hope and despair until the day she died.

And what then, if I lost her forever?

I held her, listening to the long sigh of her breath, to the fragile rhythm of her heart.

I held her and ached with the awful loneliness that I had come to realize was special to my kind.

I held her and could have wept from it.

These were the tough times. When it's the deepest part of a midwinter night and you know you'll never sleep again, it's all too easy to fall into a bleak mood and think it'll last forever. Tonight I was especially vulnerable because I was contemplating another man's death and felt the memory of my own stir in fretful sympathy.

There wasn't much I could do about it, not here and now.

I faded away and floated clear of the sheets and blankets. The bed hardly creaked as my weight simply vanished and the covers caved in on the space my body had occupied. Bobbi lay undisturbed until after I re-formed and bent to kiss her lightly on the temple. She smiled and snuggled more deeply into the pillows.

Demon lover, indeed, I thought as I dressed, shut off the light, and silently glided out.

Escott and Gordy were still in the office. Escott had turned up an ice bag and held it to his eye to bring down the swelling. The stacks of money were gone, replaced by coffee and sandwiches. The air was thick with cigarette smoke. The number of discarded butts in the desk ashtray indicated that they'd gone through at least one pack while I'd been saying good-bye to Bobbi.

"Any more calls from Kyler?" I asked.

Gordy answered. "No, but there's a couple of cars covering the club that don't belong out there. He knows what's going on."

That was a hint I couldn't ignore. "Okay, no sense dragging you into this more than necessary. I'll make sure they see me leaving."

Escott put the ice bag down. "You've decided what to do?"

"Yeah." Then there was a long pause as they waited for me to go on, only I didn't want to. "I'll call later . . . let you know what happens."

"Do you wish some company?"

I was tempted to say yes, but shook my head. Danger to him aside, something like this would have to be done alone. "Just keep an eye on Bobbi. Don't let those goons come anywhere near her."

No more questions after that. None were needed. I took the steps downstairs slowly, as though I were going to my own execution, not Kyler's.

The kitchen was deserted, so I didn't bother opening the door, and just seeped right through it. The outside air seemed harsher than before. Between the high black bulks of the buildings a gray slice of night sky pressed down upon me. The Nash was long gone, presumably parked in some safer spot than the club's back alley.

Covering the right-hand exit to the street was a black Ford. I studied it a moment and checked my immediate surroundings. It was dark enough that they probably hadn't noticed how I'd left the club. I drew in a long breath of sharp air and puffed it out again, producing a long plume of vapor, then wrapped up in the muffler and walked toward them. I halfway expected—and maybe hoped—to see the passenger window roll down and a gun to poke out. It would be so simple to mime taking a fatal shot and let them charge eagerly back to Kyler to report their success.

But they weren't about to make it that easy for me and they'd be too suspicious if I returned the favor by directly approaching them. As soon as my foot hit the sidewalk I turned south and moved away rapidly, the back of my neck prickling. After I crossed the street and kept going, their motor whined and caught. I glanced back. They were keeping pace some yards behind . . . maybe setting me up for a hit-and-run? Well, I'd been through that before and survived, though a repeat of the experience was nothing to look forward to. The second car pulled up behind them. Better and better; I wanted us all well away from the Nightcrawler before the party started.

By the time I'd crossed another street to the next block they were ready to move in. I broke into a run, fast, but nothing the Ford couldn't easily overtake. They let me get halfway down, then whipped past and stopped square in my path. The second car closed in behind.

No cover presented itself. On my right was the brick face of a tall building, showing windows only, and those too high up for a normal man to break into. On the left was more of the same with a broad bare street between. They'd picked their spot well. I skidded to a stop and waited for them.

The two men in the Ford were the first out. Their guns were ready and covered me while two more emerged from a familiar-looking Olds. The driver of that car knew me right away.

"He's the one," he told the others. "Think you're a smart-ass, don't you?" He was still stinging from my successful con back at the Top Hat.

I offered no opinion as he slapped me down for weapons. I was clean. It wouldn't have made much sense to pack something only to have it taken away again. All he did find was a rather slim money belt that I'd thought to carry. It contained no money, though. In the event that I got caught away from my usual daylight sanctuaries, the narrow pockets of the belt were loaded with oilcloth-wrapped packets of my home earth. It was a sufficient quantity to keep the dreams at bay and allow me full rest. The man only recognized the belt for what it appeared to be and started to remove it.

"Never mind that," I said. "Let's just get going."

He paused, holding his gun steady on my gut. "Tough guy," he said, pretending to be impressed. Then I looked him full in the face and his sarcasm abruptly melted off. He automatically put some space between us.

"Your boss still want to see me?" I prompted.

That got him back on balance. "Yeah," he said. "He's been waiting all night to see to you personally."

He jerked his head toward the Olds. I was in no hurry and moved reluctantly in the right direction. Before I'd taken three steps, the rough murmur of a heavy motor drifted in on the wind. Another car was turning onto our street. Correction, it was a big paneled truck. Kyler's men paused and two of them turned away from the glare of its headlights, their bodies shielding their drawn guns from obvious view. Our whole group must have looked odd, but not enough to inspire any investigation. Probably just as well. It pulled around the parked Olds, gears grinding.

As it came even with us, it downshifted and the brakes suddenly squawked. The thing rolled another dozen feet, then stopped. The rear door was wide open, framing three men. All three were armed. The short one on the end took quick aim and fired. The man next to me gave out with a wordless yell and ducked. He got off a return shot that went wild and had no time for a second. Something invisible knocked into his chest and he spun to the pavement.

I dropped flat, eyes shut, and partially dematerialized. I didn't care who saw. Explosions and shouts roared above and around me for what seemed like a very long time but couldn't have been more than a few seconds. Ringing silence followed. I found myself solid once more, eyes blinking against the acrid smoke from their guns.

The men from the truck were out and checking the four bodies that sprawled around me. One of Kyler's men still moved, trying to crawl away. The small newcomer stood over him, taking precise aim at the back of his head. I stared and breathed in the sharp metallic warmth of the blood. I had to swallow hard to keep down the rising knot of bile in my throat. My flash thought that maybe Gordy had decided at the last moment to join in the war went away. None of these faces were familiar or friendly.

The wounded man sensed something and twisted to look up. He froze, his eyebrows high and his eyes popping. It would have been comical except for all the blood.

He started whimpering. "Please . . . I didn't . . ."

"Shut up, Vic," said one of the newcomers. "Jerk never did have any spine. Get him inside."

While the short one kept me covered, Vic was lifted and quickly loaded into the truck. Another of Kyler's men moaned and moved a little. We both noticed at the same time. One fast step and my guard was over him. Without hesitation, he pulled the trigger. The man's body spasmed in time to the blast of the gun, then quivered a few times after the echoes faded, but that didn't mean anything; he was dead.

The other two came out to check on the noise. Neither of them seemed surprised or very upset that their friend's action had taken away half of the guy's head. This was business as usual as far as they were concerned.

The guns were all pointed at me now.

More sudden silence as the one who'd delivered the coup d'grace gestured for me to climb in the back of the truck. I was given no chance to do anything else. The other two each grabbed an arm and hoisted me up. I was dragged in. The doors slammed, shutting us into near darkness, and the driver got things moving. The total elapsed time of the whole business couldn't have been more than forty seconds.

The short one turned on an overhead light and they all sorted themselves onto benches lining either side of the truck. Vic was curled into a silent bundle against the front wall. I remained on the floor, not so much because they wanted me there, but because I was still too stunned by what had just happened. I stared at each of them in turn, trying to separate them into individual faces rather than pale oval blurs that killed.

That's when the next shock set in as I realized that their leader was female.

She wore male clothing, except for the shoes, which were better suited for a tennis court. It was all a little large for her, but practical, once she'd pinned up the cuffs on the pants and overcoat. Her hair was covered by a flat cloth cap. Beneath it was a clean white face with a cupid's bow mouth. A small mole accented her left cheek. She had dark liquid eyes, and didn't look much older than twenty. She took her semi-auto off cock and tucked it into a shoulder holster as though it were something she was used to doing. She watched me watching her and didn't appear to be overly concerned about it.

The two men were older and more obviously tough looking, one with a badly broken nose, the other with a scar like an old burn marring his chin. He tapped out a cigarette and stuffed it in his face with one hand; the other was busy holding a gun on me. He offered one to his buddy and then to the girl, who took it absently, as if her mind were on something else. Probably me. She looked like a starved cat at feeding time and I was the first course.

"Gotta match, Angela?" he asked, not moving his eyes from his target.

She shook her head once, plucked the cigarette from her mouth, and gave it back to him. He took it without comment and returned it to his pack. His buddy produced a match and the air soon got cloudy as they puffed away.

If they meant to unnerve me with their combined stares, it was working pretty well, though once I became aware of my own reaction it lost some of its power. Cautiously, I got to my feet and sat on the bench opposite them. No one objected. No one said anything at all during the whole ride. We were sealed in without windows; I had no clue to our route or destination. Only by a few moments of uncomfortable pressure, mitigated somewhat by the close presence of my earth, did I know we'd crossed water. I could make a reasonable guess that we were somewhere west of the city. Maybe. I asked them no questions, figuring that that opportunity would come when we finally stopped.

So there were more guests at this party than me and Kyler. I could, of course, take care of these three if I chose. I was fast enough in a fight, or could just vanish. They gave me the creeps—hell, Angela was positively terrifying—but I was in no real danger unless they knew about my problem with wood. I was willing to take that chance to find out what they were after.

Our silent ride went on. I didn't bother looking at my watch, not wanting to drop my guard. We took a few more turns, enough for me to lose any sense of our direction and come dangerously close to one of my occasional attacks of claustrophobia.

Another turn. Our speed dropped and the road surface changed, growing rougher. My companions were as stone faced as ever, but I got the feeling that we'd arrived.

The brakes whined for the last time and the motor stuttered to nothing. I'd grown so used to all the vibration that it still felt as if we were moving—that or I just didn't want to get out and face anything new. The one nearest the door opened it and jumped down. Angela jerked her chin at me and I shifted to my feet and followed, a little unsteadily. I kept thinking about how easily she'd killed off that wounded man. There had been deliberate thought behind it, but no feeling that I could see. Reflexive, like smashing a roach.

The third man dragged Vic out. He stumbled from the truck bed and collapsed on his face.

The driver came around to join us. He was a big mug with a lantern jaw who looked vaguely familiar. He checked me up and down once, but registered no return recognition, then helped pull Vic to his feet.

We stood on a white graveled drive next to the back door of a very large house. I made out two stories of expensive architecture that, again, was familiar. The driver, half carrying Vic, led us inside. Angela remained by me, on guard and looking like she wasn't. The other two brought up the rear. We walked through a plain entry—no frills for deliveries—took a few turns, and found a long hall lined with doors. It was dingy and our feet scraped against stiff, water-damaged carpet. We went through the last door. My stomach started to itch from the inside out as I began to realize where I was.

The room was a vast office, cleaner than the hall, and rich with leather and velvet furniture. The walls were lined with landscapes, traditional, solid, and giving the impression that money wasn't all that important to the people here. I drifted to a halt, Angela and the others pausing with me as I took in the office's showpiece: a larger-than-life portrait hanging behind the desk. The artist had painted to flatter, but I knew the stocky form and large, protruding eyes. In memory and—if I was caught away from my earth—in dark dreams his face haunted me with the recollection of shattering pain and death.

My death. I was standing in the home of Frank Paco, the man who had murdered me.

4

I STARED SHARPLY at Angela's profile, comparing it to the flat representation on the wall. The resemblance was sufficiently close to prompt my first question.

"Your father?"

Her eyes flicked quickly over to mine. She pointed to an overstuffed chair and one of her men gave me a nudge forward. The chair was too mushy and low for comfort, apparently designed to make a fast exit from its velvet depths difficult. I accepted it as part of their game and settled in for the time being.

Vic was dropped onto a sofa like a bag of laundry with legs. He moaned, clutching his left shoulder with a red-stained hand.

"Go get Doc," Angela told the driver. He grunted once and left.

Newton. That was his name. Six months ago he'd been guarding a phony laboratory in Paco's basement. He didn't recognize me, but he'd never had the opportunity for a good look. I'd gone in behind him then and knocked him cold. Not too sporting, but necessary in order to get him out before all hell broke loose. Reminding myself about good intentions and certain downhill roads, I wondered if tonight I'd end up regretting my past action.

Angela swept over to the desk and whipped off her cloth cap. Her sooty black hair had been scraped away from her face and pinned up. Without the additional head covering she looked somewhat smaller, but not at all vulnerable. She tore out the pins and stabbed at her hair with impatient fingers. Though a long way from beauty-parlor perfect, it more or less fell into place.

She hitched one hip on the desk, then changed her mind and paced the room, her fists shoved deep into the pockets of her man's coat. She stopped once to look out the door for Newton, then resumed, frowning at the thick rug beneath her soft shoes. The pacing did nothing to alleviate her restless energy or increase her patience at the wait. After her second trip to the door, she returned to the desk and shrugged out of the coat, tossing it onto the sea of oak in front of her. Beneath it was her shoulder holster, the black leather blending well over a dark blouse. Her gun had a bright nickel finish. It might have been a piece of fashionable jewelry the way she wore it.

The two men had taken up stations on either side of me. No one seemed inclined to start a conversation. Except for Angela, we all kept still and watched each other breathe for the next few minutes. As was usual in a very quiet room with strangers, I had to consciously imitate them to avoid attracting notice.

The place—or at least this part of it—must have been thoroughly scrubbed out since the fire. The house had not been totally destroyed, after all, and what was left had proved to be salvageable. There was no trace of the smoke damage in here, only the lingering smell of new paint. Furniture polish, overlaid with stale cigarette smoke and some faint perfume, filled up the corners.

Newton finally returned, bringing company. He held the door for an older man wearing slippers and a black-and-blue-striped bathrobe. His bloodshot eyes were puffy from disturbed sleep and he looked more than a little annoyed with Angela.

"Couldn't this have waited until morning?" he complained, making his unsteady way to her. There was a chair on one side of the desk and he sank into it with a long-suffering groan.

"We had to go when Kyler's boys made their move." She gestured at the sofa. "Fix him up."

He noticed Vic for the first time. That a wounded man lay sprawled and bleeding not ten feet away from him in such a genteel setting didn't seem to alarm or surprise him much. With a pessimistic sigh, he lurched from the chair for a closer look. "What happened?"

"Kyler's going to be three short the next time he takes roll call. Four, unless you take care of this one."

"What did you do?"

She slapped the butt of her gun with her fingers. "What do you think? This wasn't a shopping trip to the five-and-dime ribbon counter. Some of his boys got in my way. They're dead."

He pursed his mouth. "I hope you're not in over your head, girl."

"Just do your job, Doc."

"Sure, sure. Newton, go get my bag."

Newton trundled out. Doc went to a cabinet and made himself a fast drink. Fast, because he didn't bother to mix it with anything. He perked up a little after his first bracing gulp and looked at me with polite curiosity. My own scrutiny took in his bleary blue eyes and red-veined nose. I knew him, sort of, having met him for a few minutes one busy night last August. He'd been pretty drunk at the time, and now I was hoping like crazy that he wouldn't remember me at all.

I relaxed with inner relief when he turned to Angela and asked, "So who's this guy?"

"The one Kyler's after," she replied, lacing her voice with obvious patience.

His eyes flashed with awakened interest. "Fleming?"

"You tell me. You're the one who was there that night."

He stood and came closer, giving every evidence of a careful examination, but anyone could tell he wasn't certain of himself. "It was a long time ago, this *could* be him. . . ."

Angela nodded to her men. "Search him."

They loomed close, ready to handle any arguments from me, but I stood up, holding my hands out in a calming gesture. They weren't buying any tonight, though, and each grabbed for an arm. I sidestepped one, getting the chair between us, and shoved a fist into the gut of the other. He folded and fell with a low grunt, totally out of breath. By the time his partner got around the chair I was ready for him.

He dodged my punch, tried a short fast one of his own, but I caught his hand in my palm and twisted hard. He cried out once—it was almost enough to cover the snapping bones—and then crumpled to the floor.

I straightened to check on Doc and Angela. He was frozen,

but she had her gun out and ready. Her eyes were wide, but she wasn't the type to go into hysterics over a little scuffle.

"You think I'd be dumb enough to carry anything for the cops to identify?" I asked, directing the question at her. "Besides, Kyler's goons have already picked me over."

"Then why bother?"

It had, indeed, been a risk, but better than having them find that telltale money belt. "I got fed up with being pushed around. So would anybody. If you're that interested all you have to do is ask. My name is Fleming, Miss Paco—if that's who you are."

"It is," she said, her big eyes narrowing.

"Charmed, I'm sure. Now, what do you want with me?"

Doc smiled and put in his two cents' worth. "Watch yourself, my dear. It looks like this one's got balls."

"That would make a change," she murmured. "He'd need 'em to go up against Kyler. Except he wasn't doing so well when we found him."

"He seems to be doing just dandy right now, and that's what really counts. Sheldon, you okay?" he asked one of the men on the floor.

Sheldon, who now had some bones to match his broken nose, muttered something obscene.

"Now, now, there's a lady present. Lester, help him up."

The guy with the burn scar nodded vaguely, looking more in need of help himself. He wheezed a few times and eventually made it to his knees.

Unassisted, Sheldon staggered to his feet, clutching his arm and biting back the pain each movement cost him. Doc got him into a chair and clucked over the damage.

"You didn't answer my question," I reminded her. "What do you want with me?"

"Sit down over there and you might live long enough to find out," she said.

"And you're irresistible, too." But I was willing to wait. Lester had gotten his breath back by now, though he looked far from well. He was standing, but in no shape to do much more than glare at me. I could survive that.

"Tell me why Kyler wants you dead," she asked.

"I crossed him a couple of times—for that he thinks I'm dangerous."

"Maybe he's got something there," observed Doc. "He's got a hell of a grip. Shel's going to need X rays for this mess."

She kept the gun level and steady. "What did you do?"

I demonstrated, forming a fist and closing over it with the other hand. "It's all in the leverage."

"I mean against Kyler."

"You don't have to do anything to get on his bad side. I exist and he doesn't like it. That's all that matters to him. Now, what's your angle?"

She didn't bother to reply to that one. Newton came in just then with a black bag and paused, uncertain about the changes made in the last few minutes.

"Trouble?" he asked, nodding at Angela's drawn gun.

"Yes. Watch him and watch yourself. He's faster than you'd think."

He gave his burden to Doc and took up a post behind and to the left of me. Doc went to work, rooting around in the bag, finally pulling out a syringe.

Alarmed, Sheldon shook off some of his pain. "What're you going to do with that?"

Doc smiled as he squinted at the printing on a small bottle. "You just look the other way and trust ol' Doc. We'll have you playing the piano again in no time."

"But I don't play the piano—*ow!*"

"I'm only rolling up your sleeve, Sheldon."

"Oh."

Angela ground her teeth, not from Doc's ministrations, but at the time spent over them. He gave the fretting Sheldon an armful of something to kill the pain, fixed up a temporary splint, then told him to go to bed. As he wandered out, Angela all but steered Doc over to his next patient.

"Nasty, but not fatal," he concluded. "Not yet, anyway. Let's haul him to the gymnasium so I can clean him up. The light in here stinks."

"I want him awake and able to talk," said Angela.

"Do my best." Doc got Vic to stand, and with Lester's shaky aid, they wobbled toward the door like a trio of chummy drunks. "One thing about all this, Angela, did you get away from there clean?"

She nodded. "Nobody saw but these two and they're not going anyplace."

"Kyler'll be mad as hell about it, though."

"We'll see."

"You can bet on it, girl." He guided Vic and Lester from the room.

Angela shut the door, turning to stare at me. She had that hungry cat expression on her face again and I didn't think it was because she thought I was attractive.

"Alone at last," I said, then glanced at Newton. "Well, almost. So why are you taking on Vaughn Kyler? Tired of living?"

She laughed, unpleasantly, and put away her gun. Somehow, I still didn't feel very safe. "You were here last summer, weren't you?"

"I don't know, I get around a lot."

"You were here the night of the fire. You set it, didn't you?"

Uh-oh. "You seem to think so."

"A young guy calling himself Fleming broke in the house that night—"

"And my name's Fleming so that closes your case. What are you going to do, send me to prison?"

"How 'bout we break his face for having so much lip?" suggested Newton.

"Maybe later," she said. Newton took that to be a promise and subsided with a satisfied nod. Angela walked behind the desk and dropped into the massive red leather chair below the portrait. Despite her small size, she looked like she belonged there.

But things were still up in the air for her and she had trouble staying in one place for long. She lighted a cigarette, quickly smoking it down to nothing. When she smashed it out in an ashtray, she started tapping her nails against the top of the desk. Possibly out of self-defense, Newton tried to open a conversation with her, but she wasn't in the mood to talk. It distracted her from the nail tapping at least, but she got up and began pacing again, checking her watch at short intervals.

The desk phone rang, startling her.

"Who's calling this late?" asked Newton.

"Probably Mac."

"Mac?"

"I've had him and Gib watching the Travis Hotel. . . ." She fairly pounced on the phone and we were treated to her side of the conversation. It wasn't too informative from my point of view, but the news was good, to judge by her pleased expression when she hung up.

Newton was just as interested. "So what'd he say?"

"Chaven went out in a big hurry a little while ago. Mac followed him to where we picked this bird up. Cops are all over the spot like flies on fresh meat, but they don't seem to be doing much."

"So they're not looking for us, then."

"Mac also said that Chaven hung around long enough to go green at all the sights, then ran straight back to the Travis."

"That means Kyler knows what happened."

"But he won't know *who* did it."

"Not yet."

"Not yet," she agreed, looking at me. "Bring him along, I want to check on Doc."

Newton was cautious, but I willingly cooperated this time around and followed Angela down the hall to a different door. It opened onto a spacious and well-lighted gym that had everything but a boxing ring. Filling the room were Indian clubs, weights, punching bags, padded mats, and several odd machines that looked more suitable for torturing people than keeping them fit.

The bloodsmell hit me square in the face. Human, of course, not animal. There's a difference—especially to me. I'd learned to discern that difference early on in my changed life. One was food and the other a complicated mix of emotion and memory guaranteed to inspire some kind of reaction within. Right now it conjured the ghost vision of a dark street, the flash of guns, and men falling around me.

Off to one side was a high table overlooked by sunlamps. Vic lay on it, flat and unmoving. His upper clothes were off and Doc was busy working on his shoulder under the hot lights. Lester was his reluctant nurse.

"I wanted him awake," said Angela, striding over. She was oblivious to the gore.

Doc didn't bother to glance up. "This fella had other ideas. He conked out so fast we almost didn't get him on the table. It's just as well or he'd be making an awful noise at what I'm having to do."

"How much longer?"

"Until I'm finished. Now stand back so I can work."

Fuming, she subsided for a whole minute before drifting over to watch his progress. With a grunt of satisfaction he straightened, holding something in one of his fancy tweezers.

"Got the bullet," he announced. "Pesky things, especially this size. Which one of you carries a forty-five?"

"That's mine," said Angela.

Doc eyed her up and down. "Like to pack a punch, don't you, girl?"

"It does the job."

"You didn't smear it with garlic, did you?"

"Don't be an idiot."

Doc laughed out loud, dropping it into a metal dish. "Just checking," he said, continuing his work. "Bullets are generally pretty clean, but they can force a lot of stuff you don't want into even a minor wound. If the bullet doesn't kill you right away, the infection can sneak up on you later. Hope this guy believed in washing his underwear."

"When can you get him moving again?"

"In a while, give him a chance to get over the shock."

"I don't have the time and you know it. I want him awake and able to talk to Kyler."

"Why?" I asked.

They all looked at me as though I'd committed a major social crime by asking a reasonable question. Angela's eyes flashed fire, throwing a signal to Newton. She pointed to a metal door set in the far wall. Newton urged me toward it. I wasn't too worried and went along with things; I could always find a way to sneak out later and eavesdrop.

I was shoved into a dim chamber with slick white tile covering the floor, walls, ceiling, and built-in benches. Frank Paco wasn't one to do things by halves. Rather than cram himself into a cabinet, he'd installed a full-sized steam room to sweat away his troubles. It was turned off, fortunately, but still smelled like old socks.

Newton slammed the door solidly behind me. The only other exit had to do with the ventilation system, such as it was, and was far too small for a human to squeeze through. I could probably give it a shot but my ingrained claustrophobia inspired me to look for something easier.

The door was locked; I tried the knob anyway, giving it a

good rattle for the benefit of my captors. It was the sort of thing they might expect and I didn't want to disappoint them. That obligation out of the way, there wasn't any reason why I should hang around in their improvised cell. Just at eye level, the door had a small window, letting in the only light. My view was limited to a wall full of Indian clubs and Newton's back as he walked away. That was good news; people tend to get upset when I vanish right in front of them, and I had no intention of upsetting this crowd. Not just yet, anyway.

I slipped out and floated free in the open space of the gym, locating the others by memory. It was easy enough to get close and listen, only no one was talking, not even Doc. Somewhat disgusted, I found the hall door and bumbled my way back to the office to make a phone call.

"Charles?"

"Speaking." His voice was tight, guarded. "Are you all right?"

"Yeah, but I got sidetracked. Are things quiet at the club?"

"Yes . . ."

"Hear any sirens in the last hour or so? Close by?"

"Yes, we did, but—"

"I'll tell you all about it later."

"What about Kyler?"

"I never got near him, so don't relax just yet. I need a ride out of here before I run out of night."

"I'm entirely sympathetic; where are you?"

"Remember that spot off the road to Frank Paco's house where you had me wait last summer?"

"Good lord, man, what are you doing out there?"

"I said I got sidetracked."

"This sounds more like a derailment."

"There's something in that. You remember the spot?"

"Vividly."

"Great, 'cause that's where I'll be waiting for you."

"With a full explanation?"

"Cross my heart and . . . hope to see you soon."

This resulted in a noise that might have been a snort or a laugh. With Escott it was sometimes hard to tell. I hung up and took a second look around the empty office.

It was unchanged, plush as ever—except for some blood-stains on the sofa where Vic had rested. High above, Frank

Paco's portrait glared at something across the room, probably his oversized fireplace. I thought briefly about Paco, the thought running in a familiar circle about where the bastard was and what he was doing. As always, I ended up with the conclusion long confirmed by Escott that my killer was drooling the rest of his life away in some loony bin. I felt distant pity for him, but no regrets.

Out of habit, I went through the desk drawers in search of anything interesting. Most were locked, but one of the open ones contained a large checkbook just begging to be flipped through. The last six months had been expensive ones for the household. The medical bills to various head-doctors were high, but nothing compared to home repairs. Couple those with the fact that Vaughn Kyler had moved in and taken over Paco's operation, cutting off a ready source of cash, and Angela Paco would have more than enough good reasons to want to take him on.

Present was the temptation to swipe the checkbook and give it over to Escott, but in the end I decided not to bother. If he really wanted the thing, I could always come back later. Tonight, or rather this morning, I was more concerned with getting to a place of daylight safety.

Staying solid so I could see and hear things, I returned to the hall, tiptoeing silently on the rough carpet. I was ready to vanish in an instant, especially as I approached the closed door of the gym, but no one jumped out to recapture me.

I had plenty of time yet before Escott arrived; a look through the house would be more comfortable than standing out in the cold waiting for him. Once past the gym, I became cautiously nosy, opening doors and generally poking around where I knew I'd be unwelcome. This job wasn't without its favorable points.

Some of the rooms were empty; perhaps the furnishings had been ruined in the fire or they'd been temporarily moved out for the painters. One of them was lined with tarps and stuffy with the stink of fresh paint; another was still tainted by smoke and water damage.

The kitchen at the other end of the house had been pretty much restored. Curiosity lured me to the basement door and down the steps to seek out the "laboratory" I'd destroyed last summer. The stairs were new, the wood sharp and clean. They led into the kind of sealed-in darkness that even my eyes couldn't penetrate. I felt around for a light switch before going any farther. Vampires—this one at least—don't like the dark any more than the next person.

I found a button and the place became less oppressive. A string of bare bulbs marched away along the ceiling, bravely fighting the gloom, only there wasn't anything for them to shine on. The basement that had once been divided up by a wine cellar, laundry area, and old furniture was now open and bare. The old walls were gone, replaced by rows and rows of pillars to support the floors above. There was no sign of the lab, only some vague scarring on the floor to indicate where the walls had stood.

Having gotten my fill of nostalgia, I returned upstairs for more prowling. The second floor boasted more restoration, or had received less damage, and several bedrooms showed signs of occupation.

Many of the doors hung open. I proceeded very carefully here, listening before poking my head inside to check each room. One of the larger ones held a comfortable jumble of feminine gear, apparently Angela's. Discarded stockings and lace-trimmed step-ins littered the floor, dresses were flung across handy chairs, and enough cosmetics crowded the dresser top to indicate that she had a softer side. She kept no important papers or correspondence, probably reserving that business for the downstairs office and the locked drawers of its desk. A brief examination of a side table confirmed the occupant's identity; there I found a gun-cleaning kit, several boxes of .45 ammunition, and a couple of spare cartridge clips. Mixed in with the hardware were several tiny bottles of nail polish and some well-thumbed women's magazines.

Quite a gal, I thought, and repressed a shudder.

I paused in my poking around, picking up a vague sound nearby. It did not repeat, but was enough to distract me into investigating.

Down the hall I found its source: Sheldon. He was rolled up on one of the beds, treating his broken hand with another kind of medicine. In addition to whatever Doc had shot into him, he'd imbibed plenty of liquid painkiller of his own. He was so far gone as to not be alarmed at seeing me.

"How you doing, Shel?" I asked.

He squinted, grunting with annoyance. "Sonnova bitch. You busted me good."

"Sorry about that. Hope it gets better."

His eyes were rolling all over the place. "Pay you back. In spades."

"Did you work for Frank Paco?"

"Still do. Not like some wise guys." His good hand closed around the flat amber bottle on the nightstand. He pulled the cork out with his teeth, spit it to one side, and drank deeply.

"What wise guys?"

"Vic. Sonnova bitch wen' over t' the big K."

"No loyalty, huh?"

"You said it."

"Are you telling me that Paco still runs things?"

"Hah?"

I repeated the question more slowly.

"He's sick fer now, but his kid's doin' okay."

"What's Angela's angle in all this?"

"She's number one, y' jerk."

"What about Kyler?"

"He'll be sunk soon enough. She's got it all figured. Gotta cute little ass, too." His mouth twisted around in a sappy leer.

"What's she got figured?"

"The whole thing," he murmured. "And her legs . . ."

"Sheldon . . ."

He woke up a bit, but his mood had soured. I was too much of an intrusion on his dreams of romance. "What're you doin' here, anyway? Newton should be beating yer head in or somethin'."

"Yeah, we have an appointment first thing tomorrow."

"Hah?"

"Never mind, Sheldon."

"Okay," he said cheerfully, and dropped off into instant sleep.

Damn. I hadn't been influencing him, either. It had to have been the combined effect of the booze and the drugs. He might not even remember our conversation the next time he woke up, which would not be soon. Any chance of getting useful information from his wandering brain was long gone. I rescued the bottle from his lax grip, returning it to the stand, and decided to get going myself.

I found the back door and quietly slipped away, hoping the

occupants wouldn't be too mystified by my disappearance. Ah, well, Houdini used to be able to walk through walls; if asked, I could always claim him for a distant cousin.

The cold felt good in my underworked lungs and I was glad to flush the smell of the place out with sweet, clean air. My feet crunched on the white gravel as I walked along the drive toward the front. No outside lights were on, nor were there any guards with dogs patrolling the grounds as on my last visit. Excluding the two watching Kyler's hotel, there seemed to be only four men in Angela's army. Three, now that Sheldon was among the wounded. Maybe she had reserves hidden elsewhere. She'd need them to hold her own against his kind of money and organization.

But that wasn't my problem; if I had enough night left and any kind of chance to get at him, then Kyler would cease to be anyone's problem. The survivors, Angela included, could go to hell in a handbasket for all I cared.

Once up on the road, I increased my pace. I wasn't worried about missing Escott; it just felt good to *move*, arms and legs swinging freely as though I'd never really walked before. My long strides quickly ate up the distance, getting me to the right spot in a disappointingly short time. I looked back with regret, not at Paco's house, but the road running past it. To turn now and walk away from the mess I was in, to just keep going until I was lost to everyone but myself . . .

Get behind me, Satan, I thought blasphemously. Stay, and at least one man would die; go, and he would certainly kill my friends and who knows how many others with them. I would stay, of course. I'd made my decision earlier and would stick to it, but damn it all, why me?

The wind was working its way through the pea jacket and really starting to bite when I caught the low murmur of a motor coming my way. I was fairly sure the headlights belonged to the Nash, but kept my head low until it downshifted and coasted to an easy stop. The bullet dents decorating its thick metal hide were clearly visible in the starlight, almost homey in their familiarity, and I emerged from my thin cover in the brush.

Escott seemed relieved to see me and waved me over. Gratefully, I opened the passenger door and climbed in, shutting out the cold. He worked the gears, wresting a U-turn out of the big car until we were on our way back to the city.

Once up to a decent speed, he took the time to give me a good look. In light of some of my past escapades, he was probably checking for damage.

"I'm all right, Charles," I assured him.

"I was rather expecting—"

"Yeah, I just figured that out. Believe me, they're in worse shape than I am. One of them, anyway."

"Indeed? Now about that explanation . . . ," he prompted.

So I started talking. Somehow, it did not shorten the trip back.

"Well, this does throw a spanner into the works," he said when I'd finished.

"Don't see how. Angela and I seem to have pretty much the same goal of getting rid of Kyler, I just have a better chance of doing it."

"Ah, but now you've two gangs to dodge and previously the one was quite enough."

"Yeah, but Angela doesn't really know what she's up against with me. Kyler's had time to read a whole library on folklore and get prepared." Not that it would do him much good, I silently added.

"You may yet find her to be a formidable force."

Formidable. That was the word for her. I'd never be able to forget how deliberately she'd blown open the back of that man's head. "No arguments there. She's her father's daughter and then some."

"And you think her plan is to regain control of the organization Kyler took over from him?"

"Yeah. That's how it looked from what little I saw. I think she wanted to use me in the bargaining, but damned if I know how. It's not as if I'd be a valuable hostage. If she threatened to kill me, Kyler'd be in the front bleachers cheering her on."

"Unless you were meant to be some sort of bait to draw Kyler into the open," he suggested.

"The problem with that is Kyler wouldn't be dumb enough to do it."

"Only if one chooses to underestimate Miss Paco. She's been able to retain the loyalty of at least some of her father's men, quite a feat for anyone, much less a young unproven woman."

"How do we know she's so unproven?"

"Point taken," he admitted. "In certain underworld circles,

this is the smallest town in the world when it comes to gossip. I am making an assumption based on the sole fact that I've simply heard nothing about her until now."

"Maybe she just got back from finishing school."

"I shall endeavor to find that out."

"But carefully, Charles."

He took that point as well with the bounce of an eyebrow and a single nod.

"You've heard my version of the shootings," I said. "What about yours?"

"I've little to add that would be useful. We heard the sirens, of course, causing us to wonder whether they had any connection to you."

"You didn't go out to check things, I hope?"

"That was the subject of quite a lot of debate between us."

"You and Gordy?"

"And a number of his men."

That must have been a show to see. I was sorry to have missed it.

Escott continued, "He was most reluctant for me to investigate personally since he felt he'd accepted the responsibility for my safety. We reached a compromise when Ernie volunteered to go just to satisfy his own curiosity. He returned quickly enough with a report on the casualties. He recognized them as belonging to Kyler's gang and concluded that you had dispatched them."

"But I—"

"We, or at least I, know that now, but you may find your reputation has grown considerably in the last few hours with Ernie and his cronies. Be prepared for a bout of hero worship on arrival."

"Hero worship," I repeated numbly. "What about the cops? Do they have any idea about what really happened?"

"According to my own sources within the department, that matter is 'under investigation.' Gordy made a few calls himself and the unofficial conclusion has to do with gang vendettas."

"Which isn't far off the mark where Angela's concerned." I checked my watch. Dawn was only an hour away, but we were within a mile of the club and its sanctuary. All too soon I'd be forced to seek the safety of my lightproof trunk. Another day would flash by with God knows what happening outside and me totally oblivious to it. I had extraordinary advantages over the rest of humanity, but the frustrating price of them was that daily ration of death that could never be ignored.

Escott drove in silence, perhaps sensing my glum mood, or more likely he was tired himself. Between his usual insomnia and the long wait for my call, he wouldn't have gotten any sleep tonight. I was about to make some kind of comment or other to him about it when his head snapped off to the left as though he'd been given a jolt of electricity.

"Damn," he said in a soft, strangled voice and slammed the gas pedal down as far as it could go.

▲ 5 ▼

THE NASH SHOT forward, but too slowly for Escott. He came out
with another curse and I joined him, hardly knowing why. Past
his head I glimpsed the black blur of a car rushing up on us.
Yellow-white flashes from its open windows raked my eyes.
There was noise: stuttering explosions coming so fast that they
merged into a single horrifying roar that deafened all thought,
stifled all movement.

Escott kept saying damn over and over again—somehow I
could still hear him—as he fought to dredge more speed from
the Nash. He clawed at the wheel and cut a right so hard that I
would have tumbled into him except for a timely grab at the
dashboard. The explosions stopped only briefly, then resumed
as the gunman came even with us once more. Huge pockmarks
clattered across the windows.

My own throat went tight and my leg muscles strained
against one another, trying to run where running was not possible. I had to trust Escott to get us out and he had to trust his car.
Its big engine pulled us ahead a bare two yards and the shooting
abruptly ceased for a few heavenly seconds, started, then
stopped again.

Escott swerved to the left; I grabbed the top of the seat so
hard that the covering ripped. We tapped something and
bounced away in reaction, then hit it again more decisively. The
Nash shuddered, but kept plowing forward at top speed until
Escott hauled us to the right and we emerged from a narrow
street to a larger one on two shrieking wheels. When the other

two landed heavily on the pavement, I was nearly blasted into the backseat by the sudden acceleration.

Through the rear window I glimpsed the other car sideswipe a lamppost and not recover from the impact. It lurched and faltered, then swung out of sight as we took another quick turn, running like hell through a stop signal and ignoring the horn blasts of an outraged trucker. He missed broadsiding us by a cat's whisker.

Escott's teeth were showing and his eyes were wild as they darted from the rearview mirror to the front, to the sides, trying to cover everything at once as we tore along the early-morning streets. He wasn't interested in using the brakes just yet. For that, he had my wholehearted support.

After the second red light he began to slow down to something like a normal speed. I pried my hands loose and watched them shake—hell, I was shaking all over after that—and asked if he was okay. He came out with one of those brief, one-syllable laughs that had nothing to do with his sense of humor.

"Did you know them?" he asked, but didn't wait for an answer. "The driver was that rat-faced fellow who took my Webley last night."

Chaven. I groaned inside. "Kyler thinks I bumped off the men he sent after me."

"That would be a logical conclusion for him to draw. It appears that Miss Paco has not taken the opportunity to inform him of his error."

"Goddammit, Charles, it came that close to killing you!"

"Yes," he agreed, and that's when I noticed the tremor in his hands as they worked the wheel and gears. His knuckles were white, the tendons taut. I faced around front and pretended not to notice. He was handling his fear in his own way and didn't need me to point out the obvious.

"I should never have let myself get sidetracked," I muttered.

"As if they gave you much choice in the matter. If you wish to put the blame for this incident upon anyone, let it be Kyler."

"Incident?" But I canned the rest of it since he was right. Except for having all but the shit scared out of us, we were unharmed. If he wanted to reduce an attempted double murder down to the level of an "incident" that was his business. Mine, I knew, was to eliminate all possibility of it happening again. Bobbi, Escott, and even Gordy were far more valuable to me than bug-house bait like Kyler. Better him and his whole organization than my only real friends.

An unpleasant but necessary job.

A shudder crawled up my spine at that thought. The last time it had brushed through my brain, I'd been out of control. To kill the way I had killed, you had to go crazy for a while. My main fear was that once there, I might not be able to find my way back.

"The sun will be up soon," Escott reminded me. "We cannot risk returning to the club."

"And home and your office are out," I concluded. "We have to find a bolt hole somewhere in this town that Kyler won't look into."

"Or even suspect. I think that might be arranged."

"Can you arrange it before sunrise? If I have to I can hide out in the trunk of the car for the day, but . . ."

"Yes, I'll see what I can do," he promised, and we picked up speed again. Then he stared into the mirror and said, "Oh, bloody hell."

"What?" I asked, looking out the back window with a fresh dose of alarm. If a simple "damn" was his reaction to a machine gun hit, "bloody hell" could only mean an earthquake was sneaking up on us.

Not quite, as it turned out. The car closing in had flashing roof lights and a siren.

"Can we lose him?" I asked, hoping he'd say yes.

Escott shook his head. "He's in a radio car. If we run, he'll only call in others to track us down. Perhaps we can reason with him."

Translated: I would be the one to "reason" with him. Wonderful. "You sure about that? I wasn't all that good at debate in school."

"My dear fellow, this night has been quite busy enough for both of us. I, for one, have no wish to top things off by collecting a traffic citation."

"Okay, okay." This was only his way of saying that I owed him one.

Escott came to a gradual stop by a streetlight and gave the motor a rest. The cop pulled up behind us and got out cautiously, hand on his gun. Escott tried to roll down his window, but something was wrong with the mechanism. He gave up and opened the door instead, which made a terrible creaking, cracking noise that echoed off the nearby buildings. It almost sounded like a gunshot and startled all of us for a moment. Escott remained seated, doing a fair imitation of polite innocence. The cop looked him over carefully, and told him to come out. Escott complied.

"Is there a problem, officer?" he asked, using his blandest tone and most formal accent.

"Your license and registration," he ordered. They attended to that ritual, then I was ordered out of the car to take my turn. "You two wanna tell me what happened here?" He gestured at the car.

Escott followed the gesture, all ready with a distracting story so I could move in for the dirty work, but he hauled up short. It was one of the few times in our association that I had ever seen him totally speechless. He couldn't have not known that the car would be a mess, but there's a wide difference between knowing in your mind and seeing with your eyes.

"Oh, bloody *hell*," he repeated, full of sincere anguish and anger.

The thick windows on his side were nearly opaque with chips and cracks where the bullets had struck; many of them were exactly level where his head had been. A fresh pattern of dimples, dents, and a long ugly scrape ran along the door panels. The paint job was a disaster, but the heavy steel glinting through it was still good for a few more miles and then some. About the only difference between his armored Nash and a tank were the headlights, wheels, and lack of mounted guns.

And if Charles Escott loved anything, he loved his car. This had left him stunned as few things would.

"Well?" The cop raised his voice to penetrate Escott's shock. No reaction. The cop then looked to me for an answer. I had enough light to work with; I smiled and got his undivided attention.

Blithely unaware that he'd ever stopped, the cop drove away. We wasted no time taking another direction until Escott spotted an open gas station and parked a little past it. He said something about a phone call and walked back to place it. I got out as well to work some of the stiffness from my tense muscles. I'd only given the cop straight inarguable suggestions—better than getting caught in the trap of deep hypnosis—but it was still disturbing for me. Walking around the car a few times and letting the icy air clean out my lungs helped ease things until Escott's return.

He walked back quickly enough and I was glad to get going again. My imagination was working too well visualizing what could happen if we didn't find a hole to pull in after us.

"I called the club and let Gordy know we wouldn't be back tonight," he said.

"You told him about the hit?"

"Yes, though he was not especially surprised. That machine gun made a devil of a row; they had no trouble hearing it."

"What about Bobbi? Is she all right?"

"Miss Smythe is still sleeping soundly. No doubt her interior room muffled most of the noise."

Between that, her club performance, and our lovemaking, it'd take more than a greeting card from a Thompson to wake her up. It was okay by me; I'd rather have her sleeping through the storm than worrying about us.

"Gordy and his men will remain on guard today. With this shift in the situation from a quiet kidnapping to an outright attack, he deems it to be the safest course of action. This presumes that you still mean to go through with—"

"I will," I said shortly, interrupting before he could put it into words and bring it that much closer to being a reality. He caught the hint and dropped the subject without further comment.

"Now, as for our own shelter, I've set something up, but we must hurry. You're running out of time."

He was right about that. The sky was starting to lighten. Invisible to Escott, perhaps, but very noticeable to me.

We headed south and kept going. I was tempted to ask him where, but he was concentrating on street signs and it was in my own interest not to disturb him. He took us into a stark section of the city that was full of the kind of shadows that could outwrestle even the noonday sun. I began to get my own general idea of what he'd planned, and as we traveled more deeply into the area, I breathed a sigh of relief.

He slowed as we approached a block full of aggressively drab buildings that only a bulldozer could have improved. Some broken windows were boarded up, others had been left to gape

helplessly at the deserted street. We coasted to a silent stop and
Escott flashed the headlights once, frowning with tension.

"There." I pointed. "Is that it?"

Halfway down, the double doors to a decrepit and outwardly
abandoned garage swung open, guided by two vague figures
wearing overalls. One turned and waved us forward. Escott
worked the gears and we quickly slipped into a cramped and
greasy repair bay. Even as he cut the motor and lights, the tall
doors closed, shutting us into a pitch black limbo.

"This is it," he confirmed in the sudden quiet.

A flashlight came out of nowhere and blinded me as the man
holding it checked first my face, then Escott's. We must have
passed because it swept down to the stained floor and we were
told to get out. Escott did so without hesitation and I copied
him. I didn't know the man's voice, but it sounded reasonably
polite, and no one seemed to be pointing anything lethal in our
direction.

We followed the flashlight beam through several tool-littered
workrooms and a place that might have served as an office. It
connected with a short bare hall that led directly to an outside
door. Waiting in the narrow alley beyond was a newer version
of the Nash we'd just left, minus the bullet scars. The back door
opened for us and we piled in, leaving our escorts behind.

Two men were in the front seat; the tall one on the passenger
side turned around and extended his hand.

"Charles, how the hell are you?" asked a rich voice, an actor's trained voice that confirmed my earlier guess about
Escott's arrangements.

Escott's white hand was engulfed in Shoe Coldfield's black
one for several seconds. "Better, now that you're here, my
friend. Thank you for coming."

"Wouldn't have missed it. How're you doing, Fleming?"

I couldn't help but grin as we shook hands in turn. "Just
fine."

"Not from what I hear. Isham, get this buggy moving," he
told the driver. The big heavy car did not roll from the alley so
much as sail, like a graceful ship on a smooth sea. We glided
down the streets, hardly making a sound.

I figured Escott to be the likely source of Coldfield's news.
"What have you heard?"

"That Vaughn Kyler's looking to turn both of you into fish

food the first chance he gets. Talk about grabbing a tiger by the tail. How did you manage to catch on to this one?" he asked Escott.

"It wasn't all that easy . . . ," he began, and gave Coldfield a summary of most of the fun and games.

Coldfield rubbed a thumbnail against the carefully trimmed beard edging his jaw. "Shit. In a way this is almost my doing. If I hadn't recommended you to Griff—"

"Someone else with fewer advantages working for them would undoubtedly be feeding the aforementioned fish."

"Let's hope they keep going hungry. And now Angela Paco mixed herself into things, huh? I knew old Frankie had a daughter, but I didn't know she was looking to take over the family business. Sounds like she's making a good job of it, too."

"If you were unaware of that, then it's unlikely for Kyler to suspect her involvement, hence his misdirected attack on us."

"That's what it looks like. You sure you're okay, both of you?"

Escott nodded. "We're only a trifle shaken, but my poor car is in fearful need of repair."

Coldfield laughed briefly. "As long as it did the job. That thing's the best investment you ever made and I'm glad I talked you into getting it."

"As am I," Escott agreed with humble sincerity. "Are we going to the Shoebox?" he asked, referring to Coldfield's nightclub in the heart of Chicago's "Bronze Belt."

"Not private enough. Kyler's going to have everyone but mediums working for him to find out what happened to you two, but I've got a spot that should be all right."

"But will you be safe as well?"

"Safe as I ever am," he replied. I got the impression that Escott wasn't all that reassured. "How long you need it for?"

"For the day at least," I said. "I don't want to make any moves until nightfall."

"And then what are you planning?"

My voice was thick. "Then I'll take care of Kyler."

A lot of obvious questions crossed Coldfield's face, but never came out. He glanced at Escott, who simply nodded.

Even through the extra thick windows, I could sense the oncoming light. I hoped that our destination was close by or

Escott would have an apparent corpse on his hands to explain away when the sun came up.

We had all of five minutes to spare when the driver brought us to a gentle stop in another alley, next to another anonymous door. Coldfield got out first to deal with the lock, then hustled us inside. I reveled in the soothing darkness there, but still felt the approach of day creeping into my bones.

Coldfield led us upstairs. The place was old and could have been designed for anything: an office, a hotel, or apartments of some sort. Perhaps he used it for all three at one time or another, but not recently. The air was cold and stale and our shoes left revealing tracks in forgotten grit on the steps. And it was quiet. I listened hard when we paused on the landing and heard no one and nothing else moving within the building.

Our host noticed and approved of my caution. "I tell you two, the lines between black and white are pretty solid in this town, each on his own side and neither caring much about the other except during elections. I know plenty of people who wouldn't mind seeing you white guys kill each other off and be glad to help things along, so you keep your heads low—and I'm talking about down to the ground. This place is just between us and Isham downstairs and he won't talk, but you don't want to take any chances."

"Words to live by," I said. "What is this place, anyway?"

"A private way station for people in trouble."

He ushered us through the first door on the right and turned on a lamp. We stood in a small, windowless room, containing four ancient folding cots, an oil heater, a pile of dusty magazines, and a lonely old telephone. Though we were out of the wind, it seemed colder in here than in the street. Coldfield lighted the heater right away to start taking the edge off the worst of it.

Always fastidious about himself and his surroundings, Escott favored the stark place with one of his rare smiles. "This is quite an improvement over those rooms we shared at Ludbury."

"Good God, yes," agreed Coldfield.

"Ludbury?" I asked.

"A railroad town in Ontario," he explained. "The noisiest, smelliest, coldest pit we ever had the rotten luck to fall into. The pulp mills were bad enough, but add on the creosote and sulfuric acid plants and you could choke to death if the wind started blowing the wrong way. It was full of workers and miners, every one of them tougher than the next, uglier than most, and itching to prove it come Saturday night."

"What were you doing there?"

"King Lear."

"It went over surprisingly well, as I recall," Escott put in brightly.

"Oh, yeah, they just loved the scene where Cornwall is tearing out Gloucester's eyes. They wanted an encore to that one. Maybe this kind of work is one hell of a lot safer."

"You may be certain of it, old man." Escott warmed his hands in front of the heater, flexing his long fingers. They were no longer shaking. "Given those circumstances, I would think twice about taking up acting again. An audience like that one would have convinced the most rigid Fundamentalist that Darwin had, indeed, some insights about our origins."

Coldfield chuckled, but it faded when he looked at me. "You all right, kid?"

Escott glanced at his watch and correctly interpreted my situation. "Yes, Jack, you must be dreadfully tired after all this. Why don't you have a lie-down?"

"He really should keep moving until this place warms up some more," Coldfield advised.

"I'll be fine," I told him, dragging my stiffening legs over to the nearest cot. Pulling a damp blanket over my shoulders, I stretched out on the old canvas, turning to face the wall. The cot swayed and creaked, but decided to hold my weight. In a few more seconds the whole thing could drop through to the basement with me and I wouldn't notice any of it. The money belt with my earth dug soothingly into my side.

"He's had a busy time . . . quite exhausted himself," came Escott's voice as I started to drift away from the daylight prison of my inert body. "Probably sleep for hours . . ."

That's for damn sure, I thought, and then I was gone.

With my condition, bunking down in a strange place is always a risk. The next time my eyes opened, I was relieved to note that the same wall was still a mere foot away from me and that all was quiet.

Escott was on a cot closer to the heater; he looked up from his magazine and nodded to me. Since his breath wasn't hanging in the air anymore, I could assume the room had finally warmed up. I usually know offhand whether any given place is hot or cold, but it takes a while for excesses to become uncomfortable.

"Easy day?" I asked, cautiously sitting up.

"Exceedingly so. I found it to be a welcome respite. Isham came by several hours ago with some sandwiches. I persuaded him to let you sleep. If he should ask if you enjoyed your late lunch, you'll know to say yes."

I spotted the sandwich wrappings, neatly folded, on a stack of old papers. "How did it taste?"

"A little heavy on the mustard, but otherwise quite nutritious."

"Any news?"

"A Manhattan criminologist has proposed establishing a criminal identification system based on the pattern of blood vessels in the eye. In these days of plastic surgery, it sounds most—"

"I meant here in town."

"Ah." He put away his two-week-old magazine. "Nothing, really. I filled Shoe in on everything, including your remarkable escape from Angela Paco—not to worry, I did not reveal the actual details, only that her people were looking the other way and you seized the opportunity. I also gave Shoe a message to pass on to Gordy and Miss Smythe to the effect that we are well and safe and they are not to worry."

"That's good, but I'll want to call her when I can. Jeez, I could use a bath and a change of clothes. What about you?" I stood and stretched out a few muscles, rubbing my chin. Escott also wore some uncharacteristic stubble, but it didn't seem to bother him. He even looked rested. Our rough surroundings must have suited him.

"Both would be welcome were they obtainable. You'll find a washroom across the hall, but the water is freezing."

And we were fresh out of towels, I discovered after rinsing my face off, but no complaints—not aloud, anyway. We were still moving and kicking and for that I was grateful.

A door creaked open downstairs. Escott and I were in the hall at the same time, both looking and listening. His revolver was ready in his hand, his heart beating a little fast.

"It's me," our visitor called.

Escott sighed in relief, but didn't put the gun away until Coldfield was actually in sight.

He stopped on the landing and raised one hand, palm out. "Hey, I'm on *your* side."

"Indeed you are. Do come up."

Coldfield carried a covered basket. "Want any supper? Straight from the club kitchen."

The basket was stuffed with the basics of a portable feast, more than enough for all of us; even the coffee was still hot. The no-doubt savory smells only inspired the usual pang of queasiness for me, though, and I had to beg off.

"Still got that bad stomach, huh?" Coldfield asked as he set out food.

"Yeah. Must be slow digestion or something. There was a lot of mustard on those sandwiches."

Escott kept a straight face, but it was a struggle.

Coldfield didn't notice. "I keep tryin' to tell Isham that not everyone likes that much heat, but it never seems to sink in. It's where he was raised. He's from Louisiana, y'know, and that kid's eaten things I wouldn't step on."

Escott nearly choked on his coffee. "This from a man who has partaken of jellied eel?"

"Only because you told me it was really salmon."

"The light was poor."

"Uh-huh."

I was tempted to ask for more details, but it would have to wait for a better time. "Anything going on outside?"

Coldfield shook his head. "Kyler got back to his hotel around two in the morning and stayed there, but his men are still looking for you, so I wouldn't get hopeful. He's got the top floor of the Travis blocked off and nobody, but nobody's getting up there."

"Not even the cleaning staff?" Escott put in.

"You figure."

"And Miss Angela Paco?"

"No one's heard a peep from her. The papers are going crazy playing up last night's shootings and so are the cops. They've got no witnesses and the bodies sure as hell aren't talking."

"What about the prisoner she took?"

"Maybe she's still holding him. If he's the same Vic I know of, he'll be lucky to come out of things with a whole skin. He used to work for her daddy and changed sides when Kyler took over. I can imagine how that's made him real popular with the old crew."

"I'd just like to know what they wanted us for," I said.

"It's bound to be for something lousy, kid. By now every hood in the Midwest knows your name. The best favor you can do yourself is to get out of the area. Mexico is just peachy this time of year. Both of you can probably use the sun."

Escott and I exchanged openmouthed looks, then broke up. His own laughter was brief and subdued, mine bordered on the lunatic. Coldfield was disgusted. Escott made a placating gesture.

"My apologies, Shoe. It is an excellent idea, but not really practical for either of us."

"And letting Kyler chop you into fish food is?"

I sobered up fast. "It won't come to that. I'm going to settle things with him tonight."

"How? Kyler's locked in his own private fort with men all over it like ants on a sugar cube. You going to ring the front bell or come down through the chimney? That's about as far as you'll get before they cut you in two the long way."

"I'll be all right." *I think,* I silently added.

Escott backed me up. "He knows what he's doing, Shoe. Otherwise, why else would Kyler be taking such elaborate precautions?"

"Elaborate, hell. He's like that all the time. It's how we all survive, and you should know it more than most after what nearly happened to you this morning."

"We both know it," I said. "But I'm handling this one and I will be careful."

"If you want to go that bad, I can't stop you, but I'd like to know what the hell you have in mind."

Not that he could be blamed for his skepticism; in his place I would have felt the same, but I could give him no real answer. Eventually I'd find Kyler, but beyond that point my imagination stopped working. It was a form of self-protection. I simply did not want to think about what would have to be done until the time came to do it.

He measured me up with a dark expression that had nothing to do with his skin color. "Charles, are you going to tear out there as well to get yourself killed?"

"Not necessary this time, Shoe. Jack should be able to handle things."

"How? What are you not telling me?"

I shrugged. "I can't go into it now and don't want to. I have to get moving, anyway."

Coldfield's frustrated curiosity could have burned a hole right through me, but he kept it under control. Maybe he was thinking of questioning Escott after I'd left. "You gonna need a ride?"

"Thanks, but I'll find a cab. Safer for all of us. Does that phone work?"

"Yeah."

I crossed over to it and memorized the number. "I'll call when I have any news."

Escott nodded slowly, correctly interpreting what I meant by "news." I tried unsuccessfully to swallow a hard knot of something that had suddenly formed in my throat. A good thing I didn't have to breathe regularly or I might have choked on it.

The time had come to leave. Coldfield led us downstairs and unlocked a different door than the one we'd come in by. I emerged in another alley, buttoning the pea jacket against the wind.

Escott wished me luck. Nobody shook hands; it wouldn't have been appropriate. As I slipped away, he murmured, "Don't underestimate him, Shoe. He'll be all right."

"Uh-huh. Where do you want to send the flowers?"

I wasn't looking forward to any of it, but the process of actually getting started made it seem like the worst was over. Not exactly true, but I was better at lying to myself than to other people. I wondered how successful Coldfield would be at getting information from Escott.

The cab could wait; I needed a walk to limber up my muscles and clear my brain of clutter. I flushed city-tainted winter air in and out of my lungs like a normal man. It had a harsh taste but I liked it. The knot in my throat began to loosen.

After a mile or so, the character of the neighborhood improved from bedraggled buildings and empty lots decorated with broken glass to small shops and other businesses. Foot traffic was light and my earlier optimism about finding a cab waned. A line waiting at the next corner told me that a bus was on the way. I stood with them, commiserating with an old lady about the weather. The talk didn't last long. I was the wrong color for the place and with my business hanging over my head, I didn't feel much like conversation no matter how banal.

The bus came, we boarded; I didn't know or care about its destination, it was enough to be moving. Pieces of the city glided by one block at a time. People crowded around me, their bits of talk and tired silences passing over my head as though I wasn't there. I stared out the dark glass of a window that gave back everyone else's reflection but my own.

It was already here, waiting, the sweet isolation that had once carried me into the darkness of my own mind. The muscles in my neck tightened for an instant as I began to resist it, and then relaxed just as abruptly. What was the point? I was going to kill a man; better to accept the fact now and get through the job quickly than fight it and have a dangerous internal distraction.

And damned if we didn't drive right past the Travis Hotel just then. The carved stone letters of its name jumped out at me like a dare. I felt a smile twitch to life in the corners of my mouth.

A respectable four-story structure on a regular city street, it gave no outer indication of inner skulduggery. Maybe I was expecting to see sinister guys with black hats and machine guns lounging around the entrances smoking cheap cigars. They were probably all waiting in the lobby. I got off at the next stop and backtracked.

This required caution; I had to keep my eyes open for Kyler's people, but not look conspicuous. Lost cause. My clothes and stubble were fine for a soup kitchen or a dockside riot, but here they only drew unwelcome attention. I crossed the street so I could view the place from a discreet doorway without offending innocent citizens.

The spot I'd picked out offered some shelter from the wind, but the awkward placement of a streetlight left me a little too visible for comfort. Since the store it led to was closed for the night, I took a chance and vanished, re-forming inside. The place sold ladies' clothes and the front windows were a busy display of some of their best items. I bent low so that my head would more or less blend in with the phony ones showing off the latest in hats, and studied the hotel opposite. Undignified, but it was out of the cold and away from immediate sight, and didn't seem to have any rabid guard dogs.

People passed back and forth across my field of view, cars did the same. The place was disappointingly normal. Except . . . the top-floor windows were all lighted. No exceptions. Kyler might have thought that leaving the lights on would scare away the boogeyman; that, or draw him into a trap. I didn't like the idea, but nothing would be resolved until I made a move. I went out the back of the shop and took the long way around to one of the hotel's service entrances.

Working with Escott had helped me develop something of an instinct for spotting the kind of human predators who would work for Kyler. I looked for them now, anticipating he'd have an army of hoods scattered around the area. Sometimes they're pretty obvious, but often it's not what you see as much as what you feel, like the way your skin creeps when a bad storm is coming. Right now, I was aware that I could not rely on that instinct. The last few nights had left me so jumpy that I was reading sinister motives off every face up to and including a couple of nuns rustling by to make their bus at the next corner.

The alley running behind the Travis had the usual loading areas and doors for the staff. It was deserted now, which surprised me; I would have expected Kyler to have someone watching his back. Again, they could be waiting inside for trouble to show up.

Invisibility has numerous advantages, but I was having second thoughts about using it now. I could—literally—slip through a door and feel my way around the place. However, there was always the chance of materializing in the wrong spot at the wrong time, giving some bystander heart failure and the hotel a reputation for harboring stray ghosts. No, thanks. On the other hand, I wasn't too crazy about the alternative I'd just thought of, given my fear of heights, but it would be better than wasting time blindly creeping through the halls.

I'd done this sort of thing before, but never for such a height. That knot in my throat, which was a solid symptom of my own fear, returned as I looked for a likely place to start.

The fire escape was promising, but too obvious. If Kyler was expecting me—or anyone else, for that matter—he'd have men covering it. Instead, I chose to try the east side of the place. The lighting was brighter, but the next building over showed only a blank face, with no inconvenient windows.

Pressing close against the hotel's outer wall, I vanished and moved slowly upward.

Distances can be very deceptive in this form, but I was prepared for that and not too surprised when it seemed to take only a moment to find the first irregularities in the wall marking the ground-floor window. I drifted over the smooth planes of glass and bumped into the next outcrop of brick above the opening. The wind got stronger the higher I went, whipped up by the narrow channels between the city's artificial canyons.

Second-floor window. If my pores had been intact, I might be sweating badly by now, fingers slick and slipping. Did human flies have this problem as they worked their stunts? Concentrate. A gust of wind hit hard just then and was gone, free and careless. I'd read somewhere that the Windy City appellation had more to do with Chicago politics than the weather. From this insecure perch, the writer would have undergone severe revision of that opinion.

Third floor. I was like a snail, sliding on an invisible foot up endless tiers of bricks. Keep going. Hold tight against the persistent tug of wind but don't go through the wall just yet. If I got dragged away I could tumble for miles, unless I panicked and went solid, which would mean a long drop lasting a very short moment. I'd survived some terrible things since my change, but that was one experience I did not want to test.

Fourth floor. The window was shut fast. Didn't matter. I plowed through it and was inside with something solid beneath me once more. Oh God, but I hate heights.

I wanted to re-form for some badly needed orientation, but couldn't chance it just yet. Waiting and listening, I swept slowly through the room, looking for company and finding none. I poured back into reality again, grateful to have a body once more, even if it was shaken and shaking.

The window had led me to a luxurious hotel room. The Travis had not stinted on comfort when it came to the owner and his guests. The bedspread looked like real silk and the carpet was thick and new, its nap still at attention from the last cleaning. Mine were the only footprints on it, magically beginning in the middle of the floor.

Behind the curtains, I noticed that the window was indeed protected by steel shutters, open now as if in invitation. That wasn't right. Kyler wouldn't be stupid enough to leave himself so vulnerable . . . not unless he'd unquestioningly swallowed Stoker's novel whole. He might just believe the stuff about vampires being unable to enter a dwelling without an invitation. Escott had—before I set him straight on that and other myths.

I checked the sill, but found no sign or smell of garlic, mustard seeds, or salt.

The place was unnaturally quiet. Some sounds of living seeped up from the other floors, but nothing else, nothing close. *Damnation,* I thought as I cautiously poked my head outside the room to check the hall. A carpet with a hypnotic pattern of stylized fans stretched away in both directions. The doors on either side were spaced well apart, indicating sizable suites. I stepped out, taking it slowly, listening for any activity behind them. Nothing. No talk, no radios playing, not even a toilet flushing. I went through one after another, but the rooms that were supposed to be crowded with Kyler's people were empty.

I should have figured he wouldn't wait around for me to come after him. The odds were strong that he hadn't left any forwarding address, though I'd search just to be certain.

Down the hall in an unexplored room, a phone began to ring. I closed on it, then hauled up short, paranoid for a trap. Better to go carefully than quickly. I vanished.

The bell drew me on like a snagged fish until I was nearly on top of it. I was about to take a turn around the room to search for company when the ringing stopped, interrupted as someone finally answered the thing.

6

"HELLO?"

A feminine voice; flat, impatient. "I *am* hurrying. . . . No, it's quiet here. . . . I tell you, I'm just finishing up. If you hadn't called I'd be in the elevator now. . . . He's down warming up the car. . . . All right, I'm on my way."

She hung up with an exasperated sigh and moved off. I returned to the hall once more and went solid, regaining sight and better-than-normal hearing. The muffling quality of the carpet and the many intervening walls had prevented me from picking up her soft movements earlier. Now I crept to the edge of the doorway, peering around for a glimpse at my unknowing hostess.

Her back was to me as she busily shrugged into her overcoat. She already had her galoshes on; both struck a chord of recognition in me. For a few seconds I debated on how to make an approach without scaring her to death, finally deciding that it couldn't be done. I simply rapped a knuckle against the door panel.

"Keep your shirt on, Chick, I'm c——" She froze in midturn. It was bad enough that I'd come out of nowhere, but I was still dressed for a dockside riot.

I put on a friendly smile and pretended hard that I was clean shaven and in a natty tux. "Opal, isn't it? We met the other night."

No bells rang for her.

"I'm here to see your boss."

"He's gone," she blurted.

"I noticed. Where is he?"

"I don't know. I don't pay attention to things like that."

Too much explanation coming too fast. "We're not off to a very good start, are we?"

No comment to that one. Maybe I wasn't her type—or Kyler had primed her with dire warnings to look out for a bloodthirsty monster. Her nervousness was understandable, but scaring women has never appealed to me. I could calm her down, influence the fear right out of her, but shied away from that all-too-easy ploy.

We stood in a well-furnished living area. Like the rest of the place, it was cleaned out. The only personal item left was her handbag, clutched protectively in white-knuckled fingers.

"Come on," I said, deciding that any action was preferable to waiting.

"What?"

"Down to the car. Chick's probably wondering what's keeping you."

The reminder that possible help was at hand wasn't enough to encourage her to move. "But I . . ."

"Come on, Opal. I'm not going to hurt you."

She took a tentative step forward on stiff legs, then balked. "No. I'm not going anywhere with you."

"You'll be all right. I'm just going to walk you to your car." I moved toward her, slowly; she was faster and backed away. Since she was determined to keep a maximum distance between us, I used that to herd her from the room.

The elevator was something of a dilemma for her, being too small for comfort. She scurried to the end of the hall and took the service stairs instead. I followed, but not too closely. I didn't want to crowd her too much or she'd trip and break something. She was wheezing badly by the time she'd reached the bottom landing. She burst into another short hall and out a metal door to the outside, going fast despite her short breath and slipping galoshes.

A new-looking DeSoto was idling across the narrow street, a heavy cloud of exhaust streaming from its tailpipe. Opal charged straight for it, screaming Chick's name.

Chick must have been primed and ready for trouble; he came boiling out of the driver's door, gun in hand. He wore a few visible lumps from last night's encounter with Udo and Jürgens, but they weren't slowing him down. He recognized me instantly and got the gun up and aimed, but Opal plowed right into him, spoiling his shot. He cursed and shoved her headfirst into the front seat to get her out of his way, then brought the gun to bear again.

I was moving too fast to stop, grabbing the gun and pushing it to the outside with my left, throwing a desperate gut punch with my right. The breath whooshed out of him and he doubled and fell, nearly dragging me down, too. But I hadn't hit him hard enough. He landed on his side and turned around just enough to sock me a solid one in the jaw with his free hand.

As socks go, it was a good one, because I felt it. I was already bent over and off balance, trying to wrest the gun away and making a lousy job of it. This one jarred me to my knees, leaving my butt up in the air. Chick seized the opportunity to awkwardly smash one of his size twelves into the seat of my pants. I sprawled, still managing to clutch the gun, and collected another punch in the ribs.

That's when I lost my temper and put the pressure on his hand. He gave out with a yell right in my ear. I kept twisting until something snapped. The yell turned into an honest-to-God shriek, and he finally let go of the gun. I swatted it well away and staggered to my feet, but he wasn't ready to give up yet and tried to belt me once more.

"Stay down, dammit," I roared at him, slapping at his head the way you do an annoying bug. He suddenly dropped flat onto the pavement and stopped moving.

Oh, shit. Had I broken his neck? I knelt next to him to see.

Fingers shaking from exertion and sheer nervousness at what they might find, I checked his throat for a pulse. Thank God. His heart was working fast, but it *was* working. Good. One less thing to worry about. Even as I straightened, he began to moan, getting ready for the second round.

Opal's initial screams had drawn a few people toward us. Three men stepped from the rest, trying to decide whether or not to interfere. They had me outnumbered, but I was a rough-looking customer. Maybe I'd had a good reason to accost an obviously respectable citizen and flatten him.

Opal had recovered and was sitting up in the seat. Once she'd realized how the fight had come out, she screamed again, noth-

ing articulate, just earsplitting and attention-drawing. The three
heroes made their decision, surging forward to protect her. Time
to get the hell out.

I forced my way into the waiting car, pushing Opal over.
There was a bad moment fumbling with the gears before the
thing finally responded. One of the men almost caught at the
handle, but I hit the gas just in time. The door swung loosely
shut as we lurched forward.

Opal made a lot of noise and attempted to crawl out the other
door. I got a handful of her coat collar and yanked her back. She
clawed blindly, fingers jabbing into my vulnerable neck. I gave
her a rough shake to stop that nonsense. She did, but the distraction was nearly enough to smash us into an inconvenient wall. I
got the wheel pulled around in time, but overcompensated. We
missed the driveway and bumped violently over a high curb
into the street. Opal bounced halfway to the roof, came down
hard, and slipped under the dashboard with an outraged
squawk.

I yelled at her to stay put as I fought to keep a straight course.
We managed to swerve away from an oncoming car, miss a
parked one, and pick up more speed. I'd need it. As far as those
people in the street were concerned, I'd just kidnapped an innocent, albeit noisy girl, no doubt for some horrible purpose. They
were probably calling the DeSoto's license number in to the
cops right now.

It had finally penetrated to Opal that this would not be a good
time to make an exit. She crouched under the dash, holding on
to the seat for balance and glaring at me, anger overriding fear
for the moment.

"Your glasses are crooked," I told her.

She straightened them automatically. "Where are you going?"

I surprised her and myself with a laugh. "Damned if I know,
sister. Your boss has made this town too hot for me to be anyplace."

"Let me out. I mean it. Let me out right now."

"Uh-uh." But I checked first before answering to make sure
she didn't have a gun to enforce her demand. More complica-
tions I did not need.

She climbed from under the dash, straightening her clothes
with jerky, frustrated movements.

"Sit on your hands," I ordered.

"What?"

More slowly. "Sit on your hands, Opal. If you don't, I'll have to deck you just like I did Chick."

She was smart enough not to argue. Grumbling, she squirmed around on the seat.

"Get them well under, put your weight on them."

"Okay, okay."

We were approaching a stop signal; she settled in just in time. The line of cars ahead indicated we'd all have a long wait. She simmered and looked longingly out her window toward escape, but behaved herself until the signal changed and our turn to move came up. While I was busy with the gears and wheel, she wrenched her hands free and tried to get out the door.

I grabbed her arm at the last second and hauled her back. "Relax, sister, or it's beddy-bye time." The threat wouldn't have fooled a ten-year-old, but worked on her. She chewed her lower lip into a fine shade of pink with her small teeth.

"Please let me go." Just beginning to understand her new situation, she was hard put to keep the whine out of her voice.

"That sounds like a good idea, honey. Where shall I take you?"

She came that close to blurting it out, but her mouth snapped shut before she could betray her boss.

"All right," I sighed. "Then we'll have to do it the hard way."

"What do you mean?"

"You'll find out." Eventually, I located the perfect spot, coasting to a stop in front of a closed gas station with an outside telephone box. Opal squeaked when I took her arm again and tried to shrug away.

"Leave me alone."

"At the first opportunity," I promised. With a little forceful coaxing, I drew her out of the car, squeezing us unhappily into the phone box. She kept as far away from me as possible, which was not easy, given the circumstances. I blocked the door and fumbled out a nickel.

Escott answered before the first ring had finished.

"It's me."

"Are you all right?" he asked cautiously. It was a loaded question. Translation: had I killed Kyler yet?

"Just peachy. Kyler's flown the coop, but it wasn't a total waste of time. I've turned up a new angle."

"What sort of angle?"

"Remember the other night at the Satchel? Kyler's accountant, Opal?" Opal glared at me, her jaw working.

"Certainly."

"I've got her."

"You've—" He broke off as the implications soaked in.

"Yeah, and I want to bring her over, but you need to warn our temporary landlord to keep out of the way so he doesn't get drawn into this mess. The fewer people she sees, the better. You know what I mean?"

"I understand perfectly."

"Okay. I'll come by in the same door that I used to leave. We'll be there in about ten minutes."

"I'll be prepared."

We hung up, then I had to expend some effort to wrestle Opal back into the car without hurting her. She started to screech, leaving me with no option but to clamp a hand over her mouth and lift her bodily up and in. She ran out of breath before I ran out of determination. The street was momentarily deserted, but enough noise could change that in short order. I hauled ass out of there.

"This stinks and I hate you," she announced, verging on tears.

"And you're the light of my life, too. Now get under the dash."

"What?"

"Just do it, Opal!" The tone of my voice got through to her. She ducked down, fast.

After a peaceful interval, she complained, "This thing's digging into my back."

"Then stop trying to sit up."

"Why can't I?"

"You don't need to know where we're going."

"But I'm getting carsick down here."

"Fine. If you puke, be sure to keep it on your side."

"You . . ." But she was too nice a girl to use that kind of language. She tried another tack. "I can sit on my hands again. I promise I won't make any trouble."

I didn't answer.

"Really, I won't. I'll even keep my eyes shut."

"Better if you stay put."

"You—you won't think so in a minute," she gasped.

Alarmed, I checked on her. A person doesn't turn that shade of light green voluntarily. She was gulping, too. I hastily pulled to the curb and rolled down my window to give her air. "Better?"

She shook her head, her eyes desperate. Damnation. I leaned over and opened the passenger door. She crawled forward and got her head out just in time. I gripped her collar to keep her from bolting, but it wasn't really necessary. When she finally finished and I pulled her back onto the seat, she was exhausted and puffing like a beached fish, tears streaming down her swollen face.

"You all right, kid?" I found a handkerchief and offered it. She glared and wrinkled her nose. "Go on, it's clean." I pushed it into her hand.

"Why don't you leave me alone?"

"Just blow your nose."

She did, several times.

"You can keep the handkerchief," I said, suddenly inspired to generosity.

"Will you *please* let me go?"

I ignored the subject. "Feel better now?"

Sniff. "I guess so."

"Good. Get back under the dash."

Her mouth popped open and as quickly snapped shut. She looked ready to burst into real tears now, not just the by-product of being sick. "You're *mean*."

"Yeah, I cheat old ladies and kick dogs all the time."

"This stinks. Vaughn's going to get you for this." But she got back down and I resumed driving.

To keep her mind off getting carsick again, I asked, "How'd you come to work for a guy like him, anyway?"

She scowled as though I were a total idiot. "I'm a great accountant. You ask me anything about numbers and I know it."

Off the top of my head I asked: "The square root of pi, what is it?"

"Pi is a transcendental number, you can't take its square root. Ferdinand Lindemann's already proved that. Since it's an irrational number its numerical representation can only be an ap-

proximation of its value, and those numbers' square roots will
also be approximations. That's algebra, anyway. I can do it, but
accounting's better. In a correctly balanced ledger, numbers are
always sensible and clean."

I gulped, knowing that I'd seriously underestimated this little
gal. "Ah ... whatever you say, but doesn't it bother you how
Kyler makes the money you're adding up for him?"

She shrugged, indifferent.

"Or that he kills people?"

"Will you let me go? I won't tell on you."

"No."

She crossed her arms, resting them on the seat cushion, and
stared at the door handle. "This stinks. Vaughn's going to get
you good for stealing his car. He'll get you good for doing this."

I shot her a look. Somewhere along the way I'd missed something and it was just now catching up with me. "What's fifty-six
times eighteen?"

"One thousand eight," she replied in a bored tone.

"Fifty-six divided by eighteen?"

"Three, remainder two or three point one one one one . . ."

"I'll take your word for it."

"Told you I was good," she said smugly.

"How old are you?"

"Twenty-three years, four months, and eleven days."

"Now you're just showing off."

"Am not. That's the truth."

I tried a few more sums and the answers poured out of her as
fast as she heard the questions. It kept her occupied until we
reached Coldfield's building. I backed the car deep into the alley shadows. Just as I cut the motor, Escott opened the side door
for us. I urged Opal to come along, aware that I sounded like a
dog owner working with an especially difficult pet. Hugging
her purse, she finally climbed out, and I guided her inside.

"Opal, this is Charles ... Charles, Opal," I said once he'd
locked the door.

"Delighted to meet you again, miss," he responded, with a
slight inclination of his head.

She pouted at him, suspicious. "You were at the Satchel. You
didn't have a black eye then."

He glanced at me. I gave him a "be careful" expression. "Yes.
That's where we met."

She put a disapproving twist to her lips, but decided not to hold it against him. "We only just met *here*; the Satchel was where I *saw* you," she stated, then pointed a finger straight at me. "*He* won't let me go. Will you?"

He instantly came out with a thin but charming smile. "Won't you come inside and warm yourself first? It's much too cold for traveling right now." He gestured upstairs, managing to get her there with no more fuss.

She glared at the sparse furnishings and kicked at the empty packing crate that served as a table. "This stinks."

I told Opal to be quiet and read a magazine. We backed out the door, but kept it open to make sure she left the phone alone.

"Jack . . . ," he murmured from the side of his mouth.

"I know. At first I thought she was just acting cute, but it's no act."

"And you're certain she's his accountant?"

"Oh, yeah. I don't know how, but she's some kind of a genius when it comes to numbers."

"Even if she is a bit wanting in the social graces. You're sure about her being the new angle you mentioned on the phone?"

"Mostly she got dragged along for the ride, and now I'm kind of stuck with her, but I think she may know where Kyler is."

"In which case it should be easy enough to persuade her to part with the information."

"I was thinking maybe you could charm it out of her with that Ronald Colman act of yours."

Instead of bristling with his usual reply to the joke, he said, "You really don't want to hypnotize her, do you?"

No use trying to hide anything from him; he was too damn sharp. This was a talk I'd been dreading, but would have to have sooner or later. God knows, I owed him an explanation.

"Something's happened," he said. He was trying to make it easy, but I was wincing inside.

"It's too dangerous."

He paused over that one. "For you or the subject?"

"Both."

"How so?"

"It's a trap. The last . . . the last time I was talking—starting to talk, starting to get information . . . I lost control."

"In what way?"

Dammit. "I nearly killed her."

"Miss Grey?" He kept his tone low and neutral, a vocal counterbalance to my obvious twitchiness.

"Yeah."

That answered a lot of questions for him, but not all. He waited for me to go on.

"We were alone in her studio and I'd just put her under to get some answers. Then it just . . . took me over. I got caught up in something I couldn't control. That's when I stopped thinking."

Stopped thinking and began feeding, draining the blood from her as though she were one of the cattle at the Stockyards. Helpless, but uncaring, she'd been swept away and submerged in the sensual pleasure of that joining. I had played upon it, used it to satisfy an appetite and desire blended together to the point of destruction for us both. She'd have lost her life and I . . . what? Illusions about myself? My sanity? My soul? None would have mattered; she'd have still been dead.

"I . . . broke away before it was too late, but it was hard. I almost didn't."

"This aspect of your condition has always bothered you," he pointed out.

"Jesus, Charles, *every* aspect of it has bothered me at one time or another; I may never get used to being what I am. But this . . . I don't want to put anyone through that risk again."

"But you've done it many times before, what made this particular one different?"

That I'd been alone with her, or mildly attracted to her, or feeling the first inevitable pangs of hunger? "It doesn't matter."

"It does, my friend, because there are other lives than your own or even hers to consider." He wasn't indifferent to Opal, or using guilt to pressure, only stating facts that I'd already considered. Opal watched us from the windowless room, trying to read our faces for a clue to her future.

"Which puts me right between a rock and a hard place," I grumbled. "So what do I do?"

"I cannot decide for you. There are other ways of finding out what we need. Shoe or Gordy can probably help, but this will be quickest."

I turned away and paced down the hall and back. My choice was no choice, not when it came between promises to myself or protecting my friends. Opal would be safe enough with Escott acting as chaperon, but it was cold comfort at best.

My hands were starting to shake.

Opal hadn't liked waiting and said as much when we came in to sit with her. With that very clear opinion out of the way, she hunched down in her coat and crossed her arms protectively against any possible counter argument. Escott gave me a silent nod to indicate that it was my show, content to melt into the background.

In an attempt to change the subject and to get her more relaxed, I said, "You know you never really answered my question about how you came to work for Kyler."

She sensed some less obvious purpose than curiosity behind the question, and used her earlier answer. "Because I'm a great accountant."

"That tells me why, but not how. When did you meet him?"

"Two years, two months, and fifteen days ago."

I should have been prepared for that one but wasn't. My expression amused her. "That's very good."

"I know."

"How did you meet him?"

"I was a cashier at a restaurant. They wanted a singing cashier, but I didn't sing, I did numbers instead."

"Did numbers?"

"Like I did for you in the car. People'd ask me to add and subtract and stuff like that in my head. I'd do numbers for the customers to make tips. Vaughn ate there one day and asked if I could do bookkeeping and I said yes."

"If you knew bookkeeping, why weren't you doing that?"

"Because bookkeepers make eight dollars a week and no tips when they start out. I was making fifteen at the restaurant . . . plus tips."

"So Vaughn offered you a new job and you took it?"

"For a thousand dollars a month."

Wow. "What's your family think of your work?"

"They don't care about me. When I finished school, they told me to move out."

"Just like that?"

She shrugged. "They never liked me."

"Your own parents?"

"I'm smart, but in my own way. I wasn't smart in the way they wanted, so they didn't like having me around. Everything I said and did was wrong. I was glad to leave."

"I'll bet you were, kid."

"Don't call me that." She pulled her shoulders tighter, the corners of her mouth turning sharply down. "You're like them, too. Treating me like I'm a baby because I'm different from everyone else. They'd talk about it and think that I didn't hear or care, but I did."

"How does Kyler treat you?"

"He doesn't laugh at me or act embarrassed or talk like I'm not in the room, or talk out in the hall so I don't hear anything." She glared at us. Justifiably so, I thought.

"I'm sorry we have to do this, Opal. We—"

"Nuts to you. This stinks." She turned her back and stared at a dingy wall.

"Yeah, it does. Kyler's probably the best thing that ever happened to you."

"He's okay."

"Even when he kills people?"

"I've never seen him do that."

"Or talk about it? He wants to kill me, you know."

She looked around sharply. "So you're the one."

There went my plan to relax her. "Yeah. He ever say anything about me?"

Her eyes went solemn; her little mouth clamped shut.

"What'd he say?"

But she only shook her head, preferring refusal over lying. At least she didn't seem to be frightened of me. It would be easy enough to push her into answering.

Too easy, as I knew it would be. Always far too easy.

We soon learned that Kyler had forsaken his downtown fortress in the Travis for a more isolated roadhouse he'd recently bought. The purchase had been so far under the table that only a select few in his organization knew about it. Opal, fortunately, had been one of them and freely parted with details on the price, location, and normal hours of operation. It was open now with business as usual to avoid attracting attention, but tonight they would have an extra patron dropping in on them.

"It is most likely that he knows about Opal's disappearance," Escott pointed out. "And he may act upon it."

"Probably so. Chick wasn't that far gone when I left, but this is all I've got for now. I'll give the place a going-over and see what's there. Kyler can't hide forever."

"He's really mad," Opal volunteered in her flat voice as she drifted softly between consciousness and sleep.

No new information there, but was she talking about Kyler's mental state or his feelings? "Mad at me?"

"Oh, yes. Really mad because of last night. Those men you killed."

"I didn't kill them."

"Okay, the men the big guy had killed for you."

"Who? You talking about Gordy?"

"Uh-huh. He's going to get it bad tonight."

"What do you mean?"

"Vaughn's going to get back at him."

I flashed a look at Escott, but he was already on the phone, dialing the Nightcrawler's number. "What's he got in mind?"

"I don't know."

"You have to, Opal. Tell me everything he said."

"I didn't hear the rest. I was busy packing to leave."

Escott had gotten through to Gordy by then. "Yes, we're all right, but we've learned that Kyler's made plans for some sort of reprisal against you. . . . Because he thinks that you were involved with the shooting of three of his men last night when they tried to kidnap Jack. . . . No, I don't know what it could be."

"When will it happen, Opal?" I asked.

"I don't know."

I shrugged at Escott. She had an exceptional memory, but there was no way I could get information that she didn't have. He relayed it to Gordy and hung up after a minute. "He's been expecting something like this since last night, when they went after us. But he appreciated the additional warning."

"What about Bobbi?"

"He said for you not to worry."

"I'm going over there, anyway."

His eyes glinted. "I rather thought you would. Your presence may be of considerable help."

"Only if I get there in time. Will you be okay baby-sitting her?" I jerked my chin at Opal.

"She seems quiet enough."

Something that wouldn't last until my return. I knelt close by her, taking care not to touch her, and did what I could to ensure that Escott would have a peaceful evening.

Her lids slid shut and she curled comfortably upon the cot. Asleep, her pinched face smoothed out, easing the creases of determined concentration that were already gathering around her mouth and brow. Escott pulled a blanket up over her legs, then removed her glasses, folding them neatly on the packing crate.

"Are you all right?" he asked.

It hadn't been as bad as I'd anticipated, but my gut felt like jelly and he could see the tremor in my hands. I balled them into fists and shoved them into the pockets of the pea jacket. Car keys scratched my knuckles. "Go ahead and call Shoe. Let him know what's going on. I'll take the DeSoto over to the club."

"But—"

"Yeah, I know it's hot, but I'll have to chance it. I'm not waiting around for a cab."

He nodded, then I was out the door and down the stairs.

I had to fight to keep within the limits of the traffic around me. Running into another cop I could handle, but it would cost time. My too-fertile imagination worked full blast throughout the trip, coming up with a variety of attacks that Kyler might try. He could strafe the place with machine-gun fire, as with Escott's car, or lob grenades through any of the windows. The aftermath would bring out the Feds like flies on a corpse. Between them and the local law . . .

And Bobbi was smack in the middle of it. I sneaked up the pressure on the gas pedal and tore around a slow truck.

Things must have also gone wrong for Angela Paco. Vic might not have been in a condition to carry whatever message she had for Kyler. He could have died on her by now or she had needed both of us and I'd slipped out and spoiled it all. Whatever the reason, Kyler didn't know about her involvement and had logically blamed Gordy for the mess she'd left in the street. That's why his goons had been waiting near the club and opened up the moment Escott's Nash showed with me in it.

But that had been last night and a full day had come and gone with no further trouble. If he was spooked enough by Gordy's apparent involvement, why had he decided to wait? It would only give his opposition time to set up defenses or a counter-attack. His hope might be that Gordy would leave rather than risk an open gang war, but he couldn't count on it.

Or maybe he was just waiting for me to turn up again and knew that would happen only after dark.

I left the car in a deserted spot a block away from the club. Going by foot was slower, but it gave me plenty of time to check the area. I kept to the shadows, becoming invisible whenever I had to cross an open space or pass under a street-light. Halfway there, I had to quit because other people were turning up, well-dressed men in polished shoes hurrying along with their polished ladies. Some looked worried, glancing back over their shoulders, others giggled with tipsy relief. Club patrons, then, and too rushed to wait in the lobby for a cab to come for them.

It looked like Kyler had started without me.

Ahead, the flash of lights played along the high walls of the buildings. I picked up the busy commotion of human voices and the grunt of car engines and moved faster against a thin tide of people flowing from the club.

Cops and cop cars everywhere, their lights snapping in endless circles. No ambulances, at least not yet, but a couple of paddy wagons blocked the front entrance and were doing a good business.

A raid?

Gordy had been through this drill more than once, but he was a good businessman and paid his bribes like everyone else to avoid such problems. But Kyler had used the police before, trying to trap me at the warehouse, so why not again to get at Gordy?

The cops were probably all over the casino tagging the slot machines for evidence or pounding them to junk with sledge-hammers just for the hell of it. Some sawhorse barricades were up to keep out the public, including me. Fat lot of good it did them as I slipped around to the side of the building and picked out a window on the club's second floor.

I re-formed in an unoccupied bath and shot out to the adjoining bedroom. Bobbi's room was just across from it. The door was wide and her things scattered about, but she was gone. That could be good or bad.

Staying solid, I left the outer bedroom for the hall. It was empty for the moment, but I heard voices coming from Gordy's office. Time to get some answers.

Three men looked up at my sudden barge through the door: Gordy standing by the far wall, a uniformed cop next to him, and a plainclothes man in front. All but Gordy jumped a little. He was deadpan by nature, but there seemed to be a hint of relief in his small eyes and an undeniable sheen of sweat clung to his temples. Something was wrong, wrong, *wrong*.

The uniform had his gun out and it hovered uncertainly between me and Gordy. I fanned both hands up in a placating gesture.

"Take it easy, boys, I'm just here to cover things for the *Trib*."

"You sure as hell don't look it," said the other man.

At least he didn't question the presence of the press, however seedily it was clothed. On raids like this, the cops don't mind having reporters around; it made good publicity for the department. "I was working a skid-row story and saw the ruckus. You can't blame me for wanting to drop in for a look."

"And that's all you'll get. Beat it."

"Aw, c'mon, Sergeant." I had to guess at his rank. "Gimme a break, I gotta wife and kids to feed. How 'bout a short interview? I'll make you the hero of the day. What's your name?" I fumbled for my notebook and pencil, stalling for time.

"That's Lieutenant Calloway, you asshole." He was keeping himself on a short leash; I'd read that from him the instant I'd walked in. The tension washing around the room was thick enough for swimming. The uniformed man was as cool as Calloway was hot. On the desk was a gun, taken from Gordy no doubt, and a stupid thing to leave lying around. There was more going on here than a simple arrest. These guys had other things on their minds.

"Lieutenant Calloway asshole . . . ," I repeated, pretending to write it down. I shouldn't have done it that way, but he'd left himself open and I couldn't resist. It was one way to bring things to a head.

"Baker, get him outta here!"

"Just joking, Lieutenant," I said as Baker closed in. "Okay, you're officer Baker and what's your badge number?"

Baker started to hustle me out. There was no time to think up anything fancy; once I was out of the room anything could happen. Shrugging off his grip, I turned for a parting shot. "And how much is Vaughn Kyler paying you for this hit?"

Calloway's eyes got big. Baker froze solid. I didn't catch Gordy's expression, but he made a small noise in the back of his throat to communicate that I'd just thrown an appallingly large hunk of shit into the fan.

"Bring him back," Calloway said. "And this time lock up."

7

BAKER SWUNG THE door firmly shut and slid home the inside bolt. I didn't like having him behind me and instinctively turned and backed away to keep him in sight. If he decided to shoot, I wanted to see it coming. Calmly alert, he remained in place, a professional wearing a cop's uniform, but not a cop.

"Who the hell are you?" Baker's face was as blank as a store window's dummy. I wondered if he was a close relation to Kyler.

I looked past them and said, "Bobbi." It sounded like a statement, but Gordy took it for the question I meant it to be. To my relief, he shut his eyes briefly and gave a minimal nod. She was okay, then, wherever she was. That concern off my mind, I was more ready to deal with these clowns.

Baker was on the ball and noticed the interplay. "He's lying."

"Search him."

He closed in cautiously. I let him slap me down without any fuss because Calloway was standing there with his hand inside his unbuttoned coat expecting trouble. The car keys, some loose change, a pencil stub, and a thin notebook were tossed on the desk next to the gun. The money belt stayed in place; he wasn't looking for money.

"He's clean." Baker sounded disappointed as well as suspicious. If I'd been one of Gordy's men, I'd have been packing something lethal as a matter of course; if a legitimate reporter, then a wallet with some kind of identification.

"Doesn't matter," said Calloway, who was coming out of his initial shock. "What do you know about Kyler?"

I kept my eyes steady. "Enough to spot a couple of his stooges while they trip over themselves. He's picked the wrong target this time. Gordy had nothing to do with last night's hit."

"So we should take your word for it? Get him over there, Baker." He gestured at Gordy's end of the room.

"But it's a pretty sharp plan," I continued, as though he hadn't spoken. "Using a real raid as cover, you two come up here for the big fish. Only you'll invent some kind of problem and be forced to kill him, say, while he's resisting arrest. His New York bosses won't pull any reprisals against the official Chicago police because you were just doing your job. Baker can disappear in the crowd and the whole business leaves Kyler totally clear of the blame. So . . . how much are you getting to do his dirty work?"

Calloway looked ready to drop back into shock again, but picked his jaw up faster this time. "What's it to you? What's your angle?"

"I figure you can lay off of Gordy, which is okay since he's not behind that shooting like I said, and just take me with you to see your boss."

"Why should we?"

Baker interrupted my answer. "Shut up, Calloway, it's him. It's Fleming."

Calloway was quick enough to understand and react; God knows what Kyler had said about me. He pulled his gun free and centered it on my chest. Baker's was already out but there was just enough of a difference in his manner to warn me that he was going to take it one step further. Having been there myself, I instantly recognized it in another. His eyes went blank as he slid into that place of non-thought that makes it possible to kill.

As his gun leveled and centered, he darkened into a gray blur. The rasp of his lungs faded and surged again as I hurled at him, fast as thought. My hands became solid once more to fasten onto his. Momentum carried us into the wall and that put an end to the fight before it could really start. His skull bounced once, he grunted out a thick breath in reaction, and slithered to the floor with his eyes rolled up.

I turned to take care of Calloway, but Gordy was there first and making a short job of it. He'd wrestled him down, using his weight to good advantage to keep him pinned. I stepped in and relieved Calloway of his gun, then dropped to one knee to better focus on him. It might not have been too safe since I had to step up the pressure to get through, but it was fast and we needed speed. He stopped struggling after a moment; seconds later, he was deeply asleep. I broke away and backed off.

Gordy looked down at Calloway, then up to me. "How'd you do that?"

"Beats me, but it works."

"Sure as hell does, kid, and that disappearing trick . . ."

"Comes in handy once in a while, I know. Are you all right?"

He found his feet and dusted his knees. "Yeah. They were all set, you came just in time. I owe you one."

"We'll call it even if you tell me where Bobbi is."

"Locked in the basement."

"Locked?"

"It was her idea. There's a hidden room down there for emergencies."

"And a secret tunnel, too?" I joked.

"How'd you know?"

"I didn't. You mean you've really got one of those?"

"Only to the building across the street. The basements connect up."

"Maybe you and Escott should compare notes."

"Yeah? Why?"

"It's sort of a hobby with him. What d'you have one for?"

"When things were jumping hot in this town between Big Al and everyone else during Prohibition, it seemed like a good idea to have another way outta the place."

"It still is. You should use it until this blows over."

"First I make some phone calls." He gestured at the two unconscious men. "Maybe they're crooked, but this raid was real enough and I'm needing my lawyer to start putting things back together."

"You got any plans for these guys?" I asked thoughtfully.

"I'm for dumping them out the nearest window, then getting away. You got something better in mind?"

"Yeah. I want them to take me to Kyler."

He shook his massive head. "Dangerous, kid. You'll end up showing your face to a lot of other cops who don't need to see it."

Nothing like an example to illustrate a point. I vanished, reappearing a few feet to his right. An ear-to-ear grin was my automatic response to Gordy's open-mouth stare. "Think again. These mugs won't even know I'm along."

After some quick phoning to start things rolling in the legal department, we unlocked the door and cautiously checked the upper hall for invaders. Clear. Gordy locked it from the outside to keep out any importune visitors, then we hustled down to the ground-floor landing. The activity here was casual; just one cop passed us and he only nodded, not so much at me but the uniform. I'd borrowed Baker's hat and overcoat, one too small and the other too short, but it had just proved its effectiveness as cover.

Oops. Wrong assumption. The cop paused, turned, and gave me a tough once-over. "When's the last time you had a shave, kid? Just because you're working this end of things doesn't mean you can run around looking like that."

"Uh . . ."

"And those ain't regulation shoes, neither. What's your name and badge number?"

I locked eyes with him and hoped for the best. It was draining to do it like this and tough on my conscience, but in for a penny, in for a pound, as Escott might have said. "Jack Sprat could eat no fat," I babbled.

"What?"

The distraction of the rhyme took him off balance. The harder he focused to understand what the hell I was talking about, the easier he made it for me. "You didn't even see us, officer. Go on with what you were doing."

"Okay," he said reasonably, and walked off, just like that.

Gordy let out his breath. "Jeez."

"That goes double for me. Let's move."

For a big man, Gordy knew how to be light on his feet; we fairly shot down the next flight of steps.

The deserted basement was as the raid had left it, with the door open, only a couple of dim lights on, and a mess littering the floor. We dodged around some overturned crates and smashed bottles, working toward the south wall. The farther we went, the happier I was to have company. Unlike the homey familiarity of my own underground room, this one was too large for comfort. The ceiling pressed close and the silence was like a vast monster watching us from the shadows.

Damn my imagination, anyway. I swallowed it back with private embarrassment. Bobbi was stuck down here with no way of knowing what was going on and I was the one trying not to be afraid of the dark. I'd once invented a mythical Vampire's Union as a joke; this kind of nervousness would be enough to get me tossed out, fangs and all. Holding on to that crumb of lunacy got me through the next few minutes.

Gordy stopped over a dip in the floor with a large square drainage grate set into its lowest point. He braced himself and lifted it out.

"My God, you put her in there?" I whispered, staring at the black pit he'd uncovered.

"Not as bad as it looks."

He sat, swung his legs over the edge, and carefully placed his feet on some thick iron rungs set into the smooth cement of the walls. The descent was short, the bottom not more than eight feet down. The hole wasn't much bigger than a phone booth. Gordy fired up a match with one hand and used the other to grip something and push. A narrow door opened away from him. He stooped low and was gone.

I scrambled down the ladder, cracking an ankle against the last rung. Gordy, holding the door for me, waved me in. I ducked and followed and he let it close up behind. His match went out.

I worked spit into my mouth. "You got another light?"

"Jack? Is it you?"

Bobbi's clear, sane, and extremely welcome voice seemed to dispel the crushing atmosphere in my overactive brain. A distant flashlight blazed smack into my face, blinding me as effectively as the total darkness. I didn't mind.

The flash wavered from side to side as she trotted up. "Jack, Gordy, is everything okay?" She threw herself into my arms and I gathered her up in a tender bear hug.

"For the moment, honey." I reluctantly eased her down. "What about you? This place is terrible."

She almost echoed Gordy's earlier comment. "It's not so bad. I just pretend I'm a Becky Thatcher who's given Tom Sawyer the slip. C'mon." She took my hand to lead away with the bobbing light down a cement tunnel with smooth walls and a level floor. It turned once to the left and went up a step. The cement changed to ancient brick and pressed closer.

"Slick's mob built all this?" I asked.

"Not Slick," Gordy answered somewhere behind us. "Pearly Garson. He was scared of Big Al, but wanted to be like him. He heard that Al had an escape tunnel, so he had to have one, too."

"Take long to dig?"

"Nah. He tied it into an old rail delivery system that the city forgot about, even got some of the labor for free. They've tightened up on some of the graft these days, but back then you could get away with murder."

True, and he wasn't just speaking figuratively. "What happened to Pearly?"

"Got shot by his girlfriend's husband, then they took off for Canada. Never did catch those two. Cops still have the case open, but Slick moved in and made sure nobody kicked about it too much. It was one hell of a funeral."

The walls widened to a circular space that resembled a hub of some kind. More cement sealed up what had once been other branches leading off to goodness knows where beneath the city. I could have sieved through and gone exploring, but that would have to wait until sometime after hell froze over.

"All the comforts of home," Bobbi said cheerfully, gesturing at a portable lantern burning on the grit-cluttered floor with a camp stool next to it. She turned the light up, revealing all the dreary details. It was fairly dry, which was the best that could be said about the place.

"Aren't you freezing down here?" I asked. I was getting cold just looking at the endless rows of brickwork encircling us.

She gave herself a hug within her heavy coat, its high fur collar bunching up her bright blond hair. "Haven't even thought about it. What I want to know is if it's safe to leave now."

Gordy shook his head. "The raid's pretty much over, but we're gonna get out of the way for a while. I called the lawyer and fixed it. We'll go to his place. He'll have a spare room for you."

"Jack, too?" she asked hopefully.

"Not yet, sweetheart," I said.

She read my face, her own clouding up in response. "Then it's not over, is it?"

"It will be soon."

"For Kyler or you? You don't look so good, Jack."

I rallied for her sake. "I just need to clean up and shave."

She nodded slowly, accepting the offered illusion, but not at all fooled by it. "What next?"

"We get you the hell out of here."

Bobbi wasn't all that in love with the place. Gordy took the flashlight, I picked up the lantern, and we started hiking. It seemed like a very long trip. I began to wonder if the tunnel ran down the length of the street instead of crossing it when a slab of iron loomed out of the dark to block our path. I hoped that it was a door; it had a handle but nothing like a lock or bolt on this side. Gordy gave it a hard twist, lifting and pulling at the same time. The thing gave and abruptly came away toward him, revealing the yawning darkness of what I could assume to be the other basement.

"Cozy," I croaked. Both of them remained diplomatically oblivious to my nerves.

"Goes up through a furniture store," Gordy laconically explained. "The lawyer's car'll be waiting for us."

"Sure it's safe?"

"Better'n any bank."

"I'll be fine," Bobbi assured me. "Will you?"

That helped to straighten me up. Once again, she read my face right and we came together like a magnet and a bar of steel, each giving the other what was needed to hold on a little longer.

Bobbi and I weren't in any hurry to say good-bye, but Gordy pointed out that there was no telling how long the two cops would stay in dreamland. Sooner or later one of them would wake up or some enterprising member of the raid might decide to break into the office to see what was on the other side. I had things to do before that happened.

We reluctantly broke off. She gave me a last smile and squeeze on the arm and ducked through ahead of Gordy. He handed me a spare key to his office and followed her. A shift of metal and a heavy clang and we were solidly separated with very different directions to take. Armed with the lantern and trying to hold my mind on more important things than claustrophobia, I quickly returned to the Nightcrawler's basement.

Neatly dropping the grate back into place, I all but galloped across to the stairs. I left the lantern behind, making a point of turning it out, then vanished and floated upward.

It was safer in this form; any cops on the lookout for trouble would miss me, and I didn't have to worry about making noise while whipping around the landings to the second floor. I reached Gordy's office and went on through. The place was quiet. I materialized.

Thankfully, Calloway was still on the rug, sprawled on his back, and just starting to snore. Baker was where I'd left him. I shrugged out of his coat. It wasn't easy wrestling it back on him again, but things had to look right. If he noticed, he'd probably attribute his rumpled condition to our brief run-in. At least he didn't wake up, which didn't worry me too much; Calloway was my prime concern.

His snores were in full swing. It seemed a shame to disturb him, except he wasn't all that aware when I started talking to him in a low, persuasive tone. He took the orders without question, same as the other cop had, and lay there like a zombie while I quietly unlocked the door from the inside. After dropping the key in the top drawer of Gordy's desk, I stood a moment to take in a last bracing breath, then snapped my fingers.

That was Calloway's cue to wake up. I disappeared just as his eyes flickered open.

He moaned, groaned, and cursed whatever aches his body had provided for the occasion, but eventually got to his feet. I kept clear of him, not wishing to advertise the least hint of my presence. He made a trip out to the hall and back, presumably to the nearby washroom for water. I heard a soft splash followed by Baker making outraged sputtering noises.

"What the hell . . . !"

"On your feet, Baker. We gotta get moving."

"What happened?"

"You let that jerk-off kid mop the floor with you, that's what happened." He'd somehow overlooked the fact that Gordy had also fallen on him like an avalanche.

"Shit, I didn't even see it coming."

"Well, too bad for you."

"Where'd they go?"

"Out. C'mon."

"Where?"

"Kyler's. He's gonna want to know about this."

"Criminey, couldn't you just phone him?"

I'd anticipated that alternative and smiled invisibly.

"He'll want to see us personally," he said, repeating my instructions to him, word for word. He made them sound normal.

More grouse, more mild objections, but in the end they straggled downstairs with me in their wake.

Calloway collared one of the regular cops and asked after Gordy.

"You kiddin', Lieutenant? We've been tearing the place apart for him. You'd think a guy that big would have turned up by now."

I recognized the voice of the officer who had stopped us on the way to the basement.

"What about another man, tall, dark hair, needs a shave?"

Long pause, or so it seemed to me. "Nah, no one like that. Check with the boys out front. Maybe they bagged him with the others."

"Got away," Baker muttered when the cop left.

"Can't help it now. Let's get out before someone spots you instead."

"You still going to . . . going to see him?"

Calloway answered by walking off. Baker reluctantly followed. I stuck with them as they went through a regular obstacle course to their car. Like a slightly colder blast of wind, I whipped inside one of the open doors and settled on the floor behind the driver's seat. With my long legs crammed up over the drive shaft hump, I cautiously went solid again, the better to get an idea of our destination.

The ride was tense for me; I had to stay alert, ready to vanish any second should one of them happen to glance back. It was also silent with Baker nursing his bruised head and Calloway concentrating on the road. Plagued as I was by occasional motion sickness, I felt a strong pang of sympathy for Opal's difficulty earlier tonight. At least I wasn't riding with my back to the motor, though being stuffed in sideways couldn't have been that much better.

And so I occupied myself with internal complaints over minor discomforts. The idea was to keep my mind off the near future and a job for which I had no enthusiasm.

A lot more driving, starts and stops, then a long steady stretch which helped to steady my stomach. Turn, then turn again onto a bumpy surface that threatened to undo everything. I had to brace myself to keep from rattling around too much and betraying my presence. We crunched to a final stop, tires sliding over gravel and gravel sliding over mud. Calloway cut the motor. I soaked in the comparative silence for only a second before disappearing. Calloway and Baker got out and I gave them plenty of time to get well away. Solid once more, I cautiously lifted for a peek out the window.

As a roadhouse, it could have qualified as anyone else's mansion, but I wouldn't have expected Kyler to invest in a shack, not after seeing his setup at the Travis. This one had a couple of sprawling stories' worth of white-trimmed brown brick with an extra-wide porch running all around. In the summer it probably sported tables, with romantic couples wanting to watch the moon rise over the surrounding trees. Music leaked out from within. It was the kind of place I'd have taken Bobbi to for a nice dinner and some close dancing. Too bad about the new owner. . . .

Never mind that for now.

I quit the car and circled the house. The front parking lot was full; the back was less crowded, but more informative. Kyler's twin Cadillacs were parked together next to the rear entrance, noses out, prepared for a fast exit.

This was the right place and the time had come, but I hesitated to move, held back by the blankness of the immediate future. No specific plan of what to do during that final confrontation had descended upon me. To be practical, not knowing the layout or circumstances ahead meant that improvisation would be a necessity . . . but the time had come, the time had come.

Before, I'd dreaded slipping into the efficient madness that had carried me through one murder; now I was afraid of not finding it again. It was far preferable to be borne comfortably along in a soothing haze of insanity than to have each action and detail burned clearly into memory as a conscious choice. If banging my head into a wall would have helped, I'd have done so; instead, I took a deep breath and walked right through it.

I usually floated in through cracks below doors or around windows, but picked the more difficult way for distraction. I felt the graininess of the mortar and the hard blocks it held together. Perhaps one night I would find a wall that I couldn't seep through and stay trapped there like Fortunato, forever out of reach of his Amontillado. But this time the bricks gave way to plaster and strips of lath and I was in the free air of a large room.

I could fumble around and try to guess my location, but now that I'd started, it was better to keep going and to go quickly. Since it seemed quiet enough to be deserted I found a corner and slowly materialized, eyes wide and ears straining.

The dance music, along with voices and the clink of dishes, grew louder now that I had real ears again. I was in a really nice billiards room. The lights were low and the cues and multicolored balls were stored in their cabinets, but one of the tables was still very much in use. A young man and woman with most of their clothes off were happily thrashing away on its sea of green felt like nobody's business—nobody being myself.

My mouth popped open and an unexpected blush seared my face. I had enough presence of mind to disappear before either of them noticed me and got the hell out. I'd long ago lost my virginity and had seen enough of life not to be a prude, but encroaching on the privacy of courting couples was not a hobby I planned to take up just yet. The temptation to return and study another's technique was very strong, though. One peril—or bonus—of my changed condition was the danger of becoming an incurable Peeping Tom. Maybe later, I told myself firmly, and left them to it.

The accidental intrusion did serve to remind me that Kyler would probably be upstairs away from the . . . uh . . . entertainment areas. I pushed up through the ceiling and drifted around enough to guess that I was in a long hall. Invisibility had its drawbacks, with no vision and limited hearing. I could be methodical and start at the back, checking out each room, which would only take half the night. Nuts to that.

Calloway and Baker would certainly be talking to Kyler by now. I floated softly along, alert for any voices, and eventually found them. The confused verbal blur sharpened into speech as I slipped into a room.

Bingo. I recognized Baker's voice.

I brushed by several people, creating a momentary chill for each . . . hard to tell how many were scattered around the room and any of them could have been Kyler. No one moved as they listened to Baker giving his story. It was very interesting to hear things from another point of view; the facts were essentially the same, except for me being larger and more ferocious, and the fight, such as it was, lasting longer.

"The next thing I know is Calloway telling me to get up," he concluded.

"Gordy and Fleming got away?" Kyler's voice. I surged toward him.

"Yeah, boss."

"And you came all the way out here just to tell me that?"

"It was Calloway's idea."

"I figured you'd want to see us personally," Calloway added from across the room.

Kyler took a while before speaking again, either to think, grind his teeth, or to make them sweat or all three. "Use the phone in the future. You could have been followed."

"Yes, sir."

"Otherwise you saw what Baker saw?"

"What do you mean?"

"About Fleming."

"I couldn't really say. Things were jumping and I was busy with Gordy . . . but it was him and he said he wanted to see you."

"Did he say why?"

"Baker interrupted before he could tell."

I had a mental picture of Baker squirming before Kyler's unblinking eyes.

"Calloway, you may leave. Better luck next time."

"You still want Gordy hit?"

"Yes, but you're off of it. We'll have to try something else."

"But I—"

"You'll get your usual payment, but without the bonus since you were unable to complete the job. I think that's fair enough."

"Yes, sir." Calloway sounded relieved. There was some shuffling and the door opened and closed.

Kyler lowered his voice, concentrating it. "All right, Baker, I want an exact account of Fleming's attack on you."

"It's just what I said. He was fast. I hardly seen him coming."

"Hardly, or did not? Give me more detail."

"I guess I must have blinked. It was like he wasn't there for a second. He was *fast*."

"Almost as though he vanished and reappeared again?"

Baker hesitated. "Yeah . . . but that can't be right. Can it?"

Kyler didn't answer that one. "You may go, too. Change out of that uniform before you frighten away the customers."

"Yeah, boss." More shuffling and door noises. I made a fast, blind sweep of the place. Only two men were left. The odds were getting better for me.

"Well?" said Kyler.

Chaven's voice: "We still don't know how he does it. Is it mass hypnosis, like those Indian guys with the rope trick, or what?"

"The method is not so important as the fact that he is capable of doing it."

"Great, so how do we deal with something like that? If he can turn it on and off like a light bulb . . ."

"Light bulbs can be broken."

"When you can see to hit 'em. How you going to hit this guy? How you going to keep him from hitting you?"

"By being prepared. We must also prepare against Gordy."

"He'll be on guard himself, thanks to those assholes screwing up."

"No doubt."

"What about that stuff about Gordy not being behind getting Red and his boys? And what happened to Vic? If Gordy didn't get 'em, who did?"

"There are others who have the means to do it, but they would know better than to try. We'll find out for certain later. As for Gordy, we'd have had to deal with him eventually. This business only caused us to move a little faster."

"But are you ready to take on him and his backers in New York?"

"I'll have to be."

"How?"

"By hitting him again, before he can hit back. This time we make sure it works. We move in and offer New York a five-percent increase on the profits. Taking over Gordy's territory will increase our present income by about four hundred percent. That will make the expenditure of the extra five worth it."

"First you gotta find him," Chaven pointed out.

"Give it to Deiter. Where is he?"

"Downstairs someplace."

"Get him."

Chaven left. The odds would never be better: one to one and no witnesses. I went solid.

The room was on a level with the rest of the place: opulent

with its velvet curtains, grass-thick rug, and overstuffed furniture. All the comforts and then some, though I'd halfway expected him to have at least a few crosses and a garland or two of garlic up in his sanctum.

Kyler had his expensively dressed back to me. He looked smaller without his vicuna overcoat, but snakes can come in all sizes and still pack enough poison to kill. He stood before a well-appointed bar. The usual mirror behind the bottles was missing, replaced by a wall of tufted black patent leather. Too bad, I could have used it to keep an eye on the door. I moved to one side to cover it. Kyler heard the shift of my clothes and whipped around, a gun ready in his hand. It was Escott's Webley. Though not fatal to me, it hurt like hell to get shot, and the .455 bullets this weapon could spit were nearly half an inch in diameter. I decided not to provoke him into anything I might regret.

"So you did follow Calloway," he said after the first surprise wore off. "What do you want?"

"Same as before: a truce, but now I don't trust you to keep your word. Is that something you only reserve for people who can't threaten you?"

That, as Escott might have said, touched a nerve, but Kyler made an effort to hold his voice even. "I kept my word last night. I was not the one after you. Lieutenant Blair—"

"Was your patsy, yeah, I figured that much."

"He was having me watched. My hands were tied."

"So tight that you couldn't have found a way around him? Never mind, it worked out fine for you. You set me up and got the cops looking someplace else for that girl's killer and we all had a good laugh."

"Some of us. You killed Hodge, so that balances things. But I'm out the price of the bracelet."

"Turning it in got you off the hook with the cops. Cheap at the price as far as you're concerned."

He acknowledged the logic with a small nod. "Perhaps, but three more of my men are dead and another's missing along with little Opal. Where is she?"

"Safe enough. You're out the bracelet and some soldiers, but you came that close to killing my friends; we could play I-did-you-did all night. What do *you* want, Kyler?"

He usually kept a poker face, but couldn't quite suppress a

minute glitter from his dark eyes. "You may have noticed that the police still don't know who you are. I could have told them, but did not. I will continue to be silent."

I still hadn't lost my initial revulsion for the man, but it was under control, more or less. He was playing me, but I knew it and was willing to go along. "In exchange for what?"

"Information about yourself."

Not unexpected. He must be eaten up with curiosity, and the questions he asked would give me a clear idea of how firmly entrenched he might be in old superstitions. "Why do you want to know?"

"I think we can be useful to one another."

"I thought you wanted me dead."

"For a situation like this, I can be flexible."

He got a cautious nod from me on that one and I experimentally paced the room. The Webley never once wavered, but he didn't try anything, giving me time to think. My real purpose was to get my easy-to-read face turned away from him and orient myself in case I had to leave fast. That's what I told myself; I was *not* trying to stall.

Bullshit.

It was that damned wall in my head. I'd gone through a real one not ten minutes ago; time to face the internal one and get down to practicalities. Get through it, get through *with* it, then get the hell out.

I could easily take away the Webley, but it would be a bad idea to use it against him: too noisy and the thing might be traced to Escott. Maybe we could alibi each other, but he wouldn't thank me for pulling off anything so clumsy.

Perhaps I could arrange for Kyler to jump out a window. Better. That way his death would at least look like a suicide. The idea of methodically breaking his neck or stabbing him sickened me. I had no desire to touch him. It's different in the heat of a fight when the instincts to survive take over and the adrenaline pushes you past thought and over the edge. I might try arranging some kind of confrontation, force him to make the first move. . . .

How? I thought sarcastically. Look him straight in the eye, insult his immediate family, and hope he'll lose his temper?

"Flexible . . . ?" I prompted at last.

"I'll stop the hit on you," he answered readily.

"And my friends?"

"All included."

"Gordy as well?"

He didn't like it, but finally nodded.

"And listening to my life story is worth losing that four-hundred-percent increase in your profits?"

That set him back a bit as he realized I'd been there for his conversation with Chaven, but his eyes continued to glitter. "I would expect it to be instructive."

I'd been down this road before and wasn't about to make a second trip. This time I turned away to pace around his desk, looking for an idea, or maybe a blunt instrument. My eyes swept over a single book lying on the blotter. A few seconds later its title impressed itself onto my busy brain with an inner jolt. I kept going as though I hadn't seen it.

"And along with the truce I am prepared to generously compensate you for your efforts," he added, inspired, possibly, by the shabby clothes I now wore.

The book changed nothing, but it did explain the dearth of crosses and garlic. Though I'd read the story as a kid, I remembered little of it; the visual impression from seeing the movie three years ago was much stronger. The sight of Claude Rains swiftly unwrapping the bandages from his apparently missing head was not something one could easily forget. Kyler wasn't chasing after Stoker's *Dracula*, but *The Invisible Man* of H.G. Wells.

I almost laughed out loud and had to disguise the intake of breath as a heavy sigh. He'd miscalculated this one, but it did make a kind of sense, considering he'd only seen me vanishing and coming back, not lurking around the Stockyards for a meal. He was close enough to the truth and deserved a few points for choosing even crazed science over superstition-ridden vampirism. But it made no difference. The information he wanted would still be useless to him and as soon as he realized that . . .

"How much?" I asked, not looking at him.

"Five thousand."

"Make it ten."

He hesitated.

"It's worth it, Kyler." I let myself fade, moving on ghostly legs until we were closer than before. Eyes filling his face, he renewed his grip on the gun. I faded completely for just a second to drive home the point, then returned. "It's well worth it."

He'd had plenty of time to dwell on the potentials in the last day or so. My demonstration only confirmed the beginning of endless advantages. "How?" he whispered.

I said nothing. His own inner arguments would persuade him better and faster than any I could invent.

"Is it a chemical process?"

It should have been Escott standing here; he was the one with an actor's training and judgment. I had to go on instinct and hope to make it work. "You'll find that out if and when we make a deal. Call off the hits, leave my friends alone, and ten thousand in cash. In exchange, I'll show you how to . . ." I illustrated by vanishing briefly once more, returning that much closer to him.

Kyler's greed hadn't been so obvious before. Moment by moment, I was learning to read him better, and now he seemed hooked. "All right." His voice was very soft. But the last time I'd heard that tone Chaven had been holding a gun to my head. I was hard put not to glance behind me.

"Deal?"

"Yes. But five thousand down, the balance when I'm able to do what you do."

"Then we start now," I told him. "The sooner we start, the sooner I get out of here."

He had no objections to that. This was his last chance and mine as well. If I couldn't break through to him he would have to die and I would have to live with that death. He was as vulnerable now as I would ever find him.

"You must listen to me very carefully. . . ."

I put everything I had into it, focusing onto his stony eyes, shutting out all other distractions. The room we stood in, the people at their games and dances in the rest of the house, the stark winter woods surrounding the place all ceased to be. The changes within that frightened me, that I had promised to keep under control, took over and rushed free once more.

"Listen to my voice. . . ."

The air was very still except for the even thump of his heart.

"You will listen and do what I tell you."

I concentrated, willing his face to slacken into blankness, quietly demanding that he hear me.

"Do you understand?"

His jaw sagged. I almost mirrored him, surprised by sudden hope. This time it just might work.

"You must listen to me."

His eyelids flickered.

"You *must*."

But he drew a steady breath and held it, giving a sharp shake with his head. "Like hell," he said thickly. "What are you doing?"

Losing the battle. "Kyler . . ."

But the harder I tried to hold it, the quicker it slipped away. Whatever it was about him that set him apart from other men and repelled me—an especially strong will or carefully controlled insanity—worked in his favor. He was throwing off my influence, waking up, and stubbornly fighting. My own concentration wavered. Details ignored before, but necessary to survival, abruptly intruded on us.

I was aware that Chaven and another man had entered the room. They'd padded in as softly as hunters after any skittish prey. If I hadn't been so mentally bound to Kyler, I might have had a chance to do something more than just sluggishly notice their presence and start to turn. But that chance came and went like a ghost's shadow. Chaven's hand darted into his coat, dragging free his first and final answer to problems like me.

Wide awake now, Kyler looked past me. His face opened with sudden horror; one arm came up in futile protection.

"*No!*"

But if Kyler had anything more to say, it was lost in the ongoing roar of Chaven's gun.

8

KYLER YELLS A last inarticulate denial. His voice blends with my own hoarse cry.

Orange-and-white flames explode from the muzzle. Endless, unbearable thunder clogs my ears to the bursting point. Doubling, tripling, the shocks tear into my side and out again.

He falls back against the bar; nodding with each bullet's impact on his body. His cold eyes suddenly blaze to life, but it's an illusion. They turn inward to fix on a place where I cannot look—where I don't want to look. He slides to the floor.

I stagger away from the dying man. Smoke and bloodsmell overtake me. We merge into nothingness, turning, tumbling, free of gravity, free of thought, free of the first awful crash of agony. I twist and soar high in blind flight.

Chaven circles below. He and the other man cast about with broken questions, curses, and anguish. Drawn by the shots, more people rush in. Like a detached spirit with only vague interest in their little problems, I hover above the confusion. Their voices fade. I seep through a wall, seeking another, more tranquil place, away from their alarms and fears.

Stumbling awkwardly into a pink marble counter, I came back to myself with a stomach-lurching jolt. Gravity reasserted its claim on my body, trying to drag me into, and perhaps through, the floor. I fought it, needing to feel my own solidity, my own movements, needing the instinctive assurance that I still lived.

My hands clawed at the cool marble as though it were a life preserver. I stayed and was numbly thankful for the privilege.

I'd wound up in a fancy lounge. A huge mirror over the counter reflected gold walls where brass lamps clung like glowing cicadas. As usual, it missed me, but I had no interest in knowing what I looked like. Turning from its emptiness, I was busy just trying to keep my shaky legs under me. I'd been shot before, but not so many times all at once, not to such a point of shattering, sickening weakness.

The bloodsmell clinging to me was my own. Morbidly, I counted four holes going into the right side of my pea jacket and another four raggedly emerging from the left, the fabric soaked with warm red stains, and my guts still churning sharply from the aftershock. Chaven had made a good grouping—too bad he couldn't have known they'd go right through me and on to kill Kyler.

He's dead.

I braced more firmly against the counter, locking my knee joints to offset their tremors. The initial shock threatened to turn into a nauseous disaster, but I gulped it back and sucked stuffy air into my neglected lungs. It shuddered out as soft, nervous laughter that did not want to stop. Some distant part of my brain was aware that it didn't sound quite right, but the restraints were broken down. It hurt too much to hold back and continued for as long as the air lasted, ugly, mirthless whispers of relief. After too many frantic nights crowded with uncomfortable thoughts, I needed the release badly. It washed over me, a wave of sweet, soothing balm for a troubled soul. It washed over and past, leaving me weary and drained, but at peace.

I was finally free of the bastard.

A last little surge of laughter flowed away from me, soft and secret.

He's dead.

He was someone else's problem, now. And I was just cynical enough to be glad about it.

Next door, the clearly audible aftermath of Chaven's mistake was just beginning.

But he was quick to adjust to the new situation, especially since his own skin was at risk. Within a very few minutes he managed to invent a plausible story of how I'd burst in with a gun to fulfill my own contract on Kyler and escaped. The room quickly cleared as he sent his cronies out to search for me and to explain away the commotion to any roadhouse patrons who might have heard something odd happening upstairs.

Then I had to disappear for a time as two of his goons charged in to check the stalls for my presence.

"You believe that b.s. he fed us?" one of them asked as they crashed around.

"Long as we get our cut of the profits, who cares? We do what he says and make him happy."

"And if we find this guy he was talking about?"

"Then we give him a bad case of lead poisoning. C'mon, what's the holdup?"

"Just lookin'. I never been in one of these places before. I thought the pots'd be shaped different or something."

"The only difference is that some of ours are on the wall and all of theirs are on the floor."

That explained the pink marble; I was in a ladies' lounge.

"Live 'n' learn."

"C'mon."

The door banged shut.

When I came back I felt much more tired than before, but better able to think. If those two were a typical example of the kind of loyalty Kyler had inspired in his troops, Chaven had little to worry about in the reprisals department from underlings. But he was still one to watch out for as far as I was concerned, since more than ever he had a damn good reason to keep it a personal fight between us. On the other hand, there was every possibility that he wasn't the same kind of crazy as his deceased boss. I might be more successful reasoning with him.

I pressed an ear to the adjoining wall to see if he was alone yet, but no such luck, and no wonder. With an invisible God-knows-what wandering around the house he'd want to have an army around him for protection. As it was, he'd settled for one man—one too many for the moment. The kind of hypnosis that I had in mind required a certain degree of privacy. I'd have to wait.

To better hear what was going on I went back through the wall, giving the spot where Kyler had dropped a wide berth. It wasn't out of respect for the dead; nervous superstition was a better description for my caution. There was no telling what, if anything, I might encounter in this ethereal form and I had no desire to find out. I found a quiet corner and listened to the hollow voices of the living that remained.

"Now what?" asked one unfamiliar to me.

"What d'ya mean?" Chaven returned. He seemed to be standing near Kyler, perhaps looking down at the corpse.

"I mean about him. You ain't callin' the cops on this. . . ."

"Hell, no."

"Then wake up and start thinking."

Chaven's voice was ragged. "Can it, Deiter, I *am*."

During the shooting, I'd had only the barest glimpse of a man standing behind Chaven. He had to have been Deiter, the specialist Kyler had ordered up to take care of the hit on Gordy, and now the only other witness to the strange circumstance of Kyler's death. One more name to put on the roster of people to be persuaded to forget all about me.

"We take him out to the boat," Chaven finally said. "We get a box and weights and sink him just like any other job. We take him way out and we do it tonight."

"What about your gun?"

"What about it?"

"The bulls got ways of tracing bullets. If they should ever—"

"Yeah, okay, it goes in the drink with him. I can always get another." Pause. "Like maybe this one."

"What the hell is it?" Deiter had to be talking about Escott's Webley. It was a unique-looking hunk of hand artillery.

"Something that shoots. I don't think the boss'll mind me taking it back again."

"Fat lotta good it did him. What happened, Chaven? How could you shoot that guy and hit the boss? What happened to the guy? I had both eyes right on him and he just stopped being there."

Chaven moved away toward the desk where the book lay. "Here. You figure it out."

Deiter followed. "Invisible? You pulling my leg?"

"The boss was checking into it. He said the guy in the book made himself invisible with chemicals. He had the idea that this guy Fleming knew how to do the same thing, only he could turn it on and off like—like a light bulb, clothes and all."

"That's crazy."

"If it ain't this, then what else?"

"You can shoot through ghosts, can't you?" Deiter hazarded.

"I don't believe in ghosts. You saw what happened. Well, didn't you?"

"Yeah, I already said so. I just wanna know what I saw."

"A guy disappearing."

"But it don't make sense."

"It don't have to—but that's how it is. And the worst part is that bastard could be in here right now."

That ominous idea must have made Deiter a sudden believer. Things got very quiet for a while. "What are you going to do about him?"

"One thing at a time. First we clean up this mess on the floor."

"You got a story ready for Kyler's bosses?"

"Just what I told the boys here; he put a hit out on Fleming, only Fleming got him first. We stick to that and we keep our skins."

"What about his family?"

"He didn't have any that he wanted. He told me he left them behind and wanted to keep it that way."

"Maybe the wife skipped to Reno," Deiter sniggered.

"Who knows? I think any skirt would have been crazy to get cozy with him. I was the closest thing he had to a friend and I didn't like him all that much."

"Guess it's just as well we're gonna sink him. You'd do a lousy job talking at his funeral."

"Can it, Deiter. In fact, you can everything you heard and saw in here. If you want to stay out of the loony bin you don't say a word about invisible men to nobody."

"This mean you're running the show now?"

"Until and unless the other bosses say otherwise. The boys'll follow my lead long as they get their money as usual . . . oh, shit."

"What?"

"We gotta get Opal back. She's the only one who can make head or tail of the books. Without them, I'm crippled."

"But you don't know where—"

"I'm laying odds that Fleming's got his partner holding her, and this town ain't so big that they can hide forever. I'll have Calloway look into things from his side. Wouldn't it be something if we got the cops to do our work for us?"

"If you can trust him."

"He's in too deep and likes the money too much to turn on us now."

"You hope. What about the problem down the hall? We can't keep that spook in private stir forever."

Chaven's new responsibilities were starting to irritate him. "Jesus, why don't you just make a list? I'll get to him when I can."

"Right, boss."

The use of his new title mollified him somewhat and they left the room to set things in motion. I went solid almost as the door shut.

Kyler had fallen on his face, but they'd rolled him over, presumably to check for signs of life, and left him that way. His eyes were still open. The rug was thick with his blood, and the cold, dizzy scent of it teased my nose. I tried to ignore it as I borrowed the phone on the desk.

It was a relief to know that my call to Escott wouldn't be long distance and therefore traceable. I'd been worried that Calloway had driven over the state line to Indiana or had at least left Cook County. The other end of the wire began ringing for attention.

And kept on ringing. Where the hell was he?

I dialed the number again, more slowly in case I'd gotten it wrong the first time. And again, to make sure. No answer. My mouth had grown very dry. Then I had to hang up and disappear when a couple of Chaven's men came in to dispose of the body. From their lazily bickering conversation, they would be taking their time on this job. I hurled out past them to find another phone. One of them complained miserably about cold drafts and began sneezing.

Random searches are neither fast nor efficient and that much more difficult when you can't see where you're going. There might have been any number of phones handy downstairs, but I wasn't dressed for fancy socializing. I'd be spotted in short order and either thrown out on my ass by the bouncers or shot again. Both possibilities would prevent me from letting Escott know what was going on, and worse, from finding out what had happened to him.

I took a turn up the hall, bumped through a door, and swept the room for occupants. Clear. Solid again, I checked the place in one fast look. No phone, dammit. I did the same thing once more, twice more, finding either people or not finding a phone. Jeez, when you're making love or taking a bath the damn things are ringing off the wall for you, but when you really need one they vanish like roaches when the lights come on.

One more try. I materialized in a vacant meeting room with a long dark table and padded chairs all around. Some unsung genius had thought to install a phone and I took immediate advantage of the fact.

Or tried to. Just as I was dialing the last number, a door at the far end slowly swung open. There was nothing else to do but drop the earpiece back and disappear. I clearly recalled that in the movie, Claude Rains had himself endured a frustrating lack of privacy.

The impromptu investigator seemed to be alone and only stayed long enough to check the place and maybe puzzle over its emptiness. Unhappily for me he left the door ajar, the better to hear any more suspicious noises. I gave out an internal and quite silent sigh and materialized to do some listening for myself. He was alone. I decided that it wouldn't hurt for him to enjoy a short nap while I completed my call.

Taking a direct and low-key approach, I just walked in on him. Leaping out of thin air might have been more dramatic, but for this kind of work, the less ruckus, the better.

My unsuspecting victim stood in the middle of a square of rug, staring at it. I was ready for him to hear me and turn, but he took no notice. He was a stocky man, but his cheap hickory shirt and rough pants hung loose on his frame as though he'd lost a lot of weight. His clothes didn't fit this place any more than mine did. Head still down, he traced the outline of the rug's pattern with the blunt toe of his shoe. This simple and childish activity in a middle-aged man brought a rush of prickles to the back of my neck. Deiter had mentioned a "spook"; maybe I'd found him. If so, then he might prove to be as immune to suggestion as Kyler.

Deciding to not take the chance, I began to quietly back out. The man, still tracing, had gradually turned. I froze, held fast by wide, wasted eyes and a scraped-out expression. He glanced at me without concern, his pasty face and subdued manner much too calm. To him, I was just another part of the furnishings, somewhat less interesting than the rug, for he continued with his infantile game.

Recognition reluctantly burst upon me. Last summer, while subjecting a man to hypnotic influence, I'd lost control of my emotions. The anger, frustration, pain, and roaring hatred buried deep by the shock of my own death had been released like a lightning bolt into another's mind, with predictable effect. This soft, helpless husk before me was all that was left of Frank Paco.

I was frozen with apprehensive shock . . . and fascinated.

"Paco?" I ventured, not really knowing why.

"Yes?" he unexpectedly replied.

After a minute I was able to speak again. "Do you know me?"

His toe began to trace a different pattern in the rug, one that only he could see. He paused to give me a good look. Something flickered over his face, perhaps the corpse light of a dead memory. "You were on the boat."

So he recalled my last hell-filled days aboard the *Elvira*. "Anywhere else?"

He shrugged. I rubbed a hand over my rough jaw. Maybe my unkempt appearance now was misleading him. He might not be able to link me with the younger-looking intruder who had dynamited his basement and subsequently blasted away his sanity. On the other hand, why was it so important to me for Paco to recall that encounter? The answer came even as I thought up the question.

Here was Kyler's other source of information on me.

I fought down the sudden tremors running out from my spine and backed away from him without thinking. Stupid reaction, I thought, and made myself stop. Paco didn't seem to notice.

The boardroom phone was as safe as any for the moment. Paco was too far gone to be much of a danger to me now. I dialed the number once more and this time got an answer, but not the one I expected. It was Shoe Coldfield and I didn't have to hear the tone of his voice to know that something was wrong.

"This is Fleming. Where's Charles?"

"Shit if I know. When he didn't answer the phone I came over to check on him and he's not here. Where the hell are you?"

"A roadhouse somewhere outta town. Was the building broken into?"

"Looks it; I don't think the s.o.b. got bored and took off leaving the door hanging open."

Damnation. "No, he wouldn't, not unless he was on the run,

and my guess is that he'd call you for help at the first chance."
My belly churned as the right idea hit me. "If he had one."

"What do you know, Fleming?" he growled.

"Did Charles tell you about me finding Opal?"

"Kyler's accountant? Yeah, he told me all about her and the
hit on Gordy. Maybe he decided to follow you—no, if he was
watching that girl, nothing would have budged him outta here."

"They must have been watching the Travis Hotel for Kyler
when I showed up. They had to have followed me while I was
busy trying to keep Opal quiet—then they got in and got to
Charles."

"Who followed you? Who got in?" he demanded.

"It has to be Angela Paco's people."

This time he said nothing and I couldn't blame him. The situation was rapidly growing beyond words.

"I've found out why Angela put herself in the middle of
things last night. It's her father. Kyler's been keeping Frank
Paco under wraps."

"Frank Paco? What the hell for?"

"Pumping him for information about me, I guess."

"But Paco's been bughouse crazy since that fire. What can he
know that would be of any use?"

"Doesn't matter anymore—Kyler's dead."

He paused a long time on that one and there was a hint of respect in his reaction. "Took care of him, huh?"

"Not me, his lieutenant. Chaven did the honors. Right now
I'm busy keeping my head down while he's covering things
up."

"How the hell did you arrange it?"

"Believe me, it was an accident. Chaven's still after my hide,
but forget him, Angela's our main worry now. I think the reason
she kidnapped me the other night was to make a trade for her father. She might be trying to do the same again, but this time
with Charles and Opal, so there's a good chance that they're all
right." I purposely skipped over the fact that of the two, Opal
was the more valuable hostage.

"Only now she won't be dealing with Kyler—if this is what
you think it is."

"You just said that Charles wouldn't budge otherwise. Check
around, see if there's anyone else besides the Kyler and Paco
factions that are after us."

"I know there aren't. Yet."

"Right. My bet's that Angela's probably got them both and will be making her demands soon. Chaven's got his hands full at the moment and I don't know which way he'll jump on this, but he'll want Opal back because he needs her for his business."

"But Charles will be in the soup if she makes that deal. How long will it take you to get back here?"

"I'm not, I'm going straight to her place."

"If she's still there."

"You know any other bolt holes Paco had that Kyler didn't take over?"

"Okay. But I'm coming out, too."

Fine with me. I wouldn't mind having Coldfield guarding my back. We made quick arrangements on where to meet and I told him to give me at least an hour to get there. I hung up, ready to race for the nearest car.

Frank Paco stood in the doorway, his eyes narrowing and a little less empty than before. "What's all this about *mia Angelina*?"

"Nothing."

"Nothing, what?" he rumbled, a faint shadow of his old authority returning.

I made a bald guess on what was expected. "Nothing, Mr. Paco."

"You goddamn well better believe it. You boys don't say nothing against Angela. She's a good girl and I taught her how to stay that way."

"Yes, Mr. Paco. Have you seen her lately?"

"She's around the house somewhere. What d'you need to know for?"

"Uh . . . I heard she had an errand for me, is all."

"You go find her, then. You don't have her look for you. Remember that working for Angela is the same as working for me."

"Yes, sir."

"What're you doing in here like this, anyway? I don't pay you punks to dress like bums. Get out and get a shave."

"Yes, Mr. Paco." I wished for the time to question him myself, but he was getting loud, and I had to be elsewhere fast. I made my escape while I could.

Initially, I thought of "borrowing" a car from some randomly unlucky patron, but once outside, Kyler's twin Cadillacs popped back to mind and were too much of a temptation to pass up. I found them as they'd been parked, nose out and all ready to go. Locked or not, I slipped inside one and fumbled around with the wires to get it started. The soft, secretive purr of its well-tuned motor was an added bonus; no one in the house would hear my departure. While it warmed, I devoted some attention to the other car.

Both were beautiful machines; it wasn't their fault they'd caught the eye of someone like Kyler, so I drew the line at breaking the headlights off or any other obvious, crippling vandalism. Deflating tires was easy and effective enough; I stuck with what I knew best. The angry hiss of compressed air was loud, but nobody came out to check things. As soon as the rims were flush with the gravel, I took off, leaving behind the roadhouse palace and its dismayed and murderous senechals.

It took a full hour and then some to get there, and then I had to cruise slowly so as not to miss the spot off the road where Coldfield said he'd be waiting. In the summer it was sheltered by thick shrubs; now only black, branchy skeletons remained, clutching their tattered leaves like precious memories being dragged along to the grave. Despite their thin ranks and my excellent night vision, I had to look carefully before finding Coldfield's Nash.

My headlights were on so as not to annoy the traffic cops, so he naturally spotted me first. But I was startled at how fast he emerged from his car and downright alarmed when he crouched behind the armored door to point his gun in my direction. One of his men dropped out the driver's side, nervously copying him.

Maybe stealing one of Kyler's highly identifiable Caddies hadn't been such a good idea, after all. Belatedly, I hit the brakes, doused the lights, and rolled down the window to shout at him.

He recognized my voice and cautiously emerged. "You alone, Fleming?" he demanded, meaning that I'd damn well better be.

"Yeah," I wheezed, recalling how he hated surprises. I cut the motor and got out slowly. "Just me, myself, and I."

He finally put away the gun and came over to glare at the Caddy. "How the hell did you manage this one?"

"The other car had bad tires."

He barked out an unexpected laugh and thumped me on the back so hard that I nearly fell over. "All right, let's work out what needs to be done."

It seemed pretty plain to me. "First I find out if they're there, then I go get them."

"While I twiddle my thumbs?"

"I know the inside of the house."

"So does Isham," he said, with a brief gesture toward the Nash, where his driver waited. "He helped with the catering of a lot of parties there, once."

I could see that we were heading for a long argument, so I gave in, up to a point. "Okay, but we can't all three go in or Angela will have more hostages than she knows what to do with." *Or targets,* I added to myself. "How about Isham comes with me and you hang back and cover us?"

"Not too far back," he rumbled. "We'll move up close to the front gate with the car. I'm not crazy about a walk through the woods in this weather."

The wind was light, but dismal to stand in. We hustled into the temporary protection of the Nash and Isham got it in gear.

"Just how did you take care of Kyler?" Coldfield asked.

I gave him an almost truthful story, leaving out a few important points about invisibility, failed hypnosis, and saying that I ducked and ran when Chaven started shooting. It was one of my more demandingly creative efforts.

"You must know how to run pretty damn fast," he commented, but left it at that. We'd once shared a nasty street brawl together and he apparently remembered that I could really move when sufficiently inspired.

Isham stopped and set the brake. "Ready," he said, his inflection so neutral that I couldn't tell if it was a statement or a question.

We got out and checked the lock on the front gates. It wasn't much, just a length of chain with a padlock holding it together, a bit down in the world from the armed guards and dogs that once patrolled the place. Maybe Angela could no longer afford them. Isham got some large bolt cutters from the trunk and snapped open a key link. Coldfield took charge of them and wished us luck as we slipped inside.

It was a long trudge down the gravel drive to the house, or perhaps the wind only made it seem so. I didn't mind much, but Isham looked pretty miserable, and things would only get worse for him before too long.

Lights glowed in some widely separated windows, but we paid more attention to the dark ones. If Angela had anyone on lookout duty, they'd be hiding here. Nobody yelled, though, so we moved on like we belonged until we came to the inadequate shelter of a work shed. It was locked up, but the clapboard sides of the building cut the wind down to nothing, which was very fortunate for Isham. Our parting conversation was brief, one-sided, but absolutely necessary. I left him awake and alert, but had persuaded him to stay behind. Better for him to wait for my return than to have both of us in the house dodging around for cover that might not exist. It worked out fine for him; he thought it was all his idea. As for me, all I got was the start of a really nasty headache.

Free of Isham, I was able to move much faster and had no need to conceal my supernatural abilities. Rounding the nearest corner of the house, I vanished and forced my way through one of the many windows. Glass isn't my favorite material to sieve past; it's like falling through the ice in a pond, only the ice doesn't actually break. I always expect it to, though, which is why I usually avoid it. Tonight I was in too much of a hurry to bother. Wish I had; the extra effort took its toll on my head when I materialized on the other side.

The room I stood in was unfamiliar, but deserted. The lights were out in this wing of the house. Angela was either saving on the bills or the repairs hadn't gotten as far as fixing the wiring here yet. I picked my way around water-damaged furniture and eased open the door. The hinges creaked, but not too loudly. The hall was clear.

Trusting my ears and eyes to keep me out of trouble with the tenants, I checked likely and unlikely rooms on the ground floor. Some were untouched by fire and water, others were still a mess, and a few were in a halfway stage of repair. None of them were presently occupied. I blamed the late hour and could guess that Angela's boys were upstairs tucked away in their beds.

Wrong. Two of them were raiding the kitchen icebox for beer and sandwiches. They sounded oddly domestic as they cut bread and searched for the bottle opener, but their talk gave no clue about Escott. I was about to slip off when instead of sitting at the table to eat, they loaded everything onto a tray and went down another hall.

Long experiences had taught me that it was anatomically impossible to kick oneself. I settled for giving them a good start and cat-footed after them.

They were going to the private gymnasium. Vanishing, I rushed ahead to scour the place and found two people there, one stretched out on a table and the other sitting close by. Neither was doing much of anything. Fine and dandy. I whipped into the steam room where Newton had stashed me earlier and got my hunch paid off.

"Jack?" came Escott's inquiring whisper as I brushed past him.

He was alone. With some difficulty, I re-formed; this time my head was so bad that I staggered smack into one of the benches, barking my shins painfully against the wood. Twisting, I dropped onto the seat with a jolt. Rough landing, but at least I was still in one piece.

"That sudden chill was not my imagination, then," he said. "Are you all right?"

"Dizzy. All this Houdini stuff takes it out of me."

"Well, it is good to see you, my friend."

I was surprised that he could. In addition to the scrapes and black eye he'd already collected, his other eye was swollen shut and he held one arm protectively against himself. His long legs were drawn up on the bench, helping him to keep his back braced in a tiled corner. He was white to the hairline and looked about as steady as a guttering candle.

I forgot about my own troubles. "Holy shit, what happened to you?"

His mouth twitched. "Opal," he said dryly. "And, to a lesser extent, Miss Paco. I fear that one day a woman may prove to be my ultimate downfall."

"It's my fault, Charles. I wasn't careful enough about watching for tails when I brought Opal in."

He gave a minimal shrug with his eyebrows. "So I deduced when they broke into the building."

"Jeez, what else did they break? Your arm?"

"I think not, bad bruise at the worst, but I've a devil of a pain along the ribs. They'll need taping, I'm sure."

"Who hit you?"

"Opal . . . with a packing crate. Damn good luck for me that she did or I'd have come to a bad end then and there. Angela Paco was that close to blasting me into the next world."

"Good God."

"No doubt He has spared me for some other purpose for which consideration I am truly thankful. No, please don't try to help, I've just got comfortable."

"I'm sorry." An apology had never seemed so inadequate before.

He waved it away. "Hardly your fault, old man. It's part of the job. I hope that you're here to help get me away from this place?"

"Only by the shortest possible route. Isham's just outside the house and Shoe's got a car waiting at the gate."

"Excellent," he sighed with quiet approval.

"Where's Opal?"

"With Miss Paco, I think. They left me in here some time ago. Is Gordy all right? And what about Miss Smythe?"

"Yeah. They're fine."

"And Vaughn Kyler?"

It was hard work to talk about that subject, but I did give him a very short summary of what I'd been through. "Chaven must have gotten the worst surprise of his life when Kyler dropped," I concluded.

Escott exhaled a long breath and tilted his head back against the wall. "What a gift for understatement the gentleman has."

"It's still not over."

"True. But you sound better able to handle it."

"I sure as hell don't feel it."

"You do look rather done in. Perhaps Shoe was right about taking a vacation. A few weeks in the Mexican sun would surely be of far less harm to you than all this bother has been."

If I'd had the energy, I might have laughed at that one. Instead, I got to my feet with a groan and went to work again.

He watched me through one slitted eye as I prowled to the small set-in window to get a look at the mugs outside. The door was secured shut this time; I had to settle for a sideways glance through the little square of double-paned glass, but it was enough. Newton, Lester, and some other guy out of the same mold were draped on various exercise benches, putting away the beer and sandwiches. They were making too much talk among themselves to notice our whispered conversation. Near them on the massage table lay Vic, lone survivor of last night's interrupted kidnapping. He was wrapped up in a ton of bandaging and looked asleep.

"Now what about you?" I asked, turning back. "What's your story?"

He frowned. "Well, it's all so bloody embarrassing, isn't it? Though I'm content now that things turned out as they did. The alternative Miss Paco had in mind hardly bears thinking about."

"Charles . . ."

"Yes. Well. They broke open the door below, and that awakened Opal from her slumber. I must say the girl recovered herself rather well. She immediately assumed that it was her employer come to rescue her and delayed me for a few crucial moments. She made a devil of a row and that brought the intruders straight up the stairs."

"No time to shoot?"

Another grimace. "More like a catastrophic lack of inclination. The first one up was Miss Paco herself. I was ready, but damn it, I just couldn't bring myself to kill a woman . . . a girl, really. While I hesitated, Opal hit me from the side with that bloody packing case and inadvertently saved my life by getting in Miss Paco's line of fire. I'm not sure what followed, but the next thing I knew I was at the bottom of the stairs with the breath knocked right out of me and unable to move. Eventually Opal realized her mistake, Miss Paco got things sorted out, and we were all bundled into a truck and brought here."

"They say why?"

"No." He correctly read my expression. "You've learned something?"

I told him about Frank Paco.

"Well, well," he said after a moment.

"Is that what you'd call 'a spanner in the works'?" I asked.

"More like the whole tool kit. No, strike that. Frank Paco's involvement only lends complete logic to his daughter's actions. If anything, it's Kyler's unexpected death that will cause the greatest disruption."

"That's what I came up with, but it might not change stuff that much. Chaven still needs Opal back, and I figure he'll want to bump you off just to make a neat package, so you two have got to get out of here before all hell breaks loose."

He readily agreed. "To that end I suggest you locate Opal next, and from there we may work out a practical exit from this place."

I wasn't crazy about leaving him alone now that I'd found him. "I don't know about that."

He made a deprecatory gesture at the bare walls. "The decor is somewhat lacking in interest, but I can survive it a while longer. As for those fellows outside, I'm content that they shall continue to ignore me as long as I remain quiet. Do go on and find the young lady; I'll be safe enough here."

My friend, the optimist. Movement outside caught my eye. I pressed my face against the glass for a better look.

"What is it?" he asked.

"Doc just came in. I may have to get scarce."

Out of his bathrobe and into a suit, Doc gave the illusion of sobriety until you saw his face. His eyes were bright but wandering, and his arms swung long and loose. His legs were still steady, so he was probably good for a few more miles, yet.

"It's time," was all he said.

Newton and Lester finished off their beer and got up. Without hurry, they went to Vic and pulled him to his feet. He wouldn't stay there. His head rolled, dropping to his chest as they dragged him out. Doc trailed after them.

I glanced at Escott. "They just took Vic for a walk. What say we do the same?"

"And Opal?"

"I'll come back for her later. Right now there's only one guy watching things. A better chance might not turn up again."

He gave out with a twitch of the lips and a very small nod. I think he was too done in to argue much on Opal's behalf; that or he figured she owed him one for braining him so hard.

I started to slip away, but the familiar dissolving of self into weightless nothing would not come. The effort brought back the dizziness, and I had to grab my now thundering head with both hands. It felt like someone had rammed a spike right into my brain.

"What is it?" Escott demanded softly.

"Tired," I mumbled. I could hardly hear myself. After a few moments, the roaring subsided a little and I pushed out a few more words. "Been doing this too much. Tired."

"Perhaps a trip to the Stockyards would not be amiss," he suggested, an uneasy tone to his voice.

"Yeah." Simple to say, hard to fulfill, but a long drink was what I needed. I thought of that while giving myself a minute to figuratively catch my breath. When I felt ready, I tried again.

Nothing.

I'd anticipated either vanishing or more pain, but not this. For the first time in months a layer of sweat broke out on me, flaring over my entire body, and settling around my flanks and groin. "They turn the heat on in here?" I whispered thinly.

But Escott could see something was seriously wrong and that the joke was meant to cover my fear. "Sit down, Jack. You look ghastly."

I didn't have much choice in the matter. My legs sagged all on their own, and with my back to the door for support, I slid right to the tiles.

Despite his damaged ribs, Escott got over to me. He knew better than to check for a pulse, but did get a hard look at my face. It must have been bad news.

"How do you feel?"

"Like hell with a hangover." I raised a lax hand to swipe at the sweat on my forehead. An abrupt whiff of my own scent came to me from the motion. It was faint, but unmistakable. You know it by instinct and you never, never forget it: the warm, sweet, rotten stink of death.

▲
9
▼

ESCOTT MAY HAVE noticed it or not, but knew instinctively that I was in more than ordinary trouble. "Come, get up on this bench by the door."

I slowly obeyed. It was better than giving in to the cold clot of fear creeping up my throat. My body seemed heavy, as though it were sunrise already, with my limbs stiffening and mind slowing. I tried to shake out of it, but that made me dizzy again.

"You're unable to vanish? Is that it?" he asked, once I was settled.

"Guess so." I was reluctant to admit it and thus make it real.

"Has this ever happened to you before?"

It was difficult to think. "That time I got stabbed. And wood does it, too."

"What about those shots you took earlier? Would they have this kind of effect on you?"

"Maybe. Lost some blood then . . . shook me up bad. It's never hit as hard as . . . I've been doing too much of the Cheshire cat stuff tonight." Far too much, I thought unhappily.

"Perhaps you've discovered your limits, after all," he mused, but he wasn't trying to be funny.

I again mopped at the uncharacteristic and disturbing sweat. Its deathsmell remained, clinging to the sleeve of my coat like some perverse perfume. "I feel like a squeezed-out sponge."

"You look it."

"Thanks."

"Right, then let's see about getting out of here for that trip to the Stockyards. I've no doubt that you need to replenish your internal supply as quickly as possible."

He started knocking on the door to get the guard's attention. It took forever. Escott kept himself close to the window so the man wouldn't see me.

"I say there," he began loudly to make himself heard. He was putting on his broadest English accent. It was a parody of his normal pattern of speech, different enough to tip me off that he was up to something, but only because I knew him. The other guy didn't.

"Yeah? Whatizit?"

"I've been in here for hours, old man, and very much need to relieve myself."

"Yeah? Well, you'll just have to hold it."

"That's exactly what I've been doing and I won't last much longer."

"Yeah? Well, too bad."

"Indeed? I don't think Miss Paco would be too terribly pleased were I to . . ."

The guy laughed. "Okay, okay. But don't you try nothing."

"I assure you that I can barely move with these ribs. I shall make no trouble at all."

Outside, the man juggled with whatever they'd fixed up to lock the room and pulled the door open. Escott was still effectively blocking the guard's view and mine as well so I couldn't see what was going on. He shuffled forward, his breath straining and his heartbeat high, so it wasn't all acting. The man kept him in front as they started across the gym.

My turn. If I could take it; but walking was less tiring than vanishing, and the chance of escape inspired me to throw off some of the weakness. I dragged to my feet and managed to get out. A few steps away was a tempting rack of Indian clubs. I gingerly lifted one out and tiptoed after Escott, who was moving slowly and complaining about his injuries. His talk was enough to cover any small noises I made.

"Yeah," said the guy with a minimum of sympathy. It must have been his favorite word. It was also the last thing he said for the time being. I thumped him once with the fat end of the club and once was more than enough. He dropped flat.

"Good man," approved Escott. "Now, let's try that window."

Moving a little faster than before, but still obviously uncomfortable, he beelined to the far side of the room.

I felt marginally better but didn't want to rely on it lasting and wasted no time in raising the window.

Somewhere, something that sounded like a continuous telephone bell went off. Escott cursed and tapped at a metal plate set into the windowsill.

"Burglar alarm. That's torn it. They'll be here straightaway."

I popped out the copper screening. The drop to the ground was only four feet, nothing to me, but awkward for Escott.

"I can manage," he assured me, as though reading my mind, but said it through his teeth as he shifted painfully on the sill to get his legs out. He bit off a strangled noise in his throat when he jolted to the ground, throwing a hand against the house to steady himself.

"Isham's waiting over there," I said, pointing at the clapboard shed across the yard.

He hugged his aching chest with both arms and shambled ahead. I crawled out after him. The alarm bell seemed louder outside than in; the night air vibrated from it. Behind, somebody called for me to stop. I glanced back and saw Newton fast struggling out with Lester following.

Isham was ready to cover us. He stepped clear of the shed and waited for Escott to pass his line of sight before taking a potshot at the pursuit. It was purposely wide in order to miss me, but I found myself ducking anyway. Newton growled something obscene and followed it up with a shot of his own. Several shots. With me smack in the middle.

I dropped and rolled, hoping the dizziness wouldn't kick up again, but was disappointed. The night world whirled and twisted; earth, sky, and earth. My stomach and head spun with them.

More gunfire. Over me. Passing me. Then a horn blowing, coming closer.

I was on my stomach and gulping air. My toes dug into the damp earth. I levered upright. Newton and Lester were ahead of me now, using the shed for cover.

Horn.

Coldfield's Nash tore over the grounds toward Escott and Isham. He swerved around them, the heavy car skidding sloppily as he put it between them and the shooting. He leaned across to open the passenger door for them. They dived in. Escott pointed at me, yelling something. Coldfield was nodding.

He slammed gears and hit the gas. The engine roared, the wheels slipped, gouged, and caught. He was coming straight for me. I moved more to the right, ready to make a grab for a door handle when it came.

Lester broke from the shed and began firing at the car. With all its armor he'd have had better luck stopping an elephant with a peashooter. Newton was more on the ball and decided to shoot at me, instead.

I dodged and staggered to make a more difficult target. He was too damned close.

Then the car was in front of me. I seized a handle and got a foot on the running board. Coldfield hardly slowed down and I could hear him cursing through the thick glass as he fought with the wheel.

Except for the handle, I had nothing else to hold. Inside the car, Isham threw himself over the backseat to get to me. He popped up immediately and rolled down the rear window. He got a handful of my coat collar and shouted for me to climb inside.

It might have worked if I'd had my full strength and if circumstances hadn't suddenly changed.

I didn't hear it so much as feel it, a heavy shock like a drumbeat hitting me from the outside in, going right through me. My bones literally rattled from it. My muscles gave in to it. Dozens of fire-hot bee stings tore at my back. Red dots splashed the car and spotted Isham's face. Involuntarily, he winced away from it. Blood. My blood. Then Isham wasn't there anymore, though I had a last impression that he'd made a futile grab for me as I slipped away.

Hard ground hit me all over. Lights too bright to exist flashed within my brain.

Silence. The thick, ringing kind you get after something's deafened you.

I raised my wobbling head and saw the red taillights of the Nash bump along and close together as the car swung around. Searing white beams from the headlights replaced them. Coldfield was coming back for another try, but I knew it wouldn't work. I got as far as my knees and frantically waved him off, telling him to get out, to get the hell out. I couldn't hear myself shout.

Something arced over my head and bounced toward the car. It was oblong, about the size of a potato. I waved once more, screaming this time.

The Nash swerved away from it. Coldfield must have known what it was, too. His car wasn't that heavily armored. I threw myself flat and covered my head the way I'd been taught in the army. Despite the deafness, I heard this one go off. Once more the shock pulverized me. I felt like an ant under a hammer.

It stuck.

Heavy clods of earth hailed on me.

Something smashed into my hand.

Silence.

I couldn't see the car anymore. The blast had flipped me right over. Groggily turning, I was just able to see its lights skimming away. He was trying to put some distance between us, correction, between himself and them. He couldn't help it and I wasn't blaming him for going. That had been the idea behind all the waving and shouting, after all.

Movement. I followed it.

Angela Paco darted past me. Her legs flashed below the flowing hem of her dark skirt. She had something heavy in one hand. She stopped, fiddled with it, and drew her arm back. The thing arced high like the others but didn't fly far. She was small and probably not strong enough to throw it with much safety for herself. As soon as it left her hand, she rushed back.

Her face was unnaturally bright. Her breath smoked freely from her open mouth. She was laughing as she dropped on the ground not ten feet from me.

Drumbeat.

Farther away. Not so bad, but enough to shake us. When I looked up again, Angela was just dragging to her feet, still laughing with childlike delight.

The last grenade hadn't landed anywhere near the retreating Nash, which was just as well. Angela had thrown it as a parting gift to keep them moving, or maybe just for the sheer fun of it. Coldfield had taken the hint. The car bolted around the bulk of the house, heading for the front gate. They were gone.

I sighed and let my head fall back onto the earth. Clouds marred the wide sky, blocking the stars. I shut my eyes miserably against their gray monotony. It would have been nice to see the stars one last time.

They stood all around me, looking down. Angela was smiling. Newton scowled. Lester slammed another clip purposefully into his gun and chambered a bullet. I had no doubt that he was planning to use it on me.

The belated realization that my condition had limits shouldn't have surprised me, but did. Tonight I'd pushed myself too far, used up too much of myself. The raw strength and powers that I'd come to take for granted were either dampened or gone.

I felt betrayed, by myself, by my changed body.

I felt hunger.

I needed blood.

With that thought, I could almost taste it again. The smell was all around me. My canines budded. I brought my hand up to cover them.

Bloodsmell. My own.

There was a gash on the back of my hand. Precious life that I couldn't afford to lose seeped out. What would otherwise be a negligible annoyance easily taken care of was now too threatening to ignore. The red stuff, even my own, had its expected effect on me.

No, don't let them see.

They were talking. I could catch a word or two as the deafness slowly faded. Lester held his gun ready, but Angela stopped him with a curt gesture. When he put it away, I felt safe enough to turn over as though to stand up. Better to be on the ground with my back to them than for them to see. Distinct points of pain flared along my back. I'd been hit by shrapnel. It had gone through me, compounding the blood loss from Chaven's bullets. Not needing to pretend weakness, I rested a moment with my wounded hand right under my mouth.

No good. The taste was wrong. Filtered through my body and the changes within that made it so different also made it wrong. I might as well have tried drinking my own sweat to quench a bottomless thirst.

Hands under my arms, lifting me. I did nothing. They dragged me into the house. Lights. Hall. Doors. Lights burning through me, burning me up.

Heat lamp. I was in the gym, sprawled on the same massage table where they'd worked on Vic. Doc loomed over me and asked a question. I couldn't answer. Didn't dare. He'd see the teeth.

Angela stood next to him, her big dark eyes interested, but without compassion. Her dress didn't have much of a collar. I stared at the slender lines of red life rushing beneath the flushed skin of her neck.

Doc peered and poked, then pressed fingers on my wrist to check the pulse. I jerked my arm away. He shrugged and let it pass.

"Just a little stunned," he pronounced, his voice distant as though coming through a wall. "Still got some fight in him, though. Should be all right after he cleans up."

So much for his medical expertise. If I closed my eyes and kept very quiet, he might declare me fit for a six-day bicycle race.

"Good," said Angela. "We can use him."

"And just what the hell were you thinking lobbing grenades all over the place, girl? This isn't the Fourth of July by a long shot."

"I had them, so why not use them? That car had more steel than a battleship, or couldn't either of you figure that out?" She looked expectantly at Newton and Lester.

Both shrugged. "Not our fault," said Newton. "Things were jumping too fast. I think it's a good thing you came in when you did."

"Uh-huh." She saw through the flattery, but in a good-natured way. "All right, get things put back together here. Lock that window shut and set the alarm again. I don't want them creeping back on us."

"There's still a hole in the works somewhere," Doc said. He nodded at me. "How else could he have gotten through?"

"Okay. Check the rest of the house, too. What I'd like to know is how he got out last night."

"Maybe your daddy put a secret passage in the steam room," he deadpanned, pulling out a sizable drinking flask. He drank deeply. I watched with a terrible envy.

"Don't be an ass. Go check on Mac. See if he's okay."

He pocketed the flask. "Yes, ma'am."

She crossed her arms, studying me narrowly. "How *did* you get out?"

I barely opened my mouth. "Wasn't easy."

"How?"

"Waited 'til no one was looking." It was the truth, more or less. I studied her in turn, drawn by her brown velvet eyes and cupid's-bow lips. Drawn by her . . . no . . . I can't do that again.

"What's wrong?"

"Nothing. Just . . . you're very beautiful." I squeezed my lids shut and tried not to breathe in her scent.

"Oh, ho," she said. "At death's door and still able to flirt. You guys are all crazy."

"Yeah. I'm crazy. Go away."

"When I'm ready, Fleming. You've cost me, so there's going to have to be a payoff and you're it."

"Only part of it."

"What do you mean?"

"Opal's the other part. She's what matters. You don't need me to make a trade for your father."

Her voice lowered and sharpened. "What do you know about him? Kyler's had a lid on the whole business from the start. Tell me."

"Wasn't on that tight. He's got your father—you want him back. You first figured to trade me and Vic for him."

"But then you got away."

"Vic's not important enough to trade?"

"Vic makes the arrangements. He thinks he'll be traded. He'll be lucky if he survives another day, the lousy, two-faced rat."

"Used to work for you, huh?"

"That's the problem, he decided not to—" She caught herself. "Why are you so interested?"

"I just want to get out of here alive, Miss Paco."

She smiled, offered a short laugh, and turned to check Doc's progress with Mac. The latter was sitting up, head between his knees. Doc probed at the damage and got a moan of outrage from his patient.

"He'll be all right. Just needs an ice bag. What'll you do with that one, Angela?" Doc gestured at me.

"Same as the other. Put him away until we set a deal with Kyler."

"You think he'll be interested in dealing after what you did to Red and the others?"

"He can buy more soldiers. And he'll deal. Opal is one of a kind for him. He doesn't dare let her go."

"Or maybe let you get away with it. It's one thing to trade somebody he wants dead for your daddy, but another to grab one of his own people. He might not be very forgiving."

"Once Daddy's back and safe, I'll be able to fix that."

"Go easy, girl."

"Ha."

Lester returned just then. "Telephone, Angela."

"Is it Kyler?"

He shrugged. "Won't say who he is."

She pushed past him to see for herself. Doc watched her leave with a fond smile, which he turned on me.

"You need anything, kid?"

"A blood transfusion?" My teeth were safely retracted by now, but I was still weak and impossibly hollow inside.

He shook his head. "Fresh out. Better luck next time. 'Course you had some luck tonight or you wouldn't be talking now."

"And how long will that last? She doesn't need me to get her father back."

"True, but Angela and I have an arrangement: I don't try to run things and she doesn't practice medicine."

"She might listen to you."

"Don't count on it." He went away to another room for a moment, returning with a damp towel, which he used to clean up my face. "You are quite a mess, boy, you know that?"

"Mm."

"Now let's see what the rest of the damage is. You've got more holes than a sweater full of moths."

I waved him off. "I'm all right."

But he was evidently used to protesting patients and Lester was there to back him up. I couldn't fight them both. The shrapnel hits in my back were closed up by now. The metal had been moving too fast and gone right through, presumably to bounce off the car's body. I hoped the stuff had missed Isham. Doc compared the holes and stains on my clothes to the unmarked skin below and asked me an obvious question about the discrepancy. I made an uncooperative grunt to indicate that I had no answer. Thankfully, he shrugged it off for the moment. I silently blessed his lack of medical skill and the booze dulling his brain.

Doc washed off the gash in my hand. It had stopped bleeding, but still looked nasty and raw. Perhaps some flying fragment of wood had caused it.

"How about some stitches?" he suggested cheerfully.

"Never mind. Just bandage it."

"You'll have a scar."

Lester laughed. "Doc, the kid ain't gonna be 'round long enough for that."

"I know, but I need the practice. I'm not so steady as I used to be." He spread his fingers flat and exaggerated a tremor.

Then they looked at me for a reaction and found much to amuse them. Doc tied some gauze around my hand, finishing up just as Newton came back.

"I couldn't find where he got in," he said. "Everything's shut and locked. He musta come in the window there." He pointed across the room.

From the floor, Mac groggily disagreed. "Then the alarm woulda gone off."

"The alarm did go off."

"Yeah, but it wasn't going when I got hit, and the only one who coulda hit me was this guy." He jerked a thumb at me.

"Maybe the other guy socked you and you don't remember. Why the hell'd you let him out?"

"He said he hadda use the can."

"Oh, great."

"You'da believed him, too. Besides, he could hardly walk."

"Yeah, he was saving it up to run."

"If you'd seen that fall he took down the stairs . . . ah, forget it. What I'm tryin' to say is that he was in front of me the whole time and I got hit from behind. It was this one, all right. So how'd you get in the house, kid?"

"Through a window," I answered truthfully. "Maybe the alarm's busted in one of 'em, huh?"

"Oughta bust you myself, smart-ass."

"Lay off," said Newton. "I mighta missed something. You and Lester go check it again. And check on Angela, too. Make sure Vic's behaving himself."

"Where's Opal?" I asked.

"Why you want to know? She your girlfriend?"

"Just wondered if she was okay, is all."

"She's just peachy. Come on, you mugs. Get the show on the road."

Lester got Mac to his feet and helped him wobble out.

I appealed to Doc. "She all right?"

"Don't worry about her, kid. She's being looked after. She likes this place a sight better than where we found her."

Angela barged in just then, her brows drawn together and her little mouth tight with a frown. "Newton, bring him along to the office." She pointed at me and whipped out again, skirt swirling.

Newton got me off the table, but my legs were not cooperating too well. The shift from horizontal to vertical didn't help my head. The ceiling swooped down, or seemed to, and I ducked in reaction.

"Hey, this ain't a marathon dance, dummy," he complained. *"Walk."*

I did my best, but God, I was weak, like a battery out of juice. My cure, I desperately hoped, was simple enough. I needed blood, but was I too far gone to get it? And where to get it?

Newton grunted as he hauled me along. His heartbeat was steady and strong.

No. I stumbled away from that one.

"Doc, f'cryin' out loud, gimme a hand with this wet noodle."

Doc came up to take my other arm. "Sure he's not malingering?"

"Huh?"

"Faking it."

"Wish I were," I gasped.

"What's wrong with you, kid?"

"Angela dropped a grenade on me, what d'you expect?"

"Got a point there," he admitted.

We reached the office and they hurried across the last few yards to dump me onto a sofa. It was crowded. Next to me and unmoved by the ruckus was Vic. He looked like I felt.

"Jeez, he's heavy," said Newton, puffing. Doc grunted agreement and headed for the liquor on the other side of the room. He poured out some whiskey and brought it over to me. I turned my head away from it, lips sealed tight with revulsion.

"Do you good, kid," he advised.

My throat constricted. "Later. I . . . I couldn't keep it down now."

"I can believe that." Doc decided not to let it go to waste and finished it off for me.

"What's the matter with him?" demanded Angela, who was at the desk.

"Bad stomach," I mumbled. "I'll be all right."

"Probably a case of the shakes," said Doc. "Just a little reaction to what he's been through."

That's for damn sure. I closed my eyes so things wouldn't slip around so badly. If only the inside of my head would stop lurching as well.

"What's going on?" he asked her.

She sank into the big chair under her father's portrait. "I got a call from that English guy who says he's Fleming's friend."

"The guy that just broke out? He's got some nerve. Where is he?"

"He'd hardly let that slip, would he?"

"You never know. What's he want?"

"He said he's got information that's going to affect my deal with Kyler. He'll trade it for Fleming. I stalled him and told him to call back later."

Doc put the glass back next to the bottle. "Must be a lie or else he'd have been using it to bargain for himself when we had him."

"That's what I'm going to find out. So what is it he knows, Fleming?"

"I couldn't say."

"Uh-huh. You'd better come up with something. I'm setting up a deal in a few hours that's going to go right or else nobody's walking back from it."

Doc added, "That includes your friend Opal, kid."

Angela picked up on his cue. "Newton, bring her down."

He lumbered out. No one said anything while he was gone. Vic seemed to be asleep or passed out. Doc poured another drink and found a chair. Angela drummed her nails on the desk. When I shifted to a somewhat more comfortable position, she opened a drawer and drew out a gun. I behaved myself, being incapable of much else for the moment. Some of the nausea passed off, but I was still light-headed.

"This stinks," came a familiar flat voice from the hall.

Newton pushed Opal into the room, still in her coat and galoshes, and shut the door, leaning against it. Opal glared at him, at all of them in turn, then, with some surprise, at me.

"You again?"

"It's your lucky day, honey."

She crossed her arms in disgust, her face set and hostile. "No, it's not."

I'd forgotten how literal she was.

Angela played with the gun, looking thoughtful. "Since she's an accountant, she doesn't need to walk much, does she?"

Opal's attention shifted. Her eyes went wide.

"Now how about you tell me a few things before I blow off one of her kneecaps?"

She was her father's daughter, all right. "Okay, you've made your point," I said. "You can put that away."

"When I'm ready. What is it your friend's talking about?"

"I figure it has to do with Kyler."

"So could any grade schooler. What is it?"

"Look, I don't care anything about your deal with him. I just want to get away from this place and be left alone. I'll trade what I know for a fast route out of here."

"That depends on what you know." Her tone was cautious, but she was interested.

"It'll help you all right. None of this is really my show now, but I'd like to see Opal back where she belongs—"

"Then *talk*."

My lids suddenly shut down. Instant day. I wasn't there for her to yell at anymore.

(*Talk, Fleming.* I swam in my own sweat, sick from fear and the stink of Morelli's damned cigar and Frank Paco breaking my ribs and laughing about it. . . .)

My head twitched, as though I'd been lightly slapped.

Liquid fire seared my tongue. A few drops got down my throat before I suddenly choked and coughed explosively.

"Shit," complained Doc, who had been in the way. "What a waste of good booze."

"What's wrong with him?" Angela irritably demanded.

"Damned if I know, girl."

Like the room, time had shifted, tossing me back to last summer for a hellish second. There's nothing in the human experience that can be fairly compared to the memory of one's own death. I'd remembered mine just then because I was facing it again.

Doc looked me over, his expression growing long and serious as he peeled back my eyelids. He tried to get my pulse again, but I yanked my arm away. He settled for putting the back of his hand on my damp brow. That's when he must have caught the deathsmell scent coming from me. If a smell could have a color, this one was *yellow*. Nothing to do with personal courage, that's just how it seemed to me.

Maybe to both of us; he straightened and turned to Angela and didn't say anything. She got the message. She came around the desk to see better. It confirmed what she'd read from Doc, and her manner changed somewhat.

Her voice softened, no longer resembling her father's buzz-saw snarl, which had helped push my memory down its unpleasant path in the first place. "Come on, Fleming. You tell me what you know and I'll send you back home, safe and sound." A softer voice and her eyes . . . Lord, I could get very seriously lost in those big brown pools.

Then it seemed as though my deafness returned for a few moments. I forgot about all the others around us. I could hear only Angela's heart, sense only her light breath whispering in the air between us. She caught and held it and leaned closer to me. Her eyes went dull, locked solidly upon mine.

This was as different from my normal hunger as a bonfire is to a candle. She was entirely desirable, but not as a woman, as food. I recognized the feeling well enough, but was too far gone to worry about the immorality of it. A starving man doesn't care much about such details; he just knows his need, and the hell with everyone else. My instinct to survive had simply taken over, trying to reach her, to bring her to me.

"Angela?"

And so Doc inadvertently cut the link I'd almost established with her. Half hypnosis, half sexual desire for beautiful Angela, all desperate, screaming appetite for me. I'd grown that hungry.

She, of course, had been unaware of any of it. "What?"

"You gonna talk with him or kiss him?"

"Don't be an ass." She automatically dismissed his suggestion rather than make a conscious admission that something out of the ordinary may have touched her. Just as well.

He gave a small shrug to indicate it was her business, not his. The damage had been done, though. The effort, slight as it was, had tired me further. Now I had just the one card left, the one Escott had managed to slip in through Angela.

She smoothly picked up where she'd left off. "How about it, Fleming? You're right, I really don't need you to pull this off, but if you can give me an edge over Kyler . . ." Then she began to shovel the snow on thick and deep and went to some trouble to pack it down solid.

"Deal," I croaked, before her generous promises to preserve and reward me for my help got too embarrassingly out of hand.

Angela smiled, sunshine with dark eyes. And for me now, in this weakened state, sunshine was a guarantee of irreversible death.

I turned from the thought, concentrating on the real business. "Okay. Just a couple of questions: have you talked to Kyler already?"

"Yeah. We used Vic to get things rolling. Kyler's thinking things over."

"And you called him just a little while ago, right?"

She nodded.

"But did you actually talk with him?"

Her face darkened. "What are you getting at?"

I glanced at Opal, but couldn't think of a way to make it easier for her. "Kyler's dead. He's been dead since before I came here."

Opal made an indignant squeak of disbelief. Angela and Doc shifted with more subdued reactions.

"How do you know?"

"Because I was there when Chaven shot him."

"Chaven?"

Then they crowded in to demand more details, first as total skeptics, then as half believers. I gave them the version I'd told Shoe Coldfield. There were a lot more questions and interruptions from them, but I had no trouble keeping my facts straight. I would not be forgetting what had happened for a very long time—if I had any left to me.

Angela may have known she wasn't getting the whole story, but looked almost ready to accept what she had. "Can you prove this?"

"Not directly. If you send someone up on the main road to town they'll find one of Kyler's Cadillacs parked on the left-hand side. I hot-wired it to get clear of them."

"Anyone can grab a car," Newton pointed out from his post by the door.

"Sure," I agreed. "Nothing direct, like I said. You tell me, Miss Paco, who *did* you talk to on the phone?"

"With Chaven," she cautiously admitted.

"As valuable as Opal is to Kyler's organization, do you think he'd trust something as important as getting her back to one of his lieutenants?"

Her eyes got a lot brighter. "No. That's the last thing he'd do."

"I'd say that this is what Escott meant about it having a direct effect on things, wouldn't you? Who you're dealing with is just as important as what the deal's all about. And if you're still using Vic as a go-between, I'd watch him a little more closely than before."

She glanced sharply at Vic, who had woken up at the news.

"He's gotta be lying," he mumbled out. "Chaven wouldn't dare kill the boss."

"Maybe not," I said. "But he's running things now and he needs Opal back."

Opal sputtered, then found some words. "I don't want to work for *him*!"

"Pipe down, cutie," Newton told her.

"No. I worked only for Vaughn. I'm not working for Chaven."

"You can hash things out with him yourself," Angela snapped. "I'm getting my father back. You're my best chance at it."

Before Opal could open her mouth and possibly make trouble for herself, I interrupted. "I saw him tonight, Miss Paco."

That grabbed her attention far better than the announcement of Kyler's death.

"They had him off by himself in one of the rooms at Kyler's roadhouse. He seemed okay."

"You're lying."

"I've got no reason to. He's a little thinner and thinks he's still running all this." I waved vaguely. "He called you *mia Angelina*."

That tore it. Angela erupted from her spot, the energy all but sparking from her. She rapidly paced the office end to end; Doc and the others backed off to give her room to move. She stopped just as abruptly in front of me, her jaw working.

"Okay," was all she said, talking more to herself than to the rest of us. She hated the fact that I'd seen him and she hadn't. She hated it, but it was the proof that she needed. I was telling the truth, or as much of it as was good for me. I got the feeling that if her deal to get her father back didn't work, she'd either keep me alive to drag out more details about him or use me as a target for another round of grenade tossing.

My distinction wasn't enough to put off Opal, though. "Miss Paco?"

She turned a hostile face toward the girl, who was quite oblivious to her irritation.

"I said I don't want to work for Chaven."

"That's your problem."

"I thought I could work for you, instead."

Angela's jaw dropped. So did a lot of others, including my own. Angela wasn't the only one who could toss a grenade. "You . . ."

Opal anticipated the first questions, her ready answers coming out in a monotone rush. "You can trade me, but I could come back. I'm good at numbers. I'm the best, that's why Vaughn hired me."

Doc came out with a noise that could be mistaken for laughter. "I'm sure that was very generous of him, little lady, but we've already got—"

"But I'm the best. You ask me anything about numbers and I know it."

Doc nearly spoke again, but Angela waved him off. "Kyler wouldn't waste his time on . . ." She struggled to come up with another way to finish her sentence.

Opal calmly finished for her. "An idiot. I know what you think. A lot of people think that way. All except Vaughn. He knew different. He *was* different. He could scare people for no reason. I'm different, but if it scares people, they hide it. That's why they've always made fun of me, to show they're not scared.

"He tell you that?" asked Angela.

"I figured it out. But I don't want to scare people. I just want work where I can do numbers."

"Damnedest job interview I ever heard of," Doc muttered. "I'm sure you're real good at those numbers, hon, but there's more to it than that."

Opal's eyes narrowed with disgust. "Don't call me 'hon'."

He sketched a mock salute. "Yes, ma'am."

The sarcasm was lost on Opal. She turned her attention back to Angela. "What about it?"

"Doc's right. In this kind of business you can't just change sides without making a lot of trouble for yourself." She looked significantly at Vic, whose jaw was still dusting the floor. "You can make a lot more trouble for me, because Chaven's not going to be happy when he learns what you've got in mind."

Literal as ever, she said, "I don't care how he feels. I don't want to work for him."

"You've got my sympathy, but there's nothing I can do to help you. No offense, but you're just not worth the trouble you'll cause."

The idea that clicked on in Opal's head was almost audible and certainly visible to all. She lobbed in her second grenade. "I can fix that. I could bring all the organization's books out with me. That would make me worth the trouble, wouldn't it?"

10

"DOUBLE-CROSSING BITCH," said Vic in the middle of an awful lot of silence.

"You should talk," snapped Newton.

" 'S not my fault. I did what I had to do. I didn't want to work for Kyler."

But Angela waved them both down, all of her attention focused on Opal. "You're serious?"

Opal nodded. "I worked for Vaughn because he didn't make fun of me. Chaven does. I don't like him and I don't want to work for him. I can take the books and bring them to you and you can run things, instead." I think we all knew that she was telling the truth. Opal's absolute literalness could be trusted.

Angela settled into an unexpected stillness, but her brain was probably racing along like a new adding machine, working out the debits and credits of Opal's offer. Then she laughed. It was the same joy-filled shout she'd burst with outside amid the destruction she'd so casually tossed around.

Opal scowled. "Don't laugh at me."

Angela caught her breath. "Oh, no, honey. I'm not laughing at you. It's Chaven. You work things right with me on this and we'll both be laughing at Chaven. Can you imagine the look on his face?"

"Then you'll hire me?"

"You're on probation," she said decisively.

"What do you mean?"

"Pull this off and you'll never have to work for a piece of

scum like Chaven ever again. We'll treat you good as Kyler did. Better."

Ever practical, Opal stated, "He paid me a thousand a month."

"Get away with those books and I'll guarantee you fifteen hundred."

"You're going to trust her, just like that?" asked Doc.

"Why not? I said she's on probation. She'll get a chance to prove herself when the time comes. Besides, I've met Chaven and I don't blame her for wanting to get away from him."

"And what if she decides she doesn't want to be here, either? Don't you think she might just as easily walk out on you like she's doing with Kyler?"

She swung back to Opal. "What about it?"

"I worked for Vaughn, not for Chaven or any of the others, just Vaughn. He's dead, so I'm not walking out on him. Here, I'll work for you, but not for him or him." She indicated Doc and Newton.

That made points with Angela. Doc only shrugged. "Well, you can't beat that with a stick, but aren't you moving just a little too fast, girl?"

Angela grinned. "That's how you get ahead of the others. I'm not going to sit on my keester waiting for people; it's up to them to catch up with me. If Chaven can't move fast enough, then too bad."

"Long as you know what you're doing."

"Long as Chaven doesn't. And he won't. Isn't that right, Vic?"

Vic turned a gray face on her, a dead man's face, though he was still breathing. "Angela, I'll do anything you want. . . ."

"Yes, I know you will. It's the only chance you'll get from me. You screw this deal up and anything happens to my father because of it, I'm going to make sure you live."

Vic puzzled over that one, his mind too foggy to make much sense of it. "Huh?"

Doc leaned forward. "What she means is that if you make a mistake, you'll wish you were dead before we're finished with you."

"I'll do whatever you say. Promise, Angela. I promise. . . ."

Her mouth twisted. "Save the whining for later. Screw up and I'll be in the mood to hear it then."

He was sweating freely. "I won't screw up—"

"Save it," she ordered, with a dangerous edge to her voice.

He shut his mouth and saved it.

Doc chuckled. "So . . . what's next?"

"I'd like to go home," I said, by way of suggestion.

He looked surprised. "Would you now?"

"Later," said Angela. "First I deal with Chaven, then with you. Understand?"

I nodded wearily. It hadn't hurt to try. If Escott called back, maybe she'd have him come pick me up, but I wasn't going to bank on her goodwill.

"God, he looks terrible." She frowned as though it were somehow my own fault.

Newton eyed me unhappily. "You don't think he's got anything catching, do you?"

"Doc?"

Doc shrugged at them. "What about it, kid?"

"No. I gotta bad stomach is all."

"You want anything for it?"

The answer to that one would only complicate things. I kept my mouth shut and shook my head.

"Maybe he wants to see your diploma from medical school," Angela said, her plump lips marred by an unkind smile. "If you haven't hocked it yet."

Doc only shrugged again. It seemed to be his ready answer for a lot of business.

"Why do you say mean things like that to him?" Opal unexpectedly asked.

The query didn't bother Angela. Her reply was simple enough. "Because I can get away with it."

Opal next turned to Doc. "Why do you let her say mean things to you?"

Doc glanced at Angela. She looked interested in the answer, as well. "Because, my dear, I can't afford to have pride these days."

"Why not?"

"Pride doesn't buy you stuff like this." He pulled out the flask and drank from it. "Once you get a taste for the old demon rum, a little thing like pride only gets in the way of your enjoyment."

"That stinks."

"I suppose it does, but you haven't got much of a leg to stand on, either."

"What do you mean?"

"Didn't you just sell yourself out to Angela so you could work with your precious numbers? I've got booze, you've got numbers, where's the difference?"

Opal took the point right away, scowled, and turned back to Angela. "Does that mean you'll be saying mean things to me?"

Angela shook her head. "No, I won't. And neither will anyone else here." She gave her men a significant look. They all acknowledged it one way or another. No one cracked anything like a smile.

The scowl abruptly relaxed. Labor relations satisfactorily settled, she took off her glasses to polish them against the hem of her dress. "I'm hungry," she announced to no one in particular.

Angela nodded at Newton. "Kitchen. Give her whatever she wants."

"Sure. Y'want anything yourself?"

She glared at the phone with disgust and waved them out.

"When's Chaven due to call?" I asked.

"Soon." Hardly an answer, so she might not know. Chaven could stall her all night if he wanted. She'd wait. I couldn't. Come morning and . . . no, I didn't want to think about that horrific possibility just yet.

"Angela?" This from Vic, who stirred painfully next to me.

She sounded bored. "What?"

"I . . . I'm in a pretty tough spot, I know that."

"All your doing, Vic, not mine."

"Yeah, I know that. I just wanted you to know that I really didn't want to go over to Kyler."

"Uh-huh."

"Honest. The man was . . ." He avoided saying "crazy," perhaps remembering at the last second about Frank Paco's own unfortunate condition. "Well, he didn't give us much of a choice. He'd just as soon skin you alive as look at you. We—"

"Uh-huh. 'Didn't want to go over.' "

"There's others who feel the same. Mort, Gabbo, lots of others. They was too scared not to. Once word gets out about Kyler being dead, they'll want to come back to work for you again."

"Like the way you want to now."

"On the level, Angela. I know the spot I'm in. After the deal

you just made with Opal, you can't send me back for fear I'll
queer her coming back with the books."

"Looks like the boy's finally grown some brains," commented Doc.

"But I don't want to queer things, I swear to you. I'll work
with you, do whatever it takes to help you get Mr. Paco back."

Her face was stone.

"Then when it's over, I'll just tell Chaven that I'm staying on
with you. When the other guys hear that, they'll come back
themselves. I could talk to 'em, tell 'em about the books. They
won't want to work with Chaven. They know he won't be able
to hold things together the same way. Not the way you can."

The stone cracked a little. After a long pause, she sighed.
"All right, Vic, you get a second chance."

Vic could hardly believe it, sputtered, and started gushing his
thanks.

"Screw it up and you're dead," she added, which helped so-
ber him.

He relaxed back on the sofa. Less subtle than the deathsmell
coming from me was the stringy scent of his nervousness and
white-faced fear. He desperately wanted—needed—to take her
at her word, but I didn't think she could afford to keep it. It being no business of mine, I kept my mouth shut. Only last night
he'd been too ready to assist in taking me to certain doom. If he
could pull this one off, good luck to him. I had my own worries.

The phone rang. Angela pounced on it.

"Yes, it is. What's he decided? . . . Yeah, he's here. Just a
minute." She held the mouthpiece against her body. "Chaven
wants to talk to you, Vic. Watch what you say."

He nodded, as pale as his bandages. "I'll be careful."

Doc helped walk him to the desk. He slumped into the chair.
Angela had picked up the gun once more and nudged it gently
against Vic's temple.

"You just remember that you don't know Kyler's dead and
turn things back over to me first thing."

Another nod. "'Lo? Chaven? Yeah, it's me . . . I'm okay.
Yeah, they're treatin' us fine. Opal's mad as a wet hen, but fine.
Angela wants to deal, what about the boss? Okay . . . Okay." He
gave the earpiece over to Angela and wearily put his head down
on the desk. She grabbed it and hunched over the phone to make
herself heard, juggling untidily with the gun.

"All right, what's Kyler decided? Uh-huh . . . uh-huh. Yeah, we can be there by then, but why there? Uh-huh. I want to talk to my father first and make sure he's all right. . . . Then I want to talk to Kyler so he can explain. . . ." She muffled the earpiece. "The lazy so-and-so didn't want to bring in Daddy."

"Bet he wants to bring in Kyler even less," mused Doc.

She tossed me a wink of acknowledgment for the news I'd given her. I didn't bother to return it. After a moment her eyes refocused and she stiffened, struggling for breath. "Daddy! Are you all right?" She laughed at his reply, sounding a little forced. "Well, those mugs will get theirs, soon as you come home again. We'll make sure. What was that? Daddy? *Daddy*?" Her expression abruptly went cold, reflecting the change in speakers. "Okay, you just keep him happy or I'll know the reason why." Angela slammed the earpiece back on its hook.

"What's the story?" asked Doc.

"We meet at the old boat dock in an hour."

"Why there?"

"He's coming in by way of the lake. He'll be in that big yacht that belonged to Morelli and will send a boat out from it. Daddy'll be in the boat."

"Why the hell does he want to do it that way? If we wanted to we could pick them off like sitting ducks when they return. Kyler would never take a chance like that." He glared at me, full of drunken suspicion. "Unless *he's* working with him, misleading us on this whole thing."

"I'm not," I answered faintly. "And you'll talk yourself into a real circle with thinking like that. Go for the simple and obvious reason behind it all: Chaven's taking the yacht so he can dump Kyler's body into the lake. As long as he's out there, he can use it to make a fairly safe exchange. He's not worried so much about you, Miss Paco, as about the cops finding him with a stiff."

It both annoyed and amused, but also reassured her. She gave out with a short laugh that turned into a sharp gasp of shock. Without warning, Vic erupted from his chair and fell onto her. They dropped out of my view behind the desk. Doc froze with indecision for a crucial moment and then I heard Angela's bellow of outrage.

Vic staggered up. He'd gotten her gun. He looked almost as

surprised about it as the rest of us. He put his back to the wall and crab-walked toward the door.

"No trouble," he gasped, eyes wild. "No trouble. I just want outta here."

Angela's reply was anything but genteel.

He ignored it and kept going for the door. He made it, made a clumsy but successful scrabble to open it, and was away. As soon as he was out of sight, Angela was on her feet and ripping open one of the desk drawers.

Doc gave a start. "My God, girl, you can't—"

"Yes, I can," she grated. She straightened, with a grenade in each fist. "Watch him!" Meaning me. Then she charged after Vic.

Doc made a halfhearted start to follow, but gave it up. He found lengthy solace in his flask.

"Quite a handful, isn't she?" I observed, seeking calm conversation in the middle of all the insanity.

He nodded tiredly. "Her whole life. Why Frank didn't raise her to be a nice girl, I don't know."

"When I saw him—at Kyler's—he said he did just that."

"You know what I mean, kid. She's no floozie, but she's sure not a regular kind of girl. Maybe it's a sign of the times."

More likely a sign of Frank Paco's skill as a father. God help Vic.

The burglar alarm bell went off. Doc jumped.

"That'll be Vic leaving the house," he concluded. He walked to the window. "He's making for the cars. I sure hope she doesn't . . ."

Drumbeat.

The glass vibrated the way it does during a bad thunderstorm. Doc blanched and let the curtain fall back. He rubbed at his eyes as though they were sore, then looked at me. He seemed about to say something, but swallowed it back like a mouthful of vomit. He cleared his throat with another long drink.

"Want one?" he asked tonelessly.

I said no. Several minutes crawled by without another word. The alarm stopped ringing, then we heard footsteps at the door. Sheldon, his hand and arm in a proper cast and sling, poked his head in.

"Hey, Doc, what the hell's going on here?" His eyes were heavy and fogged from whatever painkiller he'd had that day.

He wore a rumpled pajama shirt, carpet slippers, and a hastily pulled on pair of trousers.

"Angela's out taking care of Vic," said Doc with a pale grin.

"That double-crossing—hey!" He had caught sight of me, waking up quite a lot. "What's *he* doing here?"

"He's helping us get Frank back."

"Like he was supposed to last night, huh? That'll be fine by me. I owe this bastard a good one for this," he said, indicating his shattered arm. "Wish I could be there to see what Kyler's going to do to you."

Doc didn't bother to give him the latest news. We heard more footsteps and Angela came in with Newton and Opal.

Angela's eyes were half closed and she wore the smooth and untroubled smile that often goes with contented accomplishment. There was a bright splash of blood on her cheek. Not hers, she explained to Doc in a brisk voice when he asked about it. She was breathing hard, but I got the impression it was from her running, not as a reaction to what she had just done. She had one grenade left and neatly shut it back into its drawer.

Watching her with something like awe, Newton and Opal kept extremely quiet. Angela observed us each in turn and liked what she saw.

"Well, I solved that problem," she stated.

I could see her point, since Vic had just shown he couldn't be trusted. Better to completely remove him as a threat than to explain why he was staying on with people who considered him a traitor. Even Chaven wouldn't have swallowed a story like that for very long without suspecting something else was brewing. I could, indeed, see the point very clearly, and concluded that I'd been hanging around this crazy house for far too long.

"What are you doing downstairs, Sheldon?" she asked, noticing him.

He was a little nervous, having correctly picked up on the tension coming off the rest of us. "I was sleeping and heard the alarm go off again. Thought I'd check things."

"Good. I'm glad to know that you're on the ball. Newton, you'll find Mac and Lester outside. I want you to help them clean up the mess there, but first put this one on ice." She indicated me. "I don't need any more surprises tonight."

"Yeah, sure thing, Angela."

"Opal, you stay with me."

"Okay."

Her eyes sharpened. "You still want to work here?"

The question genuinely puzzled Opal. "Yes, I do."

She made a gesture toward the window to indicate Vic. "Even after that?"

Opal was indifferent. "I work with numbers. That's what I'm best at. That's what I want to stick with."

Angela broke into a grin of sly delight. "You're okay, Opal."

Still indifferent, Opal simply nodded, but some of the stiffness went out of the rest of us. Doc drank some color back into his face and assumed a semblance of his version of normality, and why not? Murder was business as usual in this household.

The phone rang again. Angela snapped it up.

"Yes? What? Oh, it's you." Her big eyes rested on me, giving me an accurate idea of the caller's identity. "Uh-huh, I've thought it over and I'll accept your offer. Uh-huh? Well, you're welcome. Now, what's this information you've got? No, it doesn't work like that. You get your friend back after I hear what it is."

Escott said something to make her smile.

"He wants to know if you're all right," she relayed to me. Great, I was expected to hobble over to the desk with words of reassurance.

I spoke loudly, hoping he could hear. "Tell him I'm fine, but"—I almost added "thirsty" but decided against it—"need some rest."

"You get that?" she asked him. "Good. Now what's your story? No, first you talk. Take it or leave it."

Escott took it and Angela listened, watching me the whole time. I didn't have to ask why she was playing such games; she was only trying to confirm what I'd told her. If Escott was on the ball—and I expected he would be—he'd interpret her lack of reaction to his news to mean that she already knew about it. That's what I fervently hoped, so he'd give her the same information. If not, then the consequences were yet another subject that I didn't want to think about.

After a few minutes, I was almost able to relax. Angela nodded restlessly, as if bored with the conversation, and finally broke in on him to cut things short.

"Okay, okay, I got all that and you'll get him back, but later tonight. Call here in two hours and we'll set it up then. No, that's the best I can do and I think you know better than to bring in the cops. Good." She hung up and frowned at her watch.

"Busy night," Doc commented.

"I can handle it."

"Never said you couldn't, girl. You'll get Frank home again."

"If they know what's good for them. Newton, I told you to get this one out of here. And don't forget about Mac and Lester."

Newton stepped forward to take me away. Once more, he had to call on Doc for help getting me down the hall.

"Third time's the charm," he said as they dragged me to the steam room. "We'll see if we can't keep you here, eh?"

"Your bedside manner stinks," I muttered, not looking forward to being locked up.

"So they keep telling me."

Someone had installed a couple of eyebolts on either side of the outward-opening door since my last stay. Propped in a corner was a steel rod borrowed from a rack of barbells and stripped of its weights. Thread the rod through the bolts and you'd have to break the door itself to make an escape. In my present state, I had serious doubts about my ability to break so much as an egg. They dropped me onto a tile bench and Doc lifted and straightened my legs along it. His face was serious again. He tried to take my pulse. I jerked my arm away.

"Lemme 'lone, will you?"

"You're mighty sick, kid. I can't fix it if you won't let me."

"Then don't bother."

He acquiesced with a pitying shrug. Maybe there'd been one too many lapses to his Hippocratic oath for him to take any extra trouble over an obviously dying man. "Come on, Newton."

Newton all but raced him out in his haste to get away. He couldn't have been in much of a hurry to help Mac and Lester; perhaps he'd caught a little of the deathsmell coming from me. They shut the door and fixed the rod between the eyebolts.

Their steps faded. Silence. Not even the sound of my heart for company, but I'd long grown used to that. I breathed every few seconds just to make sure I still could. It was more than Vic was doing.

Two hours to go. Two hours plus whatever time it might take to drive to the Stockyards; I had to last that long. The waiting would be pretty awful, but at least Angela had set a definite limit for it . . . if I could take her at her word. No doubt she'd be glad to be rid of me, dead or alive.

Despite the lack of real air circulation in the room, the sweat eventually cooled and dried except where it had soaked into my clothes. Unpleasantly damp, but nothing I couldn't put up with. I drifted in my cocoon of skin and resisted the urge to check the time every other minute. Doing that would only make the wait seem longer.

Dry, painful swallow. My throat and mouth might have been coated with dust. I stopped the irregular breathing to conserve what little moisture remained. Shut away from the others, I had no distractions from the internal discomforts. The cut on my hand burned, my stomach was knotting up again, and my head kept wanting to float off by itself.

Since I was still stuck here, Escott would know that I was in a bad way. Maybe he could manage to have some blood on hand for me, as he'd done before when I'd been in trouble. Of course, he was hardly fit for climbing fences at the Stockyards himself. It was nice to think about, but not something I could count on. Coldfield was very much in the way on that one. He wouldn't be fobbed off with a made-up story about a rare medical condition. On the other hand, tell him the truth and he might take it as an insult to his intelligence.

Someone quietly slid the rod from its eyebolts. I allowed myself a glimpse at the time. It was still far too soon. Angela wouldn't even have left to make her meeting with Chaven yet. Hope jumped within me. Perhaps Escott's call had been meant to test things out. Coldfield or Isham could have somehow slipped past the alarm system. . . .

Sheldon walked in.

So much for a daring rescue.

He stood high over me and stared down and said nothing and he did this for a very long moment. Sweat popped out on the back of my neck, making it itch. I didn't move, because in his good hand was one of those damned wooden Indian clubs.

"Doc says not to worry, but I know better," he informed me, lifting his cast a little so I'd know what he was talking about. His voice was as flat as Opal's, but subtly different. Where she instantly said what was on her mind, he'd been thinking things over. He wanted to be certain I understood him.

I said nothing.

He leaned in close. The thick stink of booze was on his breath. "I can tell when that quack is feeding out a line of bull. I seen him makin' those kind of promises to other guys that didn't come true. You know how that feels when it's your turn?"

I tried to focus on him. No good. He was just too drunk for it to work, even if I'd been up to full strength.

"It's a lot of shit. They're already startin' to call me names for it; Lefty, Crab Claw. They think it's pretty damn funny when a guy needs help to get dressed. You think it's funny?"

An answer to that one would only make things worse. I kept my mouth shut tight.

"It ain't funny at all. Can't do anything worth doing now. Takes twice as long for everything else. And it hurts. Don't think it doesn't. That's how I know. It hurts deep down in the bones, in between the bones. Doc says I'll get better but I know I won't. Won't be able to handle a gun as good, sure as hell can't fight. About all I've got left is this."

He hefted the club and tapped it experimentally against the white tile near my head. It made a small, hollow echo in the little room.

"Don't take much practice for one of these. You crippled me, you son of a bitch, and I'm gonna pay you back."

I caught his eyes once more. I had to break through or die. That sickening realization didn't help my concentration, but did heighten the emotions involved.

He wavered. I pushed.

This was worse than it had been with Kyler, infinitely harder. Even with his drunkenness getting in the way, Sheldon was easily the more vulnerable, but I was weak and getting worse as I used up what little was left to me. Fear kept me going.

He shook his head, eyes blinking as though struck with a too-bright light.

"Wha . . . you . . ."

I spoke his name. Softly. Names have power, more than we care to admit to ourselves. I spoke again, steady whispers to cloud his brain with dreams of rest and peace. He stopped blinking. I stepped up the pressure, keeping my voice even and low the way I did with the cattle in the yards. Eyes fixed and growing dull, he began to gradually slip into sleep.

The club dropped as his fingers relaxed, making a shattering crack as it landed. He jumped as though from an electric shock, snapping wide awake, tearing free of my influence.

No. I was too near it now to give up. The blood pulsing through his veins was *mine*.

Before he could make another move, think another thought, I had both hands on his neck. It was like another shock to him. He tried to pull away. I held on. He tried to break my grip. I held on. A minute was all I needed to knock him out, maybe less. He heaved backward. I held on. This was as even a fight as I'd ever had with a man since my change. The sheer terror of what would happen to me if I lost this one kept me going. A minute, just a minute more of strength . . . a few . . . seconds . . . longer . . .

But he got his good arm up between us and managed to pry one of my hands loose. I instantly grabbed his arm before he could slip away, and despite the poor leverage and bad angle pulled him over and down. His slippered feet went out from under him on the smooth floor. The crown of his head smacked solidly into the wall on my left.

He dropped flat across my chest like a bag full of anvils. Any breath left inside me whooshed out and stayed there; it was just as well that I didn't really need it. His cast dug into my gut. I tried to shove him off, but couldn't budge him.

This was it. I was too far gone to move now. Within a foot of his throat and I hadn't the strength to reach it.

Wait. Rest.

God, the bloodsmell was coming right through his skin and clothes. I was going crazy from it.

Rest. He's not going anywhere, either.

His uninjured arm was close enough. It would do. Better a trickle than nothing at all. I worked first one hand free and then another, resting from each effort, but not for long; a disturbing mental picture of sand streaming out of an hourglass kept popping into my brain.

I twisted his arm up, pushing back the thin cloth of his sleeve. My teeth were out and ready. Considering my haste and desperation, I made a surprisingly clean cut on the inside of his elbow.

I drank without thought, without control. Bitter hot strength slowly soaked into my exhausted body, killing the hunger, easing the thirst. I was blind and deaf to everything as liquid life flowed into me from toes to fingertips.

Instinct combined with long practice told me when I'd had enough. I drew away, leaving behind little more than a red mark and two small holes hardly worth noticing. All would fade away soon enough. He was alive, but wouldn't be feeling well for the next few days, not so much from the blood loss, but from a concussion. The tile wall I'd slammed his head into was unforgivingly hard.

With a thankful heave, I boosted Sheldon's limp body off, letting him slump to the floor. I could almost smile at him. He'd come in to either kill or cripple me and ended up saving my life. Perhaps that was why I felt no guilt taking human blood for food this time. I wasn't proud of it, and not about to make a habit of it, but the crushing weight of conscious irresponsibility wasn't there now. I'd done what was necessary. No regrets.

Besides, I had other things to worry about, like getting the hell out of here.

My head felt heavier than before; not uncomfortable, but not normal. As I got to my feet, the feeling became more pronounced. It didn't stop me from stumbling out the door, though.

Decision time. Try the window again, or sneak out through one of the doors? Walls. I could walk through them now, but didn't like doing that, to seep through the wood and plaster like some kind of water leak. . . .

I shook my head. It would have to be practicality over preference. Going out any other way would set off the alarms. Okay, right through one of the walls, and Angela and her merry men could spend the rest of the night trying to figure it out. Jack Fleming, the new Houdini, special midnight shows only, children half price. . . .

Bumped into Doc's makeshift operating table. Bloodsmell lingered on it. My own. Vic's. Somehow knew the difference. Poor old Vic, blown to bits . . . bit . . . no rhyme there. Blown to bit . . . bit . . . bit right into . . . bit off more than I could . . . poor old Vic, dead and no one to mourn him. A sudden tear burned down my cheek, followed by another, and a groan of despair that seemed to belong to someone else.

I pushed the table away, staggering into a bicycle with only one wheel mounted on a special stand. It teetered and crashed over. I stared and decided it wasn't my fault. The owner shouldn't have left it out like that. Maybe he'd been trying to fix it; the damn thing wouldn't be going very far until he put the other wheel on. The groan changed into a sluggish laugh that only ran down after I forgot what was so funny.

Time. Wasting time. Gotta get away.

The air had become thick and heavy, like water. The harder I plowed through it, the more resistance I met. Had to ignore it. Had to find a wall. I blundered into one, knocking down some framed pictures and a plaster ornament. Wrong spot. Needed one to take me outside the house. Which? I'd known a minute ago. Maybe the guy in the steam room could tell me.

I called to him a few times before giving it up as a bad job. He was out for the count, dead drunk, or drugged. Doc had probably shot him full of something to keep him quiet.

Oh, God.

A small portion of my brain that hadn't yet succumbed screamed out a belated warning against the poison I'd so gratefully taken in. Too late now to cough it up. It was in me.

I tried to vanish, with some idea that it might help. Nothing happened. The heaviness in my head traveled down my neck, into my arms, tugged at my legs. My eyes rolled up and closed with artificial sleep. Fresh fear clogged my mind when they refused to open. I tried to force the lids back with my hands, but my fingers were clumsy and wouldn't work right. Once I used to have a nightmare about being unable to wake up, but now I seemed to be in the middle of the worst of it: asleep, knowing I was asleep, and fighting to get out of it.

Hardly able to stand, I felt my way along the wall, with no real thought left to guide me beyond the desire to escape. And then even that was lost as I fell over some obstacle and fought to untangle from it. It won.

My bones were like lead. I had no strength left to move anymore. There seemed no reason to do so. I was content to lie still and wait for . . . I forget what. I forgot everything, how to move, breathe, think.

Voices.

Men came into the gym.

"What the hell's going on here?"

Newton. He could find his own answers. I was fresh out.

"Shit. Come look at this."

He'd found Sheldon in the steam room.

"Is he okay?"

Lester.

"Out cold. Go get Doc."

Footsteps. I forgot them as quickly as they faded.

Newton returned to me, finished the untangling. I sprawled on the floor, unable to move, not wanting to, not caring about it.

Footsteps. Exclamations of surprise. Questions. In his role as a healer, Doc took over, checking Sheldon first.

"Out cold," he pronounced.

Newton snorted. "No kiddin'. Can you do something for him?"

"Hmm." Doc made a longer examination. "What do you want me to do? Bring him around?"

"Well . . ."

"First he gets his hand torn up and because he thinks he knows more than I do about what's good for him starts topping off his morphine shots with his favorite rotgut. Now he seems to have run headfirst into a truck. Next thing you know someone's gonna drop him from an upstairs window. If you ask me—and I'm taking it that you have—he's better off missing out on the rest of the evening. Got some pennies for his eyes? The way he's going, he'll need 'em."

"You just gonna leave him there?"

"Of course not, but you can't expect me to wade into a mess like that without my bag. Jeez, much more of this and I'll have to hang out a shingle and start charging for house calls."

"How did this happen?"

Angela.

"Looks to me like Sheldon came in to work off a grudge. He opens the door, but the kid's waiting for him, gets the jump on him."

"Uh-huh. So what's Fleming still doing here?"

"Probably ran out of gas, girl. He was looking pretty bad when we left him."

She gave an exasperated sigh. "Too tough for him, then. Newton, get Sheldon up to his room."

Doc's hands poked and prodded me. He noisily sucked a tooth, making a loud "tch" sound.

"What is it?" she demanded irritably. "Lester, lock this one up again and stick around to make sure he stays put."

"Too late for that sort of thing," Doc drawled.

"What d'you mean?"

"Girl, this kid's deader'n Dixie."

11

I COULD HAVE laughed, but that, of course, was impossible.

Angela came over to see for herself. "What killed him?"

"Hard to say. It's funny, but he looks better than when he was alive. He was sweating buckets and his color was all gone and now look at him."

"Okay, so he makes a handsome corpse; we've still got to get rid of him."

"Give him back to his English friend, then."

"Sure, and he'd have the cops out here tearing the place apart. There's tire tracks all over the place, holes in the ground from the grenades, and the mess Vic left of himself. . . ."

"Okay, okay, I take it back. Do what you like."

Angela paced rapidly a few times, coming to an abrupt halt. "I've got it, but the boys will have to hurry if we're going to make it out to the dock in time. Lester, go find Mac and get some really sharp knives. I want you to cut up a couple of big sections of the hall carpet. The stuff's going to be ripped out anyway, we'll get a start on things. Make 'em long enough to hold—"

Lester interrupted, a grin in his voice. "Yeah, I know, that old rug bit."

"I want them long enough so that the ends can be tied off and roomy so we can load them with weights. You'll need plenty of rope or some heavy twine."

"Okay, I got it now. You wanta sink 'em both in the lake, huh?"

"No, I thought we could stick wings on 'em and drop 'em off the Wrigley building. Get moving."

Chuckling, Lester got out.

"Two down, one to go," said Angela.

"What one?" asked Doc.

"The English guy. I still expect him to raise a stink when we don't turn over his friend, so he'll have to be shut down, too."

"Angela . . ."

"No lectures, Doc, I know what I'm doing. Anyway, go help Newton and I'll check on Lester. We're running out of time."

She whisked off one way, Doc ambled another, and I was left like so much luggage where I lay. None of it mattered to me. The idea of being rolled up in a hunk of rug like an overgrown hot dog caused no alarm. I was already comfortably wrapped in a sweet cottony cushion of well-being and couldn't care less about the things that happened beyond its limits. The people walking and talking around me were no more important than some radio left on to make noise in an otherwise empty house.

So I drifted and dreamed without sleep on Sheldon's poisoned blood while he was carried out and tended. Newton was then drafted to help with the carpet cutting. Their voices blended together in a pleasant, meaningless drone, occasionally punctuated by a laugh or Angela's urgings to hurry. They were all easily ignored as I floated in and out of the black and purple mists spinning lazily in my mind. No thoughts, no needs, no problems, no pleasures, no pains.

Angela and Newton returned and dropped something large on the floor near me. It made a mushy thump and I was treated to a puff of stale, dusty air. They took a moment to arrange it properly, then knelt next to me and rolled me over onto it. I didn't resist, couldn't resist, didn't care.

"He hasn't lightened any," Newton grumbled. "Gonna be hell getting him out to the truck."

"More than you think," said Angela. "Help me with these barbell weights."

"Easy, now, that one's too heavy for you."

"I'm just undoing the thing, you can carry it. How many will we need?"

"At least three of the fifty-pound ones for Vic. Maybe four for this guy. It's gotta be more than their own weight or they can float once they start to rot."

"Okay. Start taking 'em out to Mac and Lester, I'll roll these over to this one."

"But that's too—"

"No, it's not. I can handle fifty pounds if I have to. Get moving."

Newton got moving, puffing hard as he carried out Vic's share of iron. Angela worked to unlock the weights from their crossbars and rolled them over to me one at a time. With a small grunt and a heave, she got the first one placed high on my chest, just under my chin.

I didn't like it.

She placed the second one just below it. By the time she was ready with the third, Newton had come back and was able to take over.

I didn't like any of it. The discomfort was an unwelcome intrusion in my cobwebby dreams. I tried to push the things away, but nothing happened.

Angela lifted her side of the rug, flopping it over me. Dust and fibers smacked against my face. Newton did the same for his side, increasing the weight and discomfort.

With no need to breathe, I couldn't suffocate, but no matter what changes the body has undergone, some instincts cannot be forgotten or suppressed. The pressure on my chest and the stiff carpet folded so tightly around me brought up old nightmares and even a few fresh ones of pain and death.

"Tie it up good," came Angela's muffled voice. "I don't want the weights slipping out when we drop him in."

Newton muttered something, busy with his work. They tied off the top end of the rug just above my head and wound the rope fast around my feet and legs. The latter made me think of my last, my very last, moments of life when Fred Sanderson had tied a weight to my ankles, just before Frank Paco had . . .

"You hear something?" asked Newton.

"Like what?"

"I heard something . . . like a whimper or a moan."

"Coming from him? Doc may be a drunk, but he knows a stiff when he sees one. I've never seen him so cross-eyed that he—"

"But I was sure I heard . . . maybe this guy had some kind of fit. He could still be alive."

"And so what if he is?" she asked pointedly.

"Okay," he said after a moment. "I get you."

They finished the job without further talk.

Lester walked in. "We got Vic loaded into the truck, Angela."

"Good. Where's Mac?"

"On his way."

"Soon as he's here, the three of you get this one out and wait for me. I have to find my coat."

"What about Doc? Is he comin'?"

"Yes. He'll be looking after Daddy when we get him back. Your job will be to look after Doc. Keep him on his feet until this is over."

That got her a laugh as she dashed out.

Mac came in and the three of them puffed and cursed and carried me with all the barbell weights to the truck. Throughout, I said nothing, did nothing. I was totally helpless, a bundle of bone and muscle unable to respond to my chaotic brain. They dropped me onto the metal floor of the truck. The fifty-pound disks had each slipped a little out of place. The one on my chest bumped painfully under my chin. Much more shifting and I'd have a crushed windpipe.

A long wait and then a stream of voices as they climbed into the truck. Its big motor turned and coughed to life, and with a rough shift of gears lurched away. I caught the full effect of the uneven road and was unable to protect myself from unexpected dips and turns.

No orderly, reasoned thoughts came to me. I was operating strictly on emotion, the primary ones of fear and anger. Each added a certain strength to my unconscious internal fight, but neither was generating any workable ideas for escape. Had I been able to vanish, no doubt I would have done so. Had I been capable of movement, I would have struggled. But my body was quite separated from my brain and my brain was barely awake. Just enough of it worked to acknowledge danger, but that was all.

Newton's voice was pitched to be heard above the rumble of the truck. "So what about it, Doc? You sure this guy's really croaked?"

"You sure you haven't been into Frank's home brew? Course he's dead."

"But what about what I heard?"

"Probably just some air wheezing out of the lungs. When you

move a body around that can happen. Spooky the first time, but you get used to it."

"Maybe you are. I thought that he might still be alive, but just had some kind of a fit."

"Like catalepsy?"

"I guess."

"No, he didn't have those symptoms or he'd have been stiff as a board when you found him. No signs of epilepsy, either."

"Then why'd he die?"

"Still worried that it might be catching?"

"Yeah, why not?"

"Good question, my friend. Wish I had an answer for you. I don't know what killed him: catalepsy, concussion, or cussedness, and I'm not ready to ask Angela if I can perform a quick autopsy just to satisfy your curiosity. None of it really matters, he's still going into the lake and the fish can worry about him for you."

"But the way he just dropped dead . . ."

"Newton, sooner or later we all drop dead, 'specially in this business. My advice is not to think about it and drink enough of this stuff down so you don't give a damn when it finally does happen."

Newton growled a dissatisfied disagreement to that and subsided.

My fingers suddenly twitched. Since my mind wasn't up to coherent thinking, I didn't notice at first, and attached little importance to it when I did.

"Think he's gonna haunt you, Newton?" asked Lester with a laugh.

"Don't be a wise-ass."

"That it, Fleming? You gonna haunt him?" He nudged me with his foot.

The weight on my chest moved, settling more firmly against my windpipe. A gagging sound that only I could hear escaped. I tried to turn from it and succeeded in easing the pressure a little.

"I think Newton reads too much."

"And you don't read at all."

"Yeah, that's why I ain't gonna be haunted like you. What's the point wasting your time on something that ain't real? You won't catch me noodling around with that kid stuff."

"Knock it off, Lester," ordered Doc. "Everyone knows what you noodle around with."

"What's that supposed to mean?"

"What do you think? And if you keep it up you'll go blind. Did you know that?"

"You drunken lush. I oughta—"

"Lay off, all of ya," complained Mac. "My head's killin' me."

"Then have a drink," said Doc. They passed the flask around, which helped restore peace.

My hands had progressed from spastic twitching to controlled clenching. As far as was possible within the mummylike wrappings of carpet and rope, I formed fists and flexed muscles. Some of the wordless fears spinning in my brain ebbed away.

"You see that?" asked Newton.

"More haunting, huh?"

"Can it, Les. I saw his feet move."

I went very still, which was a conscious decision, the first real one I'd made in what seemed like hours.

"It was just the truck bouncing," said Doc.

"But did you see it?"

"Yeah, and it was the truck and this lousy light playing around."

"You wanna really be spooked, you shoulda helped me and Mac with Vic. What a mess. Had to line his rug up with old newspapers to keep the blood from soaking straight through."

"Les, will you shut the hell up about it!"

"Sorry, Mac," he snickered.

The gears ground and we slowed and turned. The road got worse, distracting them from their conversation. I took the opportunity and chanced a limited stretch. No one noticed.

"This is it," said Newton. "Everyone check your hardware."

The truck rolled to a stop, the brakes squealing crankily. The motor cut off and the front doors opened and slammed.

"Douse the light."

The back doors were also opened and the men filed out. Their voices became fainter and less identifiable.

"See anything?"

"Yeah, he's already here. There's the running lights of the yacht."

"For what we are about to receive . . ."

"They're putting out a boat."

". . . may we be truly thankful."

"Can it."

Their attention elsewhere, I flexed and stretched again, reveling in the return of feeling. Because of the weights and rug, it wasn't at all pleasant, but I knew I was still alive.

"Wish they'd hurry."

"Spread out and check the place for anybody who don't belong."

Then their voices faded altogether. I was alone in the stuffiest, most claustrophobic darkness that I'd ever known. Oddly enough, I no longer minded. The imminent alternative was Angela's completion of the job her father began last summer—dropping me to the bottom of Lake Michigan.

Without Newton and the others bickering around me, it was easy to lose track of time. I lay quietly and waited for more of my mind to clear. It was like struggling awake from a thick and restless sleep, the illusion compounded by the stuff I was wrapped in.

"Sez you, I want to see for myself." Chaven's voice, coming up fast. My muscles tightened.

"And I want to see my father," said Angela, equally demanding.

"Don't worry, he's in good hands."

"He better be or I'll—"

"First things first." He climbed up into the truck. "Which one is he?"

"There."

He began tugging at the ropes. Then I heard the snick of a knife and a snap as he sawed through one.

"You're messing it up," Angela complained. "We had him all ready to—"

"Save it, babe. If this is him, I'll do you a favor and take him off your hands."

"What?"

He cut quickly and forced apart the top half of the folded-up rug. I wisely remained as still as possible. Orange stains flickered over my eyelids as he checked my face with a flashlight. The cold, damp air coming in from the lake felt absolutely wonderful.

"It's him, all right." He slapped my face once, then removed a glove and checked my neck for a pulse. Nothing there, of course.

"Satisfied?" she asked.

"More than you think. Ever since I laid eyes on this s.o.b. he's been nothing but trouble. How'd you get him?"

"I didn't. We found him like that."

"Like what?"

"Dead, lame brain."

"Just like that?"

"Uh-huh."

"You mean he just waltzed into your house and dropped dead?"

"That's how it looked to Doc."

"That quack. Listen, Angela, nobody just drops dead. It's too convenient."

"Miracles happen."

"Come on, you plugged him and just don't want to say."

"I didn't and if I had, I wouldn't need to hide it from you. He looked god-awful for a while, said he had a bad stomach, and then he must have keeled over."

"A bad stomach? Who dies of a bad stomach?"

"Who gives a damn?" she said, her voice rising. "We're here to make a trade, so let's get on with it."

But he was still digesting the news and tapped me again for assurance. "Don't know how you did this, Angela, but I owe you one."

"Then get my father."

"You got him and welcome to him. Who's the other stiff?"

"Never mind him."

"I'll just bet it's Vic. Ah, don't worry, I never trusted the creep, anyway. Here, you have your boys load these two up on the boat and I'll save you the trouble of dumping them."

"Why are you so anxious to help?"

"Because it's something the boss wants to have done. I'm all set up for it and I think it's about time things got a little nicer between us—your bunch and mine, that is."

Angela had a smile in her tone. "Don't you mean my bunch and Kyler?"

"Yeah, that's what I meant. What d'ya say?"

"I'll talk it over with my father when he gets back."

"You got a one-track mind, but that's okay. I'll get things

started. Deiter, give these guys a hand, just to show we're all friends."

First Vic was dragged away, then came my turn. Bumpier and less secure than traveling in the trunk, they carried me to the dock. The top barbell weight finally slipped, coming out the top end of my rug. I was nearly dropped as the guy lugging my shoulders got his feet out of the way with a sharp curse. Somewhat out of breath, they agreed to keep going and come back for it later. My eyes were shut tight, but I knew when we'd moved out over the water. Right then and there I attempted to vanish and damn the consequences, but I hadn't quite recovered enough for it to work.

At least it was faceup, but the shock of impact against the wood was pretty bad when I landed, especially with the remaining weights on top. It was an effort holding in the grunts and groans resulting from their carelessness; now was not the time to effect a miraculous resurrection.

When it seemed safe, I cracked an eye for a peek at things. No one was in view, so I opened both and drew in a full breath of sweet, damp air. The clouds had broken up; I could see the stars I'd missed before, a thousand tiny suns to dispel the last shadows in my mind. I wasn't free yet, but they gave me hope.

Crowded next to me was Vic, anonymous and shapeless in his improvised shroud. If nothing else, I knew him by his bloodsmell. Despite the inner lining of newspapers, the stuff was seeping through, creating huge red patches on the outer side of the rug. Rest in pieces, I thought, and promptly had to stifle my own sudden gagging.

"What's that?" came Newton's sharp voice.

"Another ghost?"

"Lay off, or I'll bust you one. I heard something."

"Yeah, the water gurgled, is all. Keep your eyes open, we ain't exactly home free with these guys."

"Ah, don't tell me my job."

Bad reaction on my part. Black humor and some stinking memories of the war that I thought I'd forgotten. Damn Angela and her grenades. Damn my own imagination for telling me what Vic must look like. Damn the Kaiser, too, and the joker who shot Archduke Ferdinand. Damn, damn, damn, damn, damn. Unable to vanish, I wrestled around to get my arms free of the rug.

Newton was pacing around on the shore and I had to watch out for him in case he decided to check on the gurgling water for himself. He and Angela had done a good job with the ropes, though, and Chaven hadn't cut away nearly enough to make much of a difference. I'd made no progress by the time he'd marched onto the dock with Opal, Angela, and the others.

Chaven clapped his hands together for warmth. "Okay, let's get things started. First trip, I take Opal back, next, I bring in your father, the last, I clean up your garbage."

Angela agreed, but only up to a point. "Two of my men go with Opal, you stay here."

"Hey, now . . ."

"We're all going to be friends, aren't we, Chaven? Doc and Newton go along to help with my father. Deiter goes with them to keep things smooth."

"They leave their gats here, then."

"No, they don't, or I'll have you leave yours, too. Let's keep things even."

"All right, but no trouble or everyone goes in the drink."

I made another attempt to vanish, a futile one. It should have been easier than this, especially since I was over water, but nothing happened. I was as solid as ever. I damned myself for a total idiot for taking in Sheldon's polluted blood, but there'd been little else I could have done. Was it permanent or did I just need more recovery time? The way they were pushing things, I wouldn't have very long to speculate.

Opal was guided forward. She was short on complaints, perhaps preoccupied by her new employment and making plans on how to leave her old job when the time came. She was helped down into the boat, followed by Doc, Newton, and Deiter, which thinned down the crowd. I'd been concerned about getting stepped on, but everyone managed to avoid it. The oars creaked and water splashed as they shoved off.

Chaven heaved a sigh that verged on the theatrical. "I'm glad this is working out so well for all of us, Angela."

Since it was a rather obvious conversational gambit, she spared him a return comment.

Chaven bulled ahead without her cooperation. "Look, I need to talk with you."

"So talk."

"In private, not with a lot of others around. Since you don't trust me, we can stay out here and your boys can watch us from the land. We'll be in plain sight the whole time."

She thought it over. "All right."

"Angela . . . ," said Lester, warningly.

"I'll be fine. Besides, I've got my chaperon with me. If Chaven tries anything I don't like, I plug him. Got that, Chaven?"

"I never argue with a lady."

Lester grumbled, but he and Mac retired to the land end of the dock.

"Okay," she said brightly. "What is it?"

"This whole deal about kidnapping your father . . . I just wanted you to know that it wasn't my idea, that I didn't want any part of it."

"Uh-huh."

"I mean that. It was all Kyler's doing. I told him not to, but he wouldn't listen."

"And now he's come to his senses with this trade?"

"You could say that. The truth is that there's a lot of changes going on right now that you don't know about."

"Really? What changes?" She sounded interested, but wary, playing it just right.

"I wanta give it to you straight about Kyler—just between us." Chaven lowered his voice slightly. "He's on the way out."

Angela took her time before saying, "Uh-huh."

"That's the straight stuff. He's . . . well, he's going nuts."

"Not funny, Chaven."

"I don't mean it to be. If you'd seen him tonight, you'd know. That Fleming guy got him so jumpy that—"

"What?"

Chaven bumped his toe against me. "Well, Kyler got the idea that this mug could turn himself invisible. Now you can figure what the other guys thought."

"I can also figure what I think."

"Hey, I said *he* was crazy, not me. I never said *I* believed him."

Liar, I thought, and had half a mind to tell him so, but was too interested in finding out his game to interrupt.

"Anyway, there's some big changes coming and you need to know about it."

"Why?"

He hesitated. "With Kyler going out, someone else has to come in."

"And you're it?" She was unimpressed.

"I know how you feel, how things were after your father's . . . accident. They really shoulda put you in charge of things, but the big boys said no, thinking that a broa—— girl couldn't cut it. I know that Frank had it planned for you to take it over a few years down the line."

"Which didn't pan out."

"Yeah, but that don't mean it couldn't now."

"What's your game?"

"With Kyler out of the way, I move into the top spot, but I need more than just Deiter and Opal to hold things together. A lot of the boys di—— don't like Kyler, but they don't dare quit."

"So what's that to me?"

"It means this is your chance to come in on the deal. We can work together on this."

"Oooh, what's next? A box of candy and a ring?"

"I'm serious, Angela. I want to cut you in on the business."

"Why do you need me?"

"For what I just told you. To hold things together."

She was quiet for a long time, probably thinking it all through very seriously, indeed. I could tell because she wasn't pacing.

"So what d'ya say?" he asked.

"Call me when Kyler's out of the way, then we'll really talk."

"Why not now?"

"You already said it: I can't trust you and I know you don't trust me."

"Of course I do, or I wouldn't be giving you this stuff."

"You don't or you would have told me right out that Kyler's dead and on that boat."

Despite the constant lap of water masking over the more subtle sounds around us, I could have sworn that I heard his heart jump. It took him a while to settle down and find his voice. "How did . . . ?"

"Your 'invisible' friend here mentioned it. I got the whole story of how you killed Kyler and put the blame on him. I like the way you tied it up, but I don't like being lied to and I'm not going to forget it if and when we do cut a deal. Are you sure you want to work with me?"

He bumped me with his toe again. "Dead and he's still making trouble. Okay, Angela, you caught me out on Kyler and I'm sorry, but it was pretty important news and I had to know which way you were pointed before I could—"

"Uh-huh. You want to talk or give excuses all night?"

"Talk," he blurted, then shut up. I could almost sympathize with him on how she'd jerked the rug right out from under his generous offer and put him on the defensive. If they did manage to work something out, I had a good idea on who would be the senior partner.

The boat came back just then and Angela's attention instantly switched to it and its passengers.

"Daddy? Are you all right?"

No answer.

"Doc, what's with him? What's the matter?"

"Nothing, he's just a little tired and boozy. They were giving him some of the hard stuff to keep him quiet. Let him sleep it off and he'll be fine."

She wasn't too reassured and fretted until he was safely out of the rowboat and up on the dock. With Doc and Mac's help she was quick to get him away into the truck. Newton and Lester remained behind.

"Last trip and then we can call it a night," said Chaven. Deiter held the boat steady while the other three struggled to lower Vic into it. "Jeez, why did you have to pack the weights inside with the stiff? You coulda tied them on afterward."

No one bothered to answer. My turn came up. They refolded the carpet over my face and hefted and heaved. I was dropped on top of Vic without ceremony or much respect for the dead. The only reason they weren't rougher was worry over tearing up the boat. The barbell weight that had slipped out was handed, not dumped in, then Chaven climbed down and we were pushed away.

The oars scraped in their locks, then Deiter got down to rhythmic rowing. The nasty, corkscrewing motion of the boat abated a bit, but my stomach still wanted to turn itself inside out in reaction.

"What's the holdup?" asked Chaven.

"Nothing, just a heavy load. I'm getting tired and these stiffs must weigh a ton. How'd Angela take your pitch?"

"She's got more brains than what's good for her, but I think we can swing something after she cools down. Give her some time with her dear old dad, then I can start sending her posies, though if that broad's anything like Frankie, money would work better."

"You're going to *give* her money?"

"No, but I'll make sure she knows the stuff is there and waiting if she wants to work with me."

"Still can't figure why you want to risk it. I'd rather sleep with a tarantula than trust her, especially after what she did to Red and the boys."

"I'm not sleeping with her and I'm not trusting her, but she is necessary. She may not have much pull yet, but she does know how to work with people and knows what people to work with. Kyler played it too close to the chest for me to get enough of a handle on things."

"But what about Red? And Vic here? You wanta end up like them?"

"No, and as long as I keep my eyes open, that won't happen. The nice part is that Angela knows she needs me, too."

"And when she don't need you no more?"

"Then she can go on a nice cruise of this beautiful lake."

"'Less she bumps you first."

"She won't."

Deiter applied his full attention to rowing and was quite out of breath by the time one of the *Elvira*'s crew hailed us. Ropes were thrown and instructions passed. Deiter and Chaven gratefully turned the problem of unloading us over to them. After some discussion, a rope net was thrown down and wrapped around us and we were hoisted up with the help of one of their loading cranes. So I deduced from their talk and the complete discomfort and sick-making swinging around that I was subjected to before they were finished.

The steadier deck of the yacht was an improvement over the rowboat, but my back hairs were still on end and the effect of all the acrobatics on my already sensitive stomach was predictable. Vic and I were rolled from the net like so much fish and a protective tarp thrown over us. He didn't mind, but I did and began fighting to get free, not caring who saw; this was pure survival.

At least my strength had returned. After enough wriggling to tear up a straitjacket, I got one arm free. This created some space for the other to come out, and I clawed at the carpet, pushing it from my face. The tarp hadn't been tied down and fresh cold air came up under it to ease the revolution in my gut. Such frantic activity had dislodged the barbells, which was something to celebrate.

I was freezing. My fingers could do little more than fumble at the knots, which I could barely feel. All this was by touch, with me folded in two to get to the ropes on my ankles. It was the kind of work designed to teach a person patience in the most exasperating way possible. I was a lousy student and went on another silent cursing streak. Finally, one of the less likely loops came loose, but it led to another that was a dead end.

With an idea of turning up something sharp, like a convenient knife, I took a cautious look from under the tarp. No one around. Lucky them. I was in a pretty foul mood by now and more than ready to work it off on anyone handy.

They'd left us piled on the aft section. Beyond the rail was a vast line of the city's lights floating above silver and black ribbons of water—not far away, but too far for me. All I wanted was to cut loose, get to the rowboat, and get to shore and to hell with everybody else.

Except that it didn't work out like that. I'd forgotten that Chaven had more to throw overboard than me and Vic. He still had Kyler on his hands and wasn't about to waste time getting rid of him. Just before ducking back under the tarp, I saw one of the crew and Deiter struggling along with a blanket-wrapped bundle of unmistakable weight and shape. Chaven was right behind them.

"Get the rail off," he ordered.

"I still think we're too close to the shore," Deiter complained.

"Opal's starting to bitch about going home soon. I have to stay on her good side until I can get her to hand over the code for the books. So let's move it."

"A punch in the kisser would work just as good."

"Come on, give us a hand."

They yanked away the tarp. I played possum once more. With my feet still tied up, I couldn't get to them, they'd have to come to me. Deiter grabbed my ankles and hauled me almost to the edge of the deck. The water was much too close. I flinched involuntarily against the uneasy movement of the yacht.

"Hey, what the hell?" He let go as if I were a hot brick.

"What is it?"

"Chaven, look at this. He's . . . come loose . . . or something."

"Who're you kidding? He's dead."

"Maybe not so dead as you think. See?" Deiter shuffled nervously back.

"Douse that light, you jerk." His voice was thinner, harsher. "The ropes didn't hold, is all."

"Don't be a stoop. *Look* at him! He had to have done it. Who else?"

Chaven looked. "This is crazy. He's dead. I know he's dead."

"Angela put one over on you, is what it is. You gotta do something about him."

"Oh, hell, get outta the way."

It was dark enough for me to risk cracking my eyes. Chaven crowded in close, right where I wanted him, but he drew his gun—Escott's stolen Webley—which I could have done without.

As I suddenly sat up and reached for him like some long-dreaded retribution, he let out an honest-to-God shriek that I didn't think could come from a human throat. Deiter and the other guy also joined the chorus, stumbling all over one another in their hurry to get away. It might have been funny if I hadn't truly been fighting for my life.

I got both hands on his arm and shoved the gun to my right. Chaven tried to pull himself away. The damn thing went off, again and again and . . .

Chaven threw himself backward. I didn't dare let go of his arm. I was dragged along.

The bullets flew wide.

Couldn't use my legs for leverage, they were still caught up in the rug. Concentrated on the gun. Another shot.

Then I got one hand over his. The thing bucked and roared as I twisted it up. This time the bullet struck. The side of his throat exploded. Blood burst from the wound, spraying me. The gun's sharp recoil took it out of his grip; it dropped on the deck with a thud. Then there was a horrible weightless second with both of us screaming as we crashed headfirst into the lake.

Headfirst into hell.

Water.

Free-flowing water.

Free-flowing death.

Chaven pushed away, the last thing he ever did. In four seconds all the life went out of him, flooding the shifting shadows around us with the black cloud of his blood.

I was upside down, my legs tied fast in the rug and the thing spreading above me, buoyant in the water. Arms out as though flying, Chaven's body drifted past in a slow downward spiral, a thick trail streaming from his throat. The darkness took him . . . and reached out for me.

It bubbled and burned like fire, tearing right through the top of my skull.

It seared and clawed and ripped at my frail flesh like a starved monster.

It smashed and smothered, crushing my final wailing hope of escape.

Ears stuffed with it, eyes blurred from it, mouth gagging on it, bones shrinking from its freezing touch.

I kicked and writhed and fought and howled and strangled against it.

EPILOGUE

I'M ALIVE.

It was the first real thought to surface in my cobweb-clogged brain since I woke up on the beach. I'd been groggy then, with only enough stuff working in my head to shakily stand and blink down at my soaked clothes. It never occurred to me to question why I was on a beach and in such a condition, and I was still in a thought-numbing state of shock when I climbed a short, sandy rise and found the road.

Loose-limbed like a cartoon scarecrow, I walked, head bowed to watch my feet because I couldn't feel them. I looked up once to check that the lights of the city were still ahead, and tripped on something, sprawling flat. I immediately scrambled up again, not daring to rest. The icy wind was cutting me in two; if I stopped moving now, I might stop moving for good.

Teeth chattering, arms clutched tight around my chest, I bowed my head again in a wordless prayer for more strength and staggered forward. I'd been down this road before, only then it hadn't been so damned cold.

I had been colder . . . out there . . . shuddering in the water, my ankles bound together . . . not suspended between heaven and hell, but very definitely *in* hell.

Headfirst.

For an age.

Until the press of water became too much and began to crush me into something that wasn't me and yet was.

I floated, just another bubble compressed into a moving plastic sphere by the water. I was going to float to heaven.

I made it as far as the surface.

Then the trip, an endless rush over a liquid desert. Realization that heaven wasn't my destination, after all, but then neither was hell. Perhaps another time, if ever.

I shivered. It was a memory now, but memories have a way of hurting you far worse than the original experience.

Road. Watch the feet. Think of other things.

Like Angela Paco, a dark little angel of death, every bit as lethal as her father had been. If not already, she'd be making plans to get rid of Escott. Not at all nice. I'd have to have a serious talk with her.

Escott. Might want to mention it to him, too.

Chaven. Better not to think about him at all.

Same for Kyler.

Dear God, it's cold. The wind sliced through my wet clothes, cutting at my puckered white skin.

Road. The one I'd taken that first night, when Sanderson tried to run me down. I'd stuck my thumb out, hoping for a ride. . . .

Motor. This time the sound coming toward me from the city, not from behind. Too bad. Could have used the lift.

Headlights separating, growing larger, had to shade my eyes from them. Not wanting to tempt fate, I moved closer to the shoulder of the road to give the driver plenty of room to pass.

He slowed instead.

Not again.

I waited for him to shift the gears, hit the gas, and hurtle down on me as Sanderson had. I waited and shook miserably in the Arctic blast off the lake.

The car coasted to a stop, motor idling softly.

It was a Nash.

The passenger door opened. A tall, lean man got out, moving slowly, his bony face pinched with concern. I glanced behind me to see what he was looking at, but saw nothing of interest.

"Jack?"

Yeah. That's my name. His was Escott. I had something to tell him. . . .

He came closer. "Shoe and I had arranged a meeting with Miss Paco—we were just en route to pick you up. Are you . . . ?"

"B-better not g-go," I choked out. My words tasted of lake water.

He stiffly shrugged out of his overcoat. "My God, man, you're freezing to death."

I grinned, which alarmed him even more. "N-not this t-time." *I'm alive.*

He draped the thing over my shoulders and guided me toward the waiting car.